GUITAR GHOST

Chanda Stelter

For my dad, Duane Lundby, who will be reading
this *finished* copy from Heaven.

Copyrights

©2023 by Chanda Stelter

Scriptures taken from The Holy Bible, New International Version®, NIV® Copyright © 1973, 1978, 1984, 2011 by Biblica, Inc.® Used by permission. All rights reserved worldwide.

Scriptures taken from the New King James Version®. Copyright © 1982 by Thomas Nelson. Used by permission. All rights reserved.

This is a work of fiction. Names, characters, places, business establishments, events, and incidents are either products of my imagination or used fictitiously.

Cover design through Canva by Chanda Stelter

Note from the Author

As I wrote this book, I took some creative liberties with the timeline of the story in regards to the Bible editions that I chose. Even though the Bible editions I used were not in print during the time of my story, the verses I chose are in the Bible versions that have spoken to me over the years and have significantly impacted my life. All scriptures in *Guitar Ghost* were taken from the New International Version or New King James Version. Many of the scriptures I chose have seen me through my own struggles in life, just like with James and Jessie May. My husband was deployed for 14 months to Iraq back in 2003/2004 during which time our daughter was born. We had doctored to conceive and then he left when I was five months pregnant and came back when our daughter was 10 months old. This was a time of great stress and trial in our lives but would become one of our greatest, most impacting and shaping chapters in *our* love story. I wove some of our own experiences into the book as I told James and Jessie's love story.

I also mention in the book that Jessie's mom Patty had a worn, red *Good News Bible*. This Bible edition also would not have been in print during this time, but I chose it to be Patty's Bible because that is my precious memory of my own mother and her Bible. I can still picture her with it in her lap as she sat in her salmon-colored Lazy Boy recliner in our living room at the farm. This image brings me great comfort and peace. It is the same comforting presence I wanted portrayed with Patty and her Bible with Jessie May.

Acknowledgments

I owe immeasurable thanks to some special people for allowing me to interview them for a palpable sense of believability in my story. These people grew up during this time. Some were seniors during 1964/1965 just like James and Jessie. Some served in the military during the Vietnam era and graciously offered me their insight and memories during that intense time to serve in our history. I owe a great deal of gratitude to each of these people for giving me a first-hand glimpse into the years for which I wrote my storyline. My sincerest thanks and appreciation go to Duane and Betty Lundby, Alton and Cleo Nygaard, Karen Pierce, Stan Stelter and Rodger Stelter. Without them, this book would be missing some heart and soul for that era.

I also want to thank my beta readers who read the first print of my book and gave me invaluable feedback: Duane and Betty Lundby, Tori Renner, Latrisha Seil, Stan Stelter, Chara Wangen, and Mary Wentz. Not only did you give me detailed editing and insightful feedback, you encouraged me and made me feel like I was already a valued "author". Your words empowered me and my gratitude is beyond what I can express on this page. Thank you for making me feel like a sequel is needed….but, let's not get ahead of ourselves!

And finally, I would like to express my heartfelt gratitude to my husband Shawn, daughter Faith, and son Samuel. Your unwavering support, unconditional love, and sincere interest throughout the journey of writing my book made this endeavor not only possible but deeply fulfilling. I truly dedicate the pages of this book to you, my precious family. Much of what I wrote was inspired from you through my experiences as a wife and mother. I love you all passionately.

Now, I will close my acknowledgements in the same way I often closed the day with my daughter, "Good night, Pickle Nose."

Chapter 1
Just the Beginning

It was a hot day, typical for mid-September in Alabama. This particular Friday afternoon at Cordova High School, the air felt extremely sultry. The ceiling fans lazily circling above merely teased the air below, not offering the room much reprieve.

 "Class, settle down please," rattled Ms. Pennysford. Energy and anticipation for the weekend was running amuck with the evident stir of the class. "Seniors! Your attention, please!" She waited, giving them a chance to listen. "Land sakes," she sighed tossing her hands in the air. "How can *senioritis* be kickin' in with y'all already! It's only September." Ms. Pennysford had a playful smirk on her face. She was a favorite of many students and seemed to bring students to their potential, building them up to believe in themselves and they learned from her that they can do or be anything.

The final minutes of the clock were ticking away. With tenacity she tapped her ruler on her desk for a bit of order and gave her last instruction for the weekend, "Don't forget y'all have a quiz Monday on verb conjugation and your *Wuthering Heights* essay responses are due as well." She barely got the last words out as the bell rang. The room exploded in a rapid motion for the doorway. "Enjoy the weekend and weather!" her words trailed after them as they bustled out of the room no longer adhering to single-file fashion. The weekend was here.

* * *

Jessie May was barely half way down the hall when she felt his hand slide into hers. "May I walk you home, Miss Clark?"

"James Theodore, you know I don't like to be addressed so formally." His hand in hers made her heart skip faster. Her feet struggled to keep up with the increased pace of her heart. She glanced at him. He looked tall and handsome in his slim, blue jeans. He wore a plaid blue short-sleeved button-down shirt. Everything about him and his looks had charm. She loved his dark brown hair which hung a little tousled over his face – a face she could hardly look at without melting. Bashfully, she let her eyes drop from his gaze. His top two buttons were unbuttoned. His skin tone was strikingly bronzed, still tanned from the summer. It glistened from the afternoon in their stuffy classroom which seemed to accent the definition of his muscle tone. Again she felt her heart rate quicken. Oh, and those eyes. His dreamy brown eyes. Eyes that stared deep into her soul. Eyes that implored her right now playfully waiting for her response. His eyes danced; he was so full of zest…and humor. He broke into a ballad that seemed somehow polished and premeditated. He was always breaking into some song. She never understood how his spontaneous singing could produce such on-the-spot lyrics and tunes. She never told him, but she loved when he sang to her. And he was singing to her right now, in the hallway. With all the other students around them hustling off into their weekend. She blushed. She couldn't maintain her *act* of control any longer. Her smile wrapping from ear to ear gave James the answer he already knew. Yes, he could walk her home.

* * *

The fall colors amidst the rolling foothills of the Appalachian Mountains seemed to radiate an amber glow that only accentuated the blossoming love of the young couple as they walked hand-in-hand. Without a care in the world, they ambled along the bank of the Mulberry Fork playfully kicking through the dampened leaves on the ground. James stooped down and picked up a rock and skipped it casually across the water. He stopped and took both her hands in his, "Let's go around through Eden's Pathway, Miss…" He paused dramatically as if being ever-so-mindful to address her less formally, "Jessie May." To which he added for convincing purposes - a wink.

Eden's Pathway was private, off the normal beat. A path that discretely wound into a lush copse of cypress trees. It was known mostly only to the locals who for years had called the secluded lush grove "Eden's Pathway" – for it was truly a walk through paradise. The splendor of fall colors was a testament to its name. The colors gave a distinction and depth to the foliage of the grove.

"You know my daddy will wonder what took me so long comin' home from school?"

"Tell him the truth. You went the long way through Eden's Pathway. You just couldn't resist seein' the colors of *paradise* this time of year! Besides," he went on, "it's not that far out of the way, and it really doesn't take that long to walk through. I just like it 'cause it's private. It's a secret when we're in there."

Her heart fluttered and her breath caught in her throat. She didn't have long to catch it. He grabbed her hand and began running, not really waiting for her answer. Before she knew it they were lying on the moss-like undergrowth of the trees. *Their* trees he liked to tell her. *Their* paradise. As she lay on her side against him – her arm across his chest – she played with the button on his shirt. She seemed completely at peace and lost in tranquil thought. A gentle breeze that barely made its way through the dense thicket lightly caressed their skin. She watched his chest rise and fall. She knew he was watching her too.

After some minutes, he broke her quiet train of thought. "When are you goin' to introduce me to your parents?"

Losing track of time which happened often when they were together, his question startled her and she hastily got up, "Oh my goodness, my parents! I have to get home! Daddy's really gonna be drillin' me now, James Patterson."

He came to a half kneel. Grabbing her waist, both of his hands wrapped around the small of her back. "But when?" Jessie could feel her knees weaken slightly with the sensation of his touch and she knew she was blushing again. She felt suddenly very warm.

"When?" he protested again. "I wanna meet the parents of the girl I love. The girl I wanna marry."

"James!" her voice was breathy.

He leaned in closer to her, "Jessie May, I can't wait to marry you and be able to do right by you. To have you be mine, completely." As he spoke the words his left hand dropped to her side against her knee, her bare skin. He gently caressed her leg. Her skin was soft and smooth.

"James Theodore!" She scolded and playfully pushed his hand away. She looked at him squarely and said, "Not yet, but soon you'll meet my parents. I know my daddy's not ready."

"Your daddy? Or you?" he asked with a smirk working its way through the corners of his mouth.

"James! Of course, my daddy! You know how he is!"

"No, I really don't since I haven't met the man. So? When?" He stood and looked down gently into her eyes, pulling her closer to him again.

Penetrating her with those eyes she couldn't resist, "Soon," she pushed the word out almost out of breath.

He paused for a moment, speaking only with his eyes. "Alright, that'll have to do. Soon!" he said with a punctuated smile and grabbed her hand as he took off running to hustle her home.

"Wait!" she said and quickly turned back to grab their school packs. "Remember, James..."

"I know, my little bookworm, the verb quiz and essay homework! Yuck!" And with that, they were off.

* * *

Robert Clark was a loyal, hard-working man. He had worked as a mechanic at Chuck's Repair for 28 years. He had started working there the summer before his junior year in high school. He had planned to go to college after he graduated, but the owner Chuck Brown was diagnosed with Multiple Sclerosis Robert's senior year. Chuck had been so impressed with Robert's work ethic that he offered for Robert to come on full-time after he graduated and help him manage the mechanic shop. So, Robert had been working there ever since.

He was a big man with a strong-looking stature. If you would run into him on the street, you'd think he was a man not to be reckoned with, but everyone who knew Robert Clark knew he had a big heart to match his large size. It just wasn't always apparent in his staunch protectiveness of his three daughters, especially his eldest daughter who happened to be of dating age.

His youngest daughter Carrie, now eight years old, was somewhat of a daddy's girl. He never had to wonder what she had been up to because she pretty much stuck close to his side. She was always ready to help with a project and loved getting her hands dirty. She delighted in doing just about anything with her father when he was home. She loved playing games and simply had a zest for life. There really wasn't anything she didn't like…well, except picking eggs. She'd do about anything to get out of that chore.

And there was Lydia, the middle of his three girls. She had just turned 14 and was becoming quite the young lady. She was quieter. She did her chores as asked without contest, being quick to finish them so she could find an empty corner and snuggle in with another book. She'd be lost for hours in a book if her father and mother didn't make her come up for air once in a while.

Robert was chopping wood and had his back to her when Jessie came home. As his eldest daughter at 17 years old, Jessie was definitely starting to test her boundaries, but she always had a way with him. A way straight to his heart through his tough facade. He was protective of her, yes, but with her being the oldest, he had to be. The day was coming when she would leave their nest, and he wanted her ready for the world. He wanted the best for her as only any loving father would.

He knew she was trying to discreetly slip by into the house unnoticed. He stopped his incessant chopping and turned towards Jessie, "Took you awhile getting home from school today?" He raised his eye brow waiting for her to reply.

"Hi, Daddy! Oh, it did, I know! Today was so hot sittin' in that stuffy classroom, and I kept daydreamin' about walkin' through the shade of Eden's Pathway. So, I took that route home today. I just had to catch the colors of fall before the wind takes it away," she rattled off her answer giving herself away with her obvious nervous chatter.

"Was *he* with you?"

She skipped over his question. "Daddy, you should've seen Eden's Pathway today! Seriously, paradise. The reds, the golds, the oranges, and last savored shades of green from the summer."

"What about brown?"

Confused, but a little relieved her daddy was following her rabbit trail to distract him, she responded, "Oh yes, and brown. Although," she pondered out loud, "brown wouldn't necessarily be my favorite color of the fall splendor. I love all the vibrant other colors. Brown is more the end of the colors for fall."

"Hmmm, I thought you enjoyed brown the most," he said with teasing in his voice. "Wasn't it the color brown you were talkin' about to your mother of *that boy's* 'dreamy eyes' that I believe you said you liked so much...or was it 'chocolate' how you described them?"

"Daddy!" she exclaimed clearly embarrassed that he must have overheard a conversation meant just for her mother's ears. She fumbled through her words, flustered with what to say. "He...*that boy*...has a name," she stuttered and stammered a bit trying to regain her composure. "And yes, *James* and his brown eyes... or chocolate...or...or whatever I said, was walkin' with me."

"You forgot 'dreamy'. Yes, I do think it was 'dreamy' you told your mama," he said without looking up, but clearly enjoying his own banter.

"You're impossible," she gushed as she swung her arms around her father breaking through his gruff outer shell.

"I can't help it. Your mama told me."

"That was just for her."

"Well, I probed her a bit. I figured I needed to try find out more about this boy since *I hear* he's courtin' my daughter."

"Daddy, you could've just asked me."

"Well, I thought maybe if he really is as *'dreamy'* as you say, you might actually bring him here to formally meet your family."

"You haven't given me much of a choice, Daddy! You don't exactly make it easy for me to bring *any* boy around here."

"Oh? How many other boys do you wanna bring around here?" Robert dropped his voice tone a bit to sound more authoritative.

"See! Impossible, Daddy!" Jesse looked at her father and shook her head. "There are no other boys. Just James. And you make it difficult to bring him home, you know. Intimidatin' actually."

"Well, now I suppose that may be true. But, it can't just be *any* boy that courts my Jessie May Clark. He better be of good stock. Needs to have a good head on his shoulders and a focus in life. My stamp of approval is needed. And in order to do that," he paused with just enough seriousness to speak his mind gently, "I need to meet him."

"Well, Daddy, we actually were just talkin' about that on our way home."

Her father raised one eyebrow again looking in her direction. He hoped with his stern disposition he could detour his daughter's ambition. But, it didn't surprise him that his eldest daughter determined both in spirit and faith with a *healthy* touch of stubbornness –as he liked to say – should press on. She was more like him than he'd often like to admit.

Without really thinking, she blabbered off an answer, "I maybe…kind of, sort of, possibly already invited him without really askin' you and Mama."

"Spit out the details."

"I possibly invited him this Sunday after church to come for Mama's fried chicken." She was making it up as she went, but her daddy didn't need to know that. "James was so thrilled to be invited."

"Jessie May, you know you should've cleared that with your mama first before invitin' someone out on a whim like that. You know how your mother likes fair warnin'. She likes things *just so* when she's hostin', everythin' in place," he spoke, disgruntled.

"I know, I will next time, Daddy. I'm sorry. Mama will understand. She's been wantin' to meet him too.

I am just so excited for you both to meet James. I will talk with Mama. If it's not okay, then I will make up some excuse and tell James we need a raincheck. Please, Daddy? And, just maybe James said he'd bring his mama's famous pecan pie to go with the fried chicken." She was going in for the kill. She knew her daddy's weakness---pie.

Robert paused clearly wanting his daughter to know he held the authority still. She stared at him, anxious for his approval and answer.

"*Famous* pecan pie, huh?" Robert cocked his head. "How come I ain't ever heard of it before?"

Again her arms swung around her father. She knew she had him. "Ohhhh, thank you, Daddy!"

"I didn't say yes."

"You didn't say no!" she squeezed her father's neck. "I know you can't resist a good pecan pie! As Mama always says, 'The best way to a man's heart is through his stomach!'"

"Oh, she does, does she? Hmmph, married 26 years and she thinks she knows me so well!" He tried to hold the upper hand, but knew he didn't have much of a poker face anymore. Robert reached for Jessie's hands with his. They were enormous compared to hers and quite dirty from chopping wood. He pulled her into a full embrace, an embrace she had known all her life. It was powerful, but gentle. He spoke warmly, "I just want the best for you."

She squeezed her father. Yes, she certainly had a way with him. They had a very special relationship. Jessie never doubted her daddy's love for her and his unconditional love and strength for their family. It grounded her…well, next to her faith in her heavenly Father. She knew she owed all her blessings to God. But yes, in this life, she was so grateful the Lord had blessed her with her daddy, who was her rock. And now she couldn't wait for him to meet James Patterson, the other man of importance in her life. She just knew he'd approve. She smiled thinking about them both. And with that, she knew she better get ahold of James to tell him he needed to bring a pie because "soon" was indeed just about to happen!

* * *

James hustled. He was late meeting his buddies. They had agreed they'd meet in the morning at Linny's Tavern at 9:00. Hustling to meet up with his cronies, he noticed some tables set up along the board walk. A sign read, "We need you!" It was a U.S. Army recruiter. James had his head turned, still reading the sign, when he felt a punch on his shoulder, "You're late," his buddy Bobby Ray poked at him. "If we're goin' to line up any gig at all, late ain't gonna get it."

His best buddies – and band members – stood staring at him. There was Bobby Ray who had no qualms about bluntly speaking his mind. And thinking he was finer than frog hair split four ways, he easily had the biggest ego of the group. Then there was Nathaniel who always kept the group on an even keel. He had a laid-back temperament and was

12

perceptive and sensitive to others. And finally, there was Ricky James who just kind of followed the gang and did whatever they wanted. He was about as easy-going as they came. They referred to Ricky James as RJ so that there wouldn't be any confusion between him and James.

"Okay, okay, sorry guys, I'm late," he tossed his hands up in the air. "Did you see if Linny is there yet, so I can go talk to him?" James was the leader of the group.

"I saw him behind the bar wipin' down glasses when I walked by. He seemed kind of crabby," Ricky said.

"I got this, RJ!" James said with a wink and shrug of one shoulder. "Be right back."

He entered Linny's Tavern. "Hey Lin, what's up?"

"Just cleanin' up last night's mess to get ready for tonight's," Linny grumbled as he continued to dry glasses and hang them on the rack above his head.

"Say, I thought I'd pop in because a couple of weeks ago when I ran into you fishin' you mentioned possibly playin' one day here and givin' my band some exposure," James said.

"Yeah, what about it?" Linny didn't look up from the glass he was polishing with his white terrycloth.

"So, how about today?"

"Kid, I said some day."

"Yeah, so why not today? Today is *some* day, ain't it?"

"Today?" Linny asked with skepticism.

"You won't be disappointed," James poured on the charm. "Neither will your patrons. We're good, Linny. You'll see. And so will they. They'll be beggin' you to have us back," he paused with the look of youthful determination. "Give us a chance? Today."

Linny could already see the tenacity in James' eyes and knew he wasn't going to give up easily. And truth be told, he also knew his pub could use a new act. Anything that could draw new customers. He was curious what this persistent kid had to offer.

"Alright, you get from 2:00-4:00 today."

"2:00-4:00?" James had a disappointed look on his face, "Lin, that's like yarn-barn time." Linny gave him an odd look. "You know… just the ladies. Broads and Bridge time!" James really wanted the prime time of the evening. The thrill of playing in the tavern when all the locals flooded into the pub for a little happy hour…when it was packed.

"You're underage, kid. Take or leave it," was the only response from Linny.

"Lin, I'm 18. I turned the end of August."

"Yeah, well your other three hoodlums aren't. So like I said, take it or leave it. That's the time I'm offerin'…today." He said the last word with emphasis. A corner of Linny's mouth lifted a little with a smile. He liked the kid whether he wanted to admit it or not.

"We're good, Linny. Really good. It'd be good for business."

Linny knew the potential of that to be true, but he held his ground. Whether he liked the kid or not, he was going out on a limb and wanted to make sure it was in fact good for his business. "You may be good, but you're underage. That's the time I got for you to play."

James could see that Linny was not going to budge on the time…for now anyway! So, he conceded and put out his hand to shake Linny's, "Deal! We'll come in at 1:00 to get set up and warm up a bit. You won't regret this, Lin. Thanks!" He waved to Linny over his shoulder and headed out the door to let his band know the plan.

* * *

When James came out of Linny's Tavern, his buddies were leaning against the wooden fence rail waiting to hear if they had a gig or not. James tried to keep a straight face and remain stoic, but he wasn't very good at hiding his excitement. A smile began to stretch across his face. His friends knew that grin. He had struck a deal.

"We get to play today, boys!"

"That's awesome!" Bobby Ray said excitedly. "I'll have to let my mama know I won't be home for supper! She's makin' catfish and hushpuppies tonight and my granny and pawpaw arc comin', but I can miss for this. This is great!"

"You'll be home for supper. We play 2:00-4:00," James said.

"What? That's when the ladies play Bridge." The disappointment was evident in Bobby Ray's tone. "Linny wouldn't give us anythin' else? I mean, I love my mama's catfish and all, but I wanna play prime time. 2:00-4:00 is nothin'."

"Yeah!" the other guys started chiming in.

"Hey, it's not nothin'. It's somethin' and it's just the start…for today," James said giving them a wink. "They'll hear us and word will spread fast. Linny will be askin' us back. For the evenin' gig. I could see it in Lin's face, but he's checkin' us out, fellas. We have to prove ourselves first. And trust me, it's not goin' to take much to convince him. He's ready for somethin' new and we're it, boys!" He let out a whoop! "Wait 'til he hears us! I told Lin we'd be back at 1:00 to set up, so let's meet back here then."

They talked with an excited buzz a bit longer before deciding they better get going if they were going to be back after dinner. "Hey, y'all go on ahead. I'll hook up with you at 1:00." The recruiter's booth that first caught his eye wouldn't quit invading his thoughts. Ricky, Bobby Ray, and Nathaniel each gave him an inquisitive look.

"Don't make us late," Bobby Ray said, knowing James and his shenanigans all too well.

"Yeah, come on, Jimbo," Nathaniel razzed him, "we gotta get all our stuff together and eat yet. We can't be late for our first gig."

"Guys, I got time," his words were drawn out with his laid-back southern accent. "We don't have to be back until 1:00. There's somethin' I wanna check out." Ricky, Bobby Ray, and Nathaniel stopped simultaneously as they each noticed the object of James' gaze.

This time Ricky was the first to speak, "James, don't. We know what you're goin' over there to check out. And we know you. You can't leave us. We're just takin' off and gettin' good. Our band needs you. We still need our bass guitar player, too, and you said you'd help us find one. And without you…well, this band ain't a band without you."

"RJ…guys," James reassured all of them, "I'm not leavin' the band. I'm just checkin' things out. Haven't you boys been payin' attention to the news?" His buddies were staring straight at him. "Things are escalatin'. That Gulf of Tonkin thing that happened about a month ago has changed things. And now that I'm 18, I might be needed. President Johnson's already been authorized to put boots on the ground."

"But why not wait? See if you're drafted?" Nathaniel asked casually.

"My cousin Jacob is 18," said Bobby Ray, "and he said there's no way he's goin' to Vietnam. He said he's goin' to live with my daddy's sister. She married a guy from Canada and lives somewhere in Vagina or somewhere like that."

Ricky, Bobby Ray, and Nathaniel laughed.

"That's Regina! And I don't find that funny at all," James was not amused. He didn't find their crude humor or making light of the situation amusing in the slightest. "That's a draft dodger, by the way, and it's illegal. I'm not a draft dodger."

"We know you're not," Nathaniel said smoothingly. "I don't think Bobby Ray was implyin' that about you, just tellin' about Jake, that's all. And, I was just askin' my daddy about it since I'm turnin' 18 next month and he said there are ways to legally defer bein' drafted. He said there's a waiver thing we can do since we are farmers. I wouldn't have to go because our occupation is essential to the country. And when I was askin' him about you, James, since you turned 18 already, he told me that you probably could get deferred, too, since you wanna go to college to become a teacher."

"And that'd be legal, by the way," Bobby Ray jabbed with a hint of sarcasm as if to imply that James wasn't the only brains in the group.

"Look, I love you boys. You're like brothers to me…the brothers I never had," James responded. He took in a deep breath, "I know you don't understand, but now that I'm 18 I just feel I need to do my part. I don't know…it's more, *I wanna do my part*." He paused with an intentional seriousness that was rare for him. "I can't turn away from that," his expression lightened again. "Besides, guys," he paused as a grin grew across his face, "maybe that's where I'd find our bass guy!" he said jabbing RJ in the ribs playfully.

"Come on!" Nathaniel tilted his head like a dog does when you speak to it. Now it was his buddies who were not the least bit amused.

James went on trying to convince them. "You were right, RJ, thanks for remindin' me. We do need a bass. I'm our lead vocals and guitar. Bobby Ray, you're great with the piano. Nathaniel, you got drums. And RJ, ain't nobody can beat you on the fiddle or your voice for harmony, but you were definitely right – we do need a bass guitar. And we haven't had any luck findin' one here, fellas. Maybe it's time I start lookin' elsewhere. You never know, I might just find one in the army, boys!" With that he gave a firm retaliating punch to Bobby Ray's arm. He gave them no time for rebuttals as he took off calling back over his shoulder, "See you at 1:00 and don't be late, dopes." He raised his fist high in the air, "We got us our first gig, boys!"

* * *

As James walked up to the tables set up for the recruiter's booth, he stared intently at the sign now that he was closer to read it fully.

**We need you. Your nation needs you. President Johnson needs you.
Sign up today and go make a difference in this war where YOU ARE NEEDED!**

There was another guy there and the recruiter was talking with him. James recognized the other guy from school, Hank Timball. He was a senior too. He wasn't in any sports, but his body physique sure said otherwise. He had a frame that looked ready for the military. He was a smart kid, but James really hadn't talked much to him. James approached the booth off to the side table. The recruiter was handing Hank a clipboard telling him to fill out the form and that he'd take care of the rest. The recruiter noticed James the same time as Hank and both glanced in James' direction. Hank gave a small head nod. James reciprocated with a nonverbal hello.

"Lookin' to sign up too?" the recruiter asked wasting no time. Any lad that the recruiter didn't have to beckon over was already a "yes" in his book.

"I can wait for you to finish with Hank," James responded.

"Here, you can read this while you wait," the recruiter said handing James a pamphlet. The pamphlet had a picture of Uncle Sam pointing straight at James with the words "I Want You For U.S. Army. Enlist Now." James started to skim the pamphlet and, before long, Hank was gone. The recruiter's full attention was now turned to James. They took their time visiting. The recruiter was in no rush. He was very polished, knowing exactly what to say to rally James' pride and patriotism. James didn't know how long they actually stood there talking, but as he walked away he had a proud smile on his face and his head held high.

* * *

James knew Jessie would be coming into town to drop off her mama's eggs. She did every Saturday. He sat down on the curb just outside Pugsy's Grocery to wait for her. When he saw her coming, he got so excited he jumped up and hustled out into the street to greet her. He didn't even look for a car. "Jessie May!" he took her in his arms.

"James!" she squealed, "You're lucky a car wasn't comin'! You're worse than Carrie Grace! And you better be careful or you're goin' to break the eggs! My mama would have your hide, James Patterson! What's got into you?" She sensed his excitement and was all too curious.

"We got ourselves our first gig!"

"What? That's great! Oh my goodness! When? Where?" She was excited now too.

"Today!" he exclaimed.

"Really? Today?" Surprise showed on her face. She was so proud of his musical talent and so thrilled to see his band finally getting its start.

"Yeah, we play at Linny's Tavern. He agreed to let us come in at 2:00 to play for a couple hours. Get some exposure. I know it's not the best time, but it's a start, Jess!"

"Oh, that's great, James! I'm so happy for you! Tell the guys that too! I wish I could be there, but there's no way Daddy would let his girl sit in a tavern alone."

"It's okay, Babe, I know you would be there if you could. I'll sing you our songs later," he picked her up off her feet and raised her up in his arms hugging her.

"James, the eggs!" she squealed with laughter. He made her so giddy.

After he put her down, she looked at him and sighed, "I have good news for you too."

"Oh, you do?" he said with an inquisitive grin. "What is it?"

"You get to meet my parents sooner rather than later."

"That's awesome. When?"

"Um, like maybe tomorrow."

"Seriously! Tomorrow? Oh Jess!" he went to pick her up again, but she just shook her head and playfully wagged her finger at him, protecting her basket of eggs.

"Yes, after church for dinner. And I maybe told my daddy you offered to bring somethin'…like your mama's pecan pie," she said sheepishly.

"Jessie May, what am I goin' to do with you?" he laughed, pausing momentarily. "I don't think we need to worry about your mama gettin' my hide. It'll be my own!"

"Sorry, James, I know. It just kind of came out. I was nervous."

"It's okay, Jess. I'll be there tomorrow…with the pie," he shook his head, "if my mama doesn't skin me first."

* * *

"Robert, please help me get this stuff picked up and put away," Patty said. "Land sakes alive! I can't believe that girl! Invitin' people over without first okayin' it with her mama." She shook her head mumbling as she tidied the kitchen. "If you could take care of this, please; I can't have this stack of old newspapers clutterin' up my cookin' space."

"Yes, yes my dear," Robert chuckled to himself being careful she didn't notice lest he strike an unwanted nerve with his wife. She always did a wonderful job of hosting. But after being married for 26 years, Robert would tell you this about his wife – she pole vaulted over mouse turds. He'd often tell her that. He'd tell his wife not to sweat such small things. He rubbed his chin. He thought he'd remind his wife of that now, but just as he turned to open his mouth…

"Carrrrrie! Did you bring this mud in here?" Patty shrieked, pressing her hands firmly on her hips. She stood there staring with disgust at the dirty floor by the back door that went to the chicken coop.

Well, on second thought – Robert reconsidered – *if he knew what was good for him, he'd better just get to this pile of newspapers he had said he would put away.* He slid the pile of newspapers from the back corner of the table. *Why didn't he just throw these papers away when he was done readin' them?* Patty had been asking him that for years and he'd always

23

told her, "Because there might be somethin' I missed." Truth was, he never went back to read them and now, each one was old news. Patty was right; it was a cluttered mess. He scooped the pile up and walked over to the garbage to toss them out. The top paper was from the first part of August. He scanned over a heading, "Johnson Antipoverty Bill Approved in House, 228-190, But Foes Balk Final Vote; Critics Repulsed." Robert half grunted. He couldn't help but balk himself, "I'll still somehow be scrapin' the bottom of the barrel tryin' to make ends meet." And with that, he tossed the papers in the garbage and set to helping his little clucking wife before the next shriek was his own name.

Chapter 2
Dinner Guest

Sunday Jessie could hardly concentrate on the sermon at church. Her stomach rolled with anticipation. James was coming for dinner. She felt badly, but she couldn't focus on anything but James. The fact that he finally was going to meet her family made her squirm inside with excitement. *He was meeting her family!* Her thoughts raced in her head. *Her daddy.* Oh, she should have prepared James more for her daddy. Though Jessie knew he was harmless, just protective, he could sure give a different impression to others. Matter of fact, often a very cold and unwelcoming impression. But if she was going to become Mrs. James Patterson someday, she needed to get this over with. She heard Pastor Mark clear his throat and begin closing his sermon: "For I know the plans I have for you, declares the LORD. Plans to prosper you and not to harm you, plans to give you hope and a future."

Ah yes, Jeremiah 29:11 – one of her favorite scriptures. She really hadn't heard any other part of Pastor Mark's sermon, but this caught her ears distinctly. She could always hear when God was speaking to her. His timing in nudging her was perfect. Surely God knew the plans He had for her…especially now as all she could think about was her family meeting James Patterson, the young man she wanted to marry. Yes, plans to give hope and a future indeed. She smiled. The service was coming to a close and that meant one thing to her.

James was comin' to dinner!

* * *

The knock on the door shouldn't have startled her. She had been waiting for him to arrive since they walked in the door from church. She tried to be helpful in the kitchen for her mother. However, the knife in her hand peeling potatoes seemed foreign. She just couldn't keep her focus. She was giddy and chatty with her mother. When the firm knock reverberated on their front door, announcing the arrival of their guest, she jumped and quickly set down her knife. She called out loudly. The whole house heard her---she would get the door. Had they lived in town, the whole town of Cordova would have heard her excited proclamation. She raced to the door, stopped abruptly, swept back the hair across her forehead and tucked it behind her ear. She took a deep breath to calm herself and opened the door. There he was, handsome as ever, still wearing his Sunday best. His brown hair was slicked off to the side, not his usual tousled hair. And there were those eyes staring back at her. Those gorgeous brown eyes. Those *dreamy eyes*. She almost giggled to herself as she quickly recalled her conversation with her daddy Friday after school. She couldn't believe her mama told her daddy that.

"You look beautiful, Miss Clark," his voice snapped her out of her thoughts. "I mean, *Jessie May*." He gave a smile and a quick wink which eased her anxious soul. She loved his humor and comfortable personality. He leaned forward and whispered in her ear, "You take my breath away."

There it was, her heart racing again. He smelled yummy. She wanted to drink in more, but she stepped back and with a long breath to regain control, she replied, "Thank you, you clean up pretty well yourself, Mr. Patterson."

"Now, why is it that you get to call me Mr. Patterson, but I cannot call you Miss Clark?" he asked teasingly.

"Because, you can't get used to callin' me Miss *Clark*…I won't be that for long." She gave a playful smile. James loved that about her. In all her seriousness, there was light-heartedness about her. He leaned in again, gave her a quick hug and then snuck a little kiss on her lips softly and stepped inside.

He was carrying the pecan pie in his hands. Clearly, his mama hadn't skinned him after all.

* * *

Jessie's mother was adding the last heaping tablespoon of flour to a bowl of cream. She was just about to make her gravy. She began to gently whisk the contents in the bowl when James walked into the kitchen behind Jessie. "Mama, this is James, the young man I've told you about. James, this is my mama, Patricia, but you can just call her Patty. Everyone else does."

"It's very nice to meet you, Miss Patty." James held out his hand to shake Patty's.

Patty wiped her hands on her apron and shook James' hand, "It's very nice to meet you as well, James." Jessie's mother spoke with a welcoming, soft and genuine tone. James nodded respectfully. She continued, "I've heard such nice things about you from Jessie May. And thank you for bringin' the pecan pie, somethin' else I've heard good things about." She smiled, "You can just set it on the counter and go on ahead in the livin' room. Robert and Carrie Grace are in there right now playin' a game of Dutch Blitz. Carrie Grace is hopin' we'll play that after dinner, so she's tryin' to brush up on her playin' skills with her father! So go on in, I've got things under control in here. Lydia Ruth is out pickin' eggs, and when she's done, she can give a hand in here. So go on now before I change my mind and put company to work!" Patty smiled and flicked her wrist in the direction of the door to shoo them out.

Jessie glanced over her shoulder to James as she walked through the hallway just before entering the living room. James was grinning. He didn't show any inkling of nerves. She wished she could say the same. Jessie felt her stomach roll. She wanted to stop and give James a crash course in the do's and don'ts of meeting her father. Why hadn't she thought to do that until now? She could hear her sister rattling away about who-knows-what with her daddy while they played their game. She was glad Carrie was in the room with her father. She was a chatterbox. And when she introduced James to her daddy, Carrie would be the ice breaker for sure. *This time* Jessie would be grateful for Carrie's nonstop chatter.

"Hi, Daddy," Jessie greeted her father upon entering the room. "I'd like you to meet a *special* friend." She seemed to emphasize the importance of James being special to her with her introduction so her father would hopefully take the hint and go easy on him. Robert stuck out his hand. A firm handshake was something her father always said would tell a lot about a person. If they didn't give a firm handshake, he took that as a bad sign right off the bat.

James without any hesitation, firmly gripped Robert's outstretched hand and giving him full eye contact replied, "Very nice to meet you, Mr. Clark. I'm honored to have the acquaintance of your daughter and to finally meet her family."

"Sit down," her father motioned to the chair beside the couch. "Tell me about yourself."

Here we go, thought Jessie. *Geez, Daddy, let him get in, take his coat off, get comfortable a bit, a few casual conversation starters…but noooo, instead, drill him right away. Let's just get right to it.*

"Yes, sir, what would you like to know?" James didn't seem a bit frazzled by Robert's direct and immediate interrogating approach.

"Your family, tell me about them. Jessie May tells me you just turned 18. What do you plan to do with your life? What are your plans after high school?"

Gosh, Daddy, why don't you just ask him if he plans to be a loser in life? Or more specifically, does he plan on ruinin' your daughter's life or in what way could he possibly intend on makin' it better? Certainly, that would be much more direct and less beatin' around the bush, Daddy. Jessie took a breath. She waited, wondering how James would respond.

Carrie interrupted. She wasn't waiting for his answer, "You didn't introduce me, Jessie May!" And again, Carrie didn't wait; she just introduced herself, "I'm Carrie Grace! I'm so excited because we're goin' to play Dutch Blitz together. I've been practicin' and I wanna beat you. Daddy said I have to be polite, but beatin' isn't bein' rude. It just means I am better at it than you. But we don't have to play right away. I can take you and give you a tour of our house. My bedroom is pink and I have new curtains. I helped Mama make them and helped Daddy hang them up. They have pink roses on them. I can show you our yard too. I'll show you the chickens…but I won't show you how to pick eggs. I don't like that. They peck your hands when you try to take their eggs."

He smiled at Carrie and stuck his hand out to meet her too, "Pleased to meet you, Miss Carrie. Jessie May has told me lots about you and that you're very good at games. And yes, I'd love to see your curtains you made. I bet they are better than any Fancy sells at her Mercantile!" Carrie proudly smiled back. "When I'm done visitin' with your daddy, I'll take you up on that tour," he winked at her. Carrie--quite pacified--nodded happily. Then he turned his attention back to Robert. He seemed to sense that

Robert was in no rush and was waiting for a complete answer---who he was, where he came from, what he wanted to do with his life. So, James cleared his throat and began by going into a full account of his whole family.

"Well, Mr. Clark, my mama is Rita and she's married to my step-daddy John. They got married about three years ago. My daddy, Bennett, died when I was seven. He had cancer of the pancreas."

"I'm sorry to hear that, son."

"Thank you, sir. I don't remember a whole lot about him, but I know he was a good man. My step-daddy is a nice enough man; he makes my mother happy and that makes me happy. I've probably given him a bit of a hard time, but we get along and I'm glad he married my mother. We live in town right behind Golden Valley Baptist church, if you know where that is?" Jessie's father nodded, his expression remaining straight and focused. James continued casually, "My step-daddy is an insurance agent. He works with Fleck's Insurance. I think it's his eighth year there. And my mama, she works at Pugsy's Grocery in their bakery. That's where she's perfected her pecan pie and I think you're goin' to enjoy your dessert today, Mr. Clark." He looked over at Jessie – a little wink and then grin of satisfaction on his face. She knew he was banking on the old adage Jessie had shared with him that her mother always said…the *best way to a man's heart is through his stomach*. But he didn't know her father. This only worked for her mother.

"I love pecan pie. It's my favorite!" Carrie to the rescue again.

Thank you, God, for my little sister. Jessie couldn't help but smile at her sister.

"What's your favorite?" Carrie wanted to know, her impulsive curiosity getting the best of her.

James smiled so warmly at Carrie it made Jessie's heart melt. He leaned forward with both elbows on his knees, his hands folded, and turned towards Carrie to give her eye contact again, "I love pecan too. That's my favorite. I guess we have somethin' in common." Carrie's grin reached ear to ear. Fully satisfied with his answer, she looked over at her daddy and smiled.

Robert smiled back at his youngest daughter and then pressed on, "And how about you, James? Tell me more about you."

"Yes, so to finish with my family first," Robert wasn't the only one who wasn't in a hurry. James wasn't intimidated in the least and he liked talking about his family. "I have only one siblin', an older sister Elizabeth, she's 21 and married. She and her husband moved to Birmin'ham. I guess they wanted more city life than country livin'. They don't have any children and I'm not sure they wanna have kids. So, I'm not an uncle, but I'd like to be. I love children and hope to be half as good of a family man as you some day." He looked over at Jessie and subtlety winked at her.

Jessie's father turned his head and looked right at her. Robert was no dummy; clearly he knew the implication of James' wink. Jessie squirmed a bit in her chair. *James had better stop that winkin' of his or it might just get him in trouble with her father. And further, flattery would get him nowhere with her father.*

James continued, "As for me, sir, I like school. I'll graduate with honors and I plan to go to college. I'm thinkin' about becomin' a teacher and maybe goin' on and teachin' at a university. I love English and music, so I think I'd like to teach in the arts. I play in a band right now, and just yesterday we played our first gig at Linny's Tavern." James broke his eye contact with Jesse's father and looked over at her. She smiled at him. The look on her face showing her pride and support always reaffirmed him. He loved that she shared his passion for his band and loved to hear him play. Although hearing about playing at Linny's Tavern, a bar, did not seem to impress her father at all.

"Well, music can only take you so far, son," Robert commented.

"Yes, but I believe bein' in a band will really make me be a better teacher. I think that my experience leadin' the band will help me to be more organized. I think that will make me more assertive when I seek to get a job at a university someday, which I hope to do." Now he was starting to sweat a little under his collar. James could feel he was going nowhere with her father. Robert's expression remained unimpressed as he slowly stroked his chin. *Jessie was right; he was a tough nut to crack.* How could he get her father to see how serious he was with his intentions for his daughter? He decided to share his other exciting news. He wanted to share it with Jessie first. That was his plan yesterday when he saw her at Pugsy's, but he was so excited to tell her about his gig first. Then she told him about coming for Sunday dinner and with that he just merely got distracted and forgot. Now it just felt like the timing was presenting itself with her father wanting to know his future plans. Jessie would understand. *She'd probably be happy he told them together.* With confidence, he continued, "And sir, well, I'm goin' to honor my country. I'm goin' to serve in the army, in the war if I have to. I signed up yesterday. The recruiter said our country needs us now more than ever. They wanna build the strength of our military. The recruiter said that with Johnson's authorization to send military forces over, it won't be long. Young men like me will be needed to go overseas. I'm goin' to do my country right, sir. And I hope that my actions would bring honor not only to my country but to you, sir, your family, and especially your daughter."

At the mention of her, both men looked over at Jessie. Jessie's face was ashen with utter shock. Her mouth hung open. Her eyes were glazed. She looked like she was going to pass out. Robert quickly picked up on the fact that this must have come as a surprise to his daughter, softened and let up for the first time since James had been introduced. "That sounds like a very honorable thing to do. Your parents must be proud," he said.

"You're a soldier!" Carrie exclaimed, "Wow! Can I get your autograph?"

James didn't turn Carrie's direction this time. He couldn't take his eyes off Jessie. Their eyes were locked. She just kept staring at him. Her eyes glistened. He couldn't tell what she was thinking.

* * *

Jessie was speechless. Had she heard James correctly? Had James really just told her father that he had enlisted in the army? She could feel her heart pounding through her chest and suddenly she felt short of breath. Her chest hurt actually. Her palms were sweating and her knees seemed to be shaking even though she was sitting. Every muscle in both her legs seemed to be tightening. Why was the room moving and her ears ringing? She tried to remember what exactly James had just told her father.

"So…can I get your autograph?" Carrie repeated.

* * *

Silence. James didn't answer. He really didn't hear Carrie. He just kept staring at Jessie. She wasn't saying anything. Her expression was blank. He wanted to know what she was thinking. Her thoughts---her opinion---meant everything to him. *Why didn't he wait to tell her first? What a fool he was.* He'd been so concerned with making the right impression with her father, but he should have told her first.

35

Jessie's father broke the unbearable silence, "Why don't we go and see if your mama needs any last bit of help gettin' the meal on the table. I think I just heard Lydia come in. James, you'll wanna meet Lydia Ruth before she goes scootin' off to some corner with a book again. She's always got her nose in a book. You'll be lucky if you see much of her today." Robert forced a smile at his attempt with humor. He patted Jessie's back gently, "Come on, sweetheart, let's go help your mama."

* * *

Dinner was delicious. Patty's fried chicken and mashed potatoes never disappointed. Typically when she served this meal, everyone ranted and raved from the first savory bite to the last morsel licked up on the plate. But this meal was oddly quieter than normal, especially with having a new guest. And Robert of all people was the one trying to make small talk. He visited casually with James, and they truly seemed to hit it off. It must have gone well before dinner, but Patty was confused because something seemed off. There was something uncomfortable in the air; she could feel it. And Jessie had hardly said a word. She was the exact opposite from what she had been prior to James' arrival. That mixed with the fact that Robert was doing most of the talking, continuously coming up with conversation topics, was a dead giveaway that something had happened and was bothering Jessie.

Patty wondered what had gone on in the living room during introductions. Had Robert crossed boundaries and been too hard on James? Was this what was troubling her daughter? But when Patty glanced at James and Robert visiting, James didn't seem put off by Robert at all. They seemed to be visiting together quite comfortably. She knew that Jessie had been nervous about her protective father meeting James. She recalled their conversation earlier in the kitchen while Jessie helped get dinner ready. *Mama, I know that Daddy is just goin' to drill James when he gets here! Why does he have to be so hard on any boy I've ever shown an interest in? This time, this is different with James, Mama. I have never felt this way about anyone. I don't want him scared away by Daddy interrogatin' him.*

She had patted her daughter's hand and calmly reassured Jessie that it was just his "Papa Bear" that came out of him and that he truly meant no harm. Robert was just protective of her, of all his girls. He didn't want anything bad to ever happen to his girls. They were his world. He wanted only the best for his girls. But now, she wondered. *Oh Robert, what did you do or say?* she fretted to herself. Had he crossed a line and put his foot in his mouth? Yet, she couldn't figure it out because James did not seem the least bit uncomfortable or offended by Robert. In fact, those two dominated the conversation and appeared to have connected quite nicely. So, what was it that was bothering her daughter? There was something. She knew it, though she couldn't quite put her finger on it. She would certainly talk with Jessie later.

* * *

After dinner, everyone pitched in and gave a hand getting things put away and cleaned up. The afternoon spun by. Carrie gave James the tour of their house she had promised, pausing extralong at her room. She proudly showed off her curtains. Then they taught James how to play Dutch Blitz. It reminded him a lot of Solitaire. Carrie soaked up every minute. She and James teased back and forth just like a big brother and little sister would do. It felt like they had known each other for a while rather than just meeting that day. But as the hour grew late, James knew he needed to be going home. His mama was expecting him for supper. James cleared his throat and stood to make his exit. Carrie who usually followed her daddy wherever he went was now following someone else. She had found a new person she was infatuated with – James. Pretty much having stuck by his side all afternoon, she stood simultaneously when he did. Carrie assumed she would help Jessie walk James to the door to say good-bye.

"Carrie Grace, I'd like to say good-bye to James," Jessie's said, her voice quiet.

Carried nodded and stood waiting.

"Alone, please," Jessie intoned.

Carrie looked almost insulted when Jessie added the last part. James squatted down to eye level with Carrie and held out his hand. Carrie put her hand in his. "It was a pleasure meetin' you, Miss Carrie," James smiled and Carrie curtseyed. James let go of her hand and suddenly tousled her hair, "Even if you did give me a good wallop in Dutch Blitz."

She busted out in laughter and took off for the kitchen, yelling over her shoulder, "Winner gets the last piece of pie!"

* * *

Standing now in the entry way, they were alone for the first time that day. James turned and met Jessie's eyes. He took both her hands in his. She still said nothing. She just looked straight into his eyes. James knew Jessie very well. She was someone who was always thinking. He loved that about her. She pondered everything. And right now, he knew there were many thoughts going on behind those soft hazel eyes of hers. I guess he shouldn't expect anything less after finding out the way she did that he had enlisted in the army. And he also knew that they didn't have time, or the privacy for that matter, to talk about it at the moment. That was killing him inside, but he knew that now was not the time. *Why hadn't he been more mindful of that earlier? He was such a doofus.* It wasn't how she should have found out, he realized now. He had known it the moment he let the cat out of the bag to her father with Carrie in the room and he had seen the look of horror on Jessie's face. But, he'd do just as he did all day. Put on a facade like nothing was wrong. For now.

He leaned forward and gently kissed her on the side of the cheek. "I had a wonderful time. Your family is great. And I guess I should say thanks, Jess, for spontaneously volunteerin' me to bring that pecan pie…even if my mama wasn't happy with me for springin' it on her last minute!" He winked and cocked a half-sided, somewhat sad-looking, grin that lifted the corner of his mouth.

* * *

There it was. That dang wink. She couldn't help but smile back. She wasn't mad at him. Just surprised…and a little hurt. She wanted to ask him about signing up for the army. Up until a few hours ago, she had no idea he had signed up for the military nor even any knowledge that he had an inkling to do so. And then, she found out *with* her father. However, now was not the time. She'd have to find another time. Maybe tomorrow in school. Or maybe walking home. Maybe they could take Eden's Pathway on the way home again. Yes, she'd ask him then.

She forced a smile on her face, though small, but there for him to see. She wanted to reassure him she wasn't mad at him and that she still loved him. He had her heart.

* * *

Relieved, the smile being just what he needed, James hugged her. He held her slightly longer this time in their entry way and held her body firm against his. He could feel her breath on his neck and he could feel her heart beating just as hard as his was. Ever so quietly he whispered in her ear, "I love you, Jessie May Clark. And, I'm goin' to honor you…all the days of my life."

She had a quick fleeting thought. *All the days of his life.* In light of the news that she had just found out---that he could possibly be heading to Vietnam after

40

he graduated---*what did that mean? All the days of his life?* She squeezed her eyes shut tightly not wanting to cry. Not here, not now.

James pulled slightly away from their hug. He gently kissed her on the tip of her nose. Then he turned and opened the front door. He paused slightly and looked back at her as if he wanted to say something, but he didn't. He turned around, stepped outside and quietly shut the door behind him.

Jessie stood motionless. She heard the door of James' car outside as he closed it. She heard the engine start. She heard his tires crunch the gravel as he drove away. She could hear the clock on the wall ticking behind her. She stood there for some time. And then, without a word, she turned and walked straight up to her room and shut her door.

Chapter 3
Restless Minds

Patty was just finishing wiping the mess of supper off the table and shifted to wipe the counter. She cleaned up the crumbs left by Carrie devouring the last piece of pecan pie. *It was a delicious pie*, Patty nodded to herself. She would have to get Rita's recipe. She smiled. It had been a lovely afternoon and James seemed to be every bit of the charming young man that Jessie had told her about. Patty liked him. Matter of fact, it seemed he made a good first impression with everyone in their family.

James was so patient with Carrie. Patty sighed. Oh goodness, her youngest daughter definitely needed some rearing on social etiquette. All afternoon Carrie had smothered him, nearly sitting on his lap the entire game of Dutch Blitz. And not just clinging to him--- but oh goodness---her nonstop prattle. Oh, that girl could talk. But, he was so good with Carrie. He teased her like she was his little sister and yet validated what she added to the conversations. She smiled again thinking about how James had made Carrie feel an important part of the conversation.

James had also connected with their middle daughter Lydia. They each shared a love of literature and reading and writing. When James asked Lydia if she had read Roald Dahl's new book *Charlie and the*

Chocolate Factory, she had never seen her daughter Lydia become so animated in conversation. Lydia had recently gotten it for her birthday and it was her new favorite. James had made a lasting impression with Lydia as well.

And, Robert. Yes, peculiar as it was, her husband had changed his disposition and was more relaxed than she'd ever seen Robert around a boy interested in his daughter. He had visited casually all afternoon with James.

That brought Patty back to her concern with how quiet Jessie had been all afternoon. And at supper, she hardly spoke a word. Her eyes were red, as if she had been crying. Patty figured she was so tuckered out from introducing James to her father. She had excused Jessie from cleaning up supper to go get ready for the evening's end. Patty stood pensive for a moment. *Somethin' wasn't right. What was botherin' her?* Patty stopped what she was doing in the kitchen. She knew right then and there that she needed to go find Jessie and talk with her.

* * *

Patty poked her head into the living room. Robert sat in his favorite tan recliner. Both his arms tucked behind his head. The television was on and he was watching *The Ed Sullivan Show*. Lydia was sitting on the davenport next to Robert's chair. Of course, her nose was in a book. She was reading *Charlie and the Chocolate Factory*. She had already read the entire book, but Patty was quite sure her enlightened conversation with James spurred her to pick it up

43

again. A re-read of a book wasn't uncommon for Lydia or herself for that matter. Carrie must be up in her room, probably playing with her Barbie dolls. She figured Jessie was upstairs too.

She walked up the stairs and could hear voices coming from the first door on the left – Carrie's room. She discretely peeked in and could see Carrie sitting on her bedroom floor by her bed. Ken was in one hand and Barbie in the other. A teddy bear sat propped up in her lap. Carrie jostled her legs a little giving the bear some animation and spoke in a husky voice, "This is my youngest daughter, Carrie Grace, and my favorite." Carrie tilted Barbie towards the bear and spoke sweetly, "Oh, Daddy, your favorite? You're too kind." Then she began to gently shake Ken and let his masculine voice come to life, "Miss Carrie, aren't you just pretty as a peach. It's lovely to meet you. I've heard *so much* about you." Moving the hand holding Barbie she gave a little giggle, "Oh, James, how nice to meet you. I can't wait to play games with you." Patty had to stifle a laugh. How fitting that she chose the bear for Robert! *Papa Bear!* Patty almost chuckled out loud. Then she shook her head, *Favorite daughter. Oh, Carrie Grace!*

Patty smiled. To be young again without a care in the world. Carrie chattered away just like she had the entire afternoon with James. Patty lifted her chin and tilted her head up to the ceiling. *Thank you, God, for remindin' me that her prattle is the blessin' of a carefree eight-year-old. Thank you for Carrie Grace and that she keeps us on our toes and has a way of makin' our hearts light.*

It would soon be time for Carrie to take her bath and get ready for bed. It was a school night after all. But right now, Patty wanted to find Jessie and didn't want Carrie interrupting them while they were talking. She tip-toed quietly past Carrie's door so as not to disturb her. She walked past the bathroom. The next door across the hall on the right was Jessie's. The door was shut. She knocked lightly. No answer. She knocked one more time and opened it slowly, "Jessie May?" She peeked inside. There on the bed lay her daughter. Face down. Sobbing. Patty sat down next to Jessie and caressed her back with the loving gentleness of a mother, "What's wrong, sweetheart?"

Jessie sat up. Her eyes, lips, and nose were puffy, showing she had been crying for a while. "Oh, Mama!" she exhaled hard and fell into her mother's waiting arms.

* * *

Robert really couldn't get into watching *The Ed Sullivan Show* and it was too much work to get up and flick the channels to find something else engaging to watch. "Lydia Ruth, would you mind turnin' off the TV for me, please?" Lydia set her book down, got up, and turned the knob. The television screen went black. Lydia resumed her reading. *Maybe he should read the newspaper* he thought as he grabbed *The Walker County Tribune* lying on the coffee table next to him. He hadn't had a chance to read it earlier in the day like he usually enjoyed on his Sunday mornings after church. They had been too busy getting ready for their dinner guest to arrive. He nodded to himself. The day had certainly been an eventful one. **Absorbed** in his thoughts, he drifted to the look on his daughter's face when James told him that he had enlisted in the army. *Did Jessie not know he had signed up? She must have at least known he was thinkin' about it?* He wondered. *Certainly she had some idea. Right?* He huffed slightly. *They'd been spendin' enough time together. Surely they had talked about it.* He stared at the paper in his lap, the words a blur as he pondered the day. He heard his wife come in and sit down on the davenport next to him. He looked up. A look of concern was evident across her face. "Lydia Ruth, why don't you go and start gettin' ready for bed?" Robert said. Lydia didn't move. He put the foot rest of his recliner down and repeated with more volume, "Lydia Ruth?"

"Huh? What? Did you say somethin'?" she set her book down in her lap.

"Time to say goodnight to the Oompa Loompas and put your book away. It's time to get ready for bed."

"How do you know what an Oompa Loompa is?" Lydia asked with piqued interest.

"Oh, you're not the only one who reads in this house," he gave his daughter a mischievous look and then shooed her off to get ready.

"But it's just barely 8:00?" Lydia whined. "I'm 14 and Carrie Grace isn't even gettin' ready yet."

"Yes, but who takes the longest in the bathroom?" Robert asked. Lydia looked down at the book in her lap. "That's right, my dear. And if you wouldn't take

46

those books of yours into the bathroom, you wouldn't take as long. So, go start now. Your sisters will need to get in there soon too."

She stuck her bookmark in her book and stood up. As she walked by, Robert reached out for her. She leaned down and gave him a hug. He patted her arm and told her he'd come up and say goodnight in a little bit.

After Lydia was out of the room, Patty got up and sat down on the floor in front of Robert. She wrapped her arms over his knees. She wondered if her eyebrows and forehead were as creased as his. As she stared up at her husband, his face was twisted in concern. Her heart was troubled and, clearly, she could see the same heaviness was upon him, "What is it, Robert? What's troublin' you?" Patty had a hunch it had to do with the conversation she just had with Jessie, but she wanted to hear what Robert had to say about it.

Robert looked at Patty, his eyes meeting hers. He sighed and his tense expression relaxed. The lighting from the lamp next to him accentuated a softness in his features that not many people got to see, "I liked him, Patty."

She laughed, "And that troubles you?"

"Yes, because I see how much she likes him," he cocked his head upstairs to mean Jessie, as if Patty didn't know that already.

"Hmmm," Patty gave a loving look towards her husband. "She is 17, Robert." Patty paused slightly, "She seems so much like me when I was that age."

"Exactly, and you already had weddin' bells in those hazel eyes of yours at that age," he sighed as he lifted his arm and gently rubbed the back of his hand alongside her face. "It's obvious she cares deeply for him, but I saw somethin' in her face today I've never seen before. Beyond the dewy-eyed look of bein' in love. A look of fear… or shock… or… I don't know, Pats. I wish you would've been there." He sighed again, "While you were gettin' dinner ready, James told me that he had enlisted in the military, just yesterday matter of fact. And if you could have seen Jessie's face right then and there, Patty, your heart would've skipped a beat." Robert swallowed a lump in his throat. "Patty, I really think she had no clue."

"You're right, Robert. She didn't. She was clueless. The topic of enlistin' had never ever come up between them, not once." This time the sigh was hers. "I just came from her bedroom. I knew somethin' was wrong already at dinner. She was unusually quiet especially for how talkative and giddy *and loud* she was before James arrived. And it's not like Jessie to get quiet when she's nervous. If anythin', she gets chattier. I knew it had to be somethin' more. I just didn't know what. Then she disappeared after James left and didn't come and help with makin' supper like she usually does. Durin' supper, I noticed her eyes were red and she didn't say a word. I just found her now in her room cryin' her eyes out." Patty laid her head on Robert's lap for a moment. Then she looked up again, "Oh Robert, you are right in presumin' our daughter has marriage on her mind just like I did at her age. She told me that she and James have already talked about gettin' married." Robert shifted uncomfortably. "Settle down, Robert, not any time soon. They've just talked…about their future together…a future that never once included the military. She's scared, very scared, and I guess I don't blame her. Oh Robert, you need to go and talk with her."

It was times like these that Robert didn't feel he was a very strong head of the house. "Patty, I don't know what to say to her. I *should* as the leader of our family. I should know what to say, but I don't. I really don't wanna say anythin'. I just wanna scoop her up and let her feel protected and shielded from her hurt. I'd like to say somethin' that gives instant comfort, like a soothin' balm to her worries...but, Patty, nothin' comes to mind right now."

"Then maybe you're not meant to say anythin' tonight," Patty responded. "Maybe that's what she needs tonight. No more words. I guess I already talked with her and she's exhausted from cryin'. Right now she probably just needs some time alone to process what happened today. I know sometimes I'm not lookin' for words…just a presence and that is comfort enough." Patty picked up Robert's big rough hand in hers. "You are here, Robert, always for our family and she knows that. So, I guess, maybe let her come to you. She always does, eventually." She rubbed his hand. "I prayed with her before I left and encouraged her to talk with James tomorrow or as soon as she can, not let too much time go."

"You are wise, my love, come here," he gently tugged her hand to pull her up to him. She sat down on his lap and laid her head on his shoulder. He put his arm around her and tucked her small frame under his arm, "Let's pray together for our daughter…and James."

With the space closed between them, in a loving embrace, they bowed their heads together and began to pray.

* * *

The house was dark and quiet. Robert pealed himself from his recliner. He should have gone to bed with Patty a couple hours ago. He yawned. As he passed by their bedroom, he could hear the soft whistle of Patty's breathing while she inhaled and exhaled in her slumber. He paused but didn't go in. Instead, he walked to the stairway just as he did many nights before going to bed. He stopped for a moment at the bottom of the stairs. He rested his hand on the newel post. It was tacky to touch and with the humidity the smell of varnish still permeated the air. He could feel the grain of the wood underneath is fingertips. He gripped the wooden railing, drew in a breath, and then placed his foot on the first step. It moaned a soft creak as he placed his weight upon it and began ascending the stairs.

He really didn't know why he did it, maybe just in case he heard his girls stir and they needed their daddy to comfort them or tuck them back in like when they were little. But many nights before crawling into his own bed, he would go upstairs to where his girls slept. When he came to each of their doors, he would stop and reach up, place his hand on the trim above their door, and pray over them. Tonight, Robert's heart was heavy for Jessie. He walked to her bedroom door and gently reached his hand up and rested it above her doorway. He closed his eyes and silently prayed to his Father as he had done so many times before. Like when Jessie had broken her arm on the playground in the first grade or the next year in second grade when she broke her other arm on the playground again. Or for Lydia when her favorite kitten, Mittens, didn't come home for three days. Robert petitioned his Father to ease their suffering…to give it to him. He could take the pain, but he could not bear to see them suffer.

As he prayed for Jessie, tears streamed down his weathered cheeks. After some time, he brought his hand down and wiped the tears from his face. He turned around and sauntered to the stairway. Slowly, he made his way back down the stairs, each wooden step now feeling chilly to his bare feet. He entered his bedroom and eased into his bed. Patty hardly stirred from her sleep. He kissed the side of his wife's face and then rested his head comfortably on his pillow. Robert peacefully fell asleep, his mind at ease knowing his Father knew the desires of his heart and was in control of everything.

* * *

Jessie was grabbing the books she needed out of her locker and putting them in her book bag. She was making small chat with her friend Karen Colter who shared a locker right next to her when James walked

51

up, "Mornin', Karen Norraine," he nodded at Karen. Then he turned solely towards Jessie, "Mornin', Babe," his voice was soft and his eyes full of concern and an intense desire to know she was okay.

Sensing awkwardness, Karen gave a quick greeting, "Hey, James!" Then she shut her locker and turned towards Jessie, "Gotta run! Talk later." She waved good-bye to them both and was off.

"How are you?" he asked as he leaned against Karen's locker, bringing himself closer to Jessie.

"Good," she said, obviously quieter than normal. She was always excited to see James after the weekend. Today wasn't any different. Yet in light of the shock of yesterday's surprising news, she didn't know what to say. The bell rang. *Saved by the bell* she thought.

"I'll walk you to class."

She only nodded.

As long as Mr. Bieberdorf, their principal, wasn't roaming the halls, he could hold her hand. He slid his hand in hers and squeezed it, "You sure you're okay?" Again she only nodded but squeezed his hand too and rubbed her thumb against the skin of his hand. Her soft touch reassured him.

"Jess, may I walk you home after school today? Or do you have to pick up Carrie Grace on your way?"

"No, remember Lydia Ruth walks her home because they get done earlier."

"So, Eden's Pathway?" he asked as he tilted his head down towards her. He was quite a bit taller than she was and somehow today with the sadness deep behind her eyes, she seemed smaller, almost fragile. *James, what have you done?* he chided himself. He hated this. He knew she was hurting inside, shocked at finding out the way she did about his decision to enlist in the army. If he could only explain it to her, maybe she wouldn't look the way she did now. He wanted to stop her right in the hallway, hug her, and tell her how much he loved her and that he was sorry. Reassure her that everything was going to be okay. The look on her face was killing him. She didn't look angry, he hoped, but she looked helplessly sad. "You didn't answer. May I walk you home?" he asked again, patiently looking her way.

"Sure," she didn't offer any other words. They walked a little further without talking, and then she turned towards him, squeezed his hand and said, "I'm goin' to be late for Trig. I'll see you later."

Before he knew it, she had hustled off. It was obvious to James that she was putting a little separation between them and that hurt him. Normally, they seized any chunk of time they could together throughout their day. Whenever they could be together, they were. He wanted to respect her desire for space right now, but 3:30 couldn't come soon enough.

* * *

It was the last period of the day and as Jessie walked into **Ms. Pennysford's room, she yawned. She felt** tired; she hadn't slept well. Ms. Pennysford greeted her and asked how her weekend was. The question had a sting to it. She tried her best to give a cheerful answer while opening her book bag to take out the *Wuthering Heights* essay questions that were due. She set them in Ms. Pennysford's metal basket on the top of her desk and turned to take her chair. She glanced in the room for James. He wasn't there yet. She went and sat down by her friend Betty Lou. She set her book bag on the floor.

Betty Lou smiled at her, "Hey Jess, you ready for the quiz?" Betty Lou had her notes out and was last-minute cramming, "I'm not!"

Jessie let out a long breath, "I guess so. Ready as I'll get."

"You okay?" Betty Lou asked.

"Yeah, just tired, I guess. It was a long weekend," she took out her notebook and was about to begin cramming when James walked in and caught her attention. Her heart fluttered. Eyeing a spot next to her, James hustled in and sat down.

"How was your day?" James asked.

"Fine," was all she replied. There was a definite elephant in the room, but right now she had no words. She was distracted with all the things she wanted to say but couldn't. What could she really say now before class? This was agonizing. She hadn't been able to focus all day and she wouldn't be able to now either, not until they could talk. *The quiz was doomed.* She shook her head. Just yesterday she had found out James had enlisted in the army and she had no idea he was even thinking about such a thing. Suddenly, a chilling thought came over her. *How well did she know James?* A twinge of fear came over her. *Maybe she was too young to be thinkin' about marryin' him.* That stung her heart.

She thought about what her mother said last night. Her mother was right. She wasn't just feeling hurt. Jessie had to admit it, she was feeling a little angry too. Her mother definitely hit the nail on the head. She needed to talk to him sooner than later. She recalled what her mother had said – if they didn't talk about things soon, her feelings would fester and turn into something neither of them had intended. She was thankful her mother had prayed with her Ephesians 4:26-27, "In your anger do not sin. Do not let the sun go down while you are still angry, and do not give the devil a foothold." Her mother had reassured her that the best thing to do was to get a good night's sleep and talk to James about it as soon as possible. She said the scripture didn't mean you couldn't sleep on it. Matter of fact, she had told Jessie that many times if she and her father had not slept on an argument or taken a little time to step away from something that was really upsetting them, they would not have survived the past 26 years of marriage. Her mother said that when the sun would rise it would bring the bright new promises of *the Son.* Her mother had explained that the scripture meant we are to deal with our feelings sooner than later so that anger doesn't fester and gain control over us.

Her mama maybe hadn't gone to college, but she was a smart woman. She was so thankful for her mother.

Yes, when they walked home together, she would talk with James. But right now, she needed to get her focus shifted back to their English quiz if she was going to pass it. She looked down at her notes on conjugating verbs and forced herself not to look at James again.

* * *

Another one-word answer. James knew her well. One-word answers weren't Jessie. *Was she mad at him?* His heart pounded. He cared more about what Jessie thought than anyone else. He glanced up at Ms. Pennysford. She was busy writing something on the chalkboard, so he quickly reached over and squeezed Jessie's hand, imploring her with his eyes. She forced a smile, but didn't look his way. She just kept looking at her notebook. He knew her small smile was her way to reassure him they were ok, but he also knew she was upset.

"Time to put everythin' away but your pencils," Ms. Pennysford announced above the stir in the classroom. She began passing out the papers. He kept his eyes on Jessie. She wasn't glancing his way at all. She just kept rolling her pencil in her hands and staring down at her notebook. As Ms. Pennysford passed out the quiz, she reminded Jessie that she needed to put her notebook away. Jessie nodded and quickly tucked her notebook into her book bag. Ms. Pennysford went to the front of the classroom and stood by her desk and began the conjugation quiz. She called out the first verb. James didn't hear. "James, are you writin' your answers? We've begun."

"Sorry, Ms. Pennysford, could you please repeat the word?" Ms. Pennysford gave him a stern look. He better concentrate; he would talk with Jessie after class.

* * *

The walk home started out very quiet as they made small chat about their day. When they came amongst the trees of Eden's Pathway the shade overhead cast a shadow on them. It seemed to mirror their mood, but it also gave the privacy that James had been longing for all day with her. He dropped his bag and turned to her, pulling her into his arms.

"Jessie May, I'm sorry I didn't tell you. I was goin' to, but it just came out while your daddy was askin' me about my future plans. I guess…I guess I was more nervous than I realized. I really wanted to make a good first impression on your father. And I guess," he paused staring into her eyes, "I guess I just wanted your father to see me as a responsible….a responsible man who could support his daughter." He was bumbling through his words. Jessie didn't say anything. She just continued to stare deeply into his brown eyes. He couldn't tell what she was thinking. Were his rambling words making any sense to her? He put both his hands on her arms squeezing her gently, "Talk to me, Jess. Your silence is killin' me. I'm sorry I didn't tell you. I should have told you first. Just please, talk to me. I'm so sorry I didn't tell you first."

After another agonizing moment of silence, she opened her mouth, hesitated slightly, and then softly

57

spoke, "James, it's not that you didn't tell me first…but you didn't tell me at all." She looked down. She was trying to keep her composure. She did not want to cry and she did not want to be short with him either. She wasn't angry really, but she didn't know what she was feeling. She tried to put her finger on why she was so upset? *Was fear knockin' at the door of her heart?* "James, I didn't even know this was somethin' you gave an inklin' of thought about. I had no idea that it was somethin' you were even considerin' and now…well, now…it's too late. It's done. And I feel I can say nothin'. I thought my input mattered."

"It does, Jess. More than anyone else," he squeezed her.

"Well, if I am goin' to be a part of your future, I thought you would have me in your future plans. I would have liked to have known when you were decidin' what those future plans are. But now," she sniffed back the tears that were trying to double-cross her. "Now, it doesn't really matter. There's no goin' back." She put her head down. Defeated. Her tears no longer obeying her will as they stained her face.

He put his hand under her chin and gently lifted her head up so he could look at her, "Jessie, I didn't even know I was goin' to do it. I didn't premeditate it." She cocked her head and gave him a questioning look. "Really, Jess, I had never thought about it before. I guess…I guess it just happened. And you have to know, I was thinkin' of you when I made this decision about my…our future."

More tears pooled below both her eyes. She tried to hold them back and keep them from spilling onto her face, but she couldn't stop them now. So many thoughts were screaming through her mind.

"Jess, remember Saturday when I got that gig for the band at Linny's?" She nodded. "Well, I saw a recruiter set up on my way to talk to Linny." She remained quiet, nodding that she was listening intently. "I hadn't planned on anythin'. I didn't even know I was goin' to go and check out his tables. Jess, believe me when I tell you that I hadn't planned on enlistin', but somethin' beyond myself, bigger than me, drew me to that booth that day." Another tear slipped down her cheek. He rubbed it with the knuckles of his hand. He put both his hands on each side of her face. Her beautiful face. How could he bring such anguish to her? His thumbs gently rubbed her tears away. Oh, he loved her. Loved her more than anything he'd ever known. Maybe more than he had even realized himself until this very moment. "Babe, I wanna marry you."

"James," she spoke his name, hardly able to push enough breath through to be heard. "You're leavin'."

"Jessie May, I'm leavin' for us."

She put her head down. She didn't want to hear that. How was he thinking of her? How could he be leaving *for them* when he was leaving her?

"I wanna spend the rest of my life with you. I'm leavin', but I will be back. This will be good for us. The recruiter gave me this pamphlet. Here, read it." He bent down and pulled the crumpled pamphlet from his book bag that the recruiter had given him on Saturday.

"*Good* for us?" Jessie took the pamphlet skeptically.

"It will be a steady paycheck, Jess. Unlike my band gigs. Think of what that will do for us startin' off gettin' married without debt from college, but instead ahead with money in our pockets? And the recruiter told me with the trainin' I'll get from the specialty I chose that I'll easily be able to get a job when I get out. I signed up to be a journalist, Jess. I'm not a combat soldier. I will be writin' for the military. Just think how that could help me get a job as an English professor at a university like I want. Then I'll be able to support you…and a family."

"When do you leave?" She clearly couldn't quit thinking about that fact in the details, the part where he left her. He was leaving. She swallowed the lump in her throat. She looked at him sorrowfully as if he was already gone. She sniffled and several more tears spilled down her cheeks.

"I get to finish school first and then I go, right after graduation."

His answer made her feel like someone had just punched her in the stomach. She dropped to her knees.

"Jessie, it's okay. It's goin' to be okay," he knelt down and held her in his arms and hugged her. They stayed that way for a while. Then he tipped her chin up and looked into her eyes that were red from crying, "I wanna marry you, Jessie May, with everythin' in me. It is all I think about. Bein' with you forever. Bein' with you always."

"Then why are you leavin' me, James?" she blurted out and began to cry without holding it back now. Her shoulders slumped and shook as she heaved the sobs she had been trying to hold back all day.

"Jess, I am not *leavin' you*. I am goin' there so I can support you. When I marry you, I wanna be strong for you and support you…like…like your daddy. Just like he does for you and your family."

"Oh James…" she had no words. Just tears.

* * *

When Jessie got home, she was surprised to see her daddy was already home from work. Monday was usually his day he worked late and stayed to close up the shop, but he was outside cleaning the windows on the family's Plymouth Fury. He was always doing things for their family. Always taking care of them. Always taking care of their mother. That thought made her sniff back more tears as she thought about how James wanted so badly to support her and take care of her just like her daddy did. She walked slowly up to her father, looking down slightly so maybe he wouldn't notice her red eyes and puffy nose and swollen lips, "Hi, Daddy." Her voice was shaky. Robert stopped his cleaning and turned. He had come home a little early from work today. His daughter had been on his mind all day and he kept thinking about Patty telling him to just give her some space and time. Let her come to him. He wanted to be available

61

if she did. And now, he could see she had been crying.

"Hi honey, how's my girl?"

His daughter said nothing. She looked straight into her father's eyes and suddenly burst into tears. She fell into his ready arms. Arms that had anticipated this very moment. He was there for her; he held her tightly. She sobbed. For a long while he held his daughter in his arms and said nothing. He just stroked her hair as she soaked his work shirt. He had nowhere else he needed to be but right there. He continued to gently stroke her hair, determined to hold her in his safe embrace for as long as she wanted.

Slowly, her crying abated. After she felt she had no more tears left to cry, she looked up at her daddy and rubbed his shirt with her hand, "I'm sorry, Daddy, about your shirt."

"Oh, sweetheart." Not too often was Robert Clark at a loss of words, but he didn't know what to say. Instead, he just waited. He listened.

Through muffled left-over sobs still causing quick successions of breath in her chest, Jessie managed to tell her father everything. That James had never even considered signing up before Saturday. That they had never even talked once about it. That it came as a total shock to her. And---she revealed her heart to her father---that she was so scared he would never come back, because she wanted to marry him. "Daddy, James and I wanna get married. He's the one I love, my forever and for always, like Mama was for you in high school and still is. He can't go, Daddy. He just can't." Her chest heaved again, her chin quivering as she sucked in a quick breath, "He may never come back."

She broke into a wave of sobs again. When she was little, Robert felt he could fix anything. He'd pick her up in his big, strong arms when she'd fall off her bike and he would kiss her skinned knee. He could fix her trike when the tire fell off and make it all better. But now, he felt utterly helpless. There was nothing he could do. Just listen. Listen to his daughter cry her heart out. Robert knew, however, that his daughter needed him to say something. Just like when she was a little girl, she was looking up at him with big, sad eyes. She needed him, his strength. And more than his strength, he knew she needed to be reminded of the *Lord's strength*, "Darlin', I wish I could take this pain away from you, but I can't. I wish I could change things, but you know I can't do that either. But what I can do is remind you of God's strength. He is greater than this. He has a plan for you. Though you don't know what lies ahead, God does. He's already written it in His plan. Always remember God's great love for you, Jess. What you and James have together," Robert paused, choking up a bit at the thought of his daughter in love with a young man. Regaining his composure, he continued, "I can see how much you care for one another. I can see you love him and I can see he loves you deeply too." He hugged his daughter and then he stepped back, loosely holding her in his arms. He looked at her squarely and said, "But Jessie May, whose love is greater?"

She knew the answer, "God's," she responded quietly.

"Remember on Sunday Pastor Mark's sermon on Jeremiah 29:11?" He waited, allowing her own revelation as the scripture and Pastor Mark's sermon began to sink in.

For I know the plans I have for you, declares the LORD. Plans to prosper you and not to harm you, plans to give you hope and a future. At the time Jessie thought that surely God was speaking to her about her future marrying James and being so nervous to introduce James to her father. But in God's infinite knowledge and omniscient ways, the message then was to give her hope now.

She looked at her daddy. She had more reassurance in her heart than she had felt the last 24 hours. And for the first time since yesterday afternoon, she felt herself calm. She took a deep breath that filled her lungs, "Thank you, Daddy, that's just what I needed to hear. You're right, God knows our plans and they are not to harm us." She leaned into his arms again, "I have to believe and trust that James will come home. Oh, Daddy…" Her daddy hugged her. She would have to trust that James would come home to her. She had to. It was the only way she could persevere through this. She let out a sigh of quiet resolve. *Yes, God had plans for them, and they were plans to prosper them and not harm them. Plans to give them hope and a future.*

* * *

"Hey dopes, so did you hear?" he had Ricky, Bobby Ray, and Nathaniel's attention. "We're the talk of the town?" James crunched down on a carrot stick as he looked across the table at his friends. Jessie sat next to him eating her lunch quietly and listening to the guys as they talked.

"How do you know?" Ricky asked just before sinking his teeth into his barbecue sandwich.

"My mama said at the bakery she overheard Natty Buckston talkin' to Mabel Frank and her husband Tom. Natty and Mabel were talkin' about their Bridge last Saturday and finally gettin' some live entertainment while they played."

"Go on!" Nathaniel chirped as he wiped a smudge of mustard from the corner of his mouth.

"Natty was tellin' Mabel's husband about this 'talented band' that had been playin' while they were there. Mama said they went on and on about us and how good we were and that they hoped Linny would get us again."

"That's plumb great!" Bobby Ray said in a muffled voice, his mouth over-stuffed with barbecue.

"Yeah, and then her husband chimed in and said if we were that good, maybe old Lin oughta look at bookin' us durin' the evenin' when they play poker and quit bein' such a cheapskate. He said it was high time that Linny booked somethin' decent for them. And he chided that if Linny had live entertainment for the ladies, he'd better for the guys' poker too."

Ricky jumped in, "Do you think he'll say somethin' to Linny?" the excitement on Ricky's face could hardly be contained.

"From what my mama said, I doubt Tom will let it go. He'll be sayin' somethin' to Linny before they deal up the cards to their next game!" James laughed light-heartedly.

Bobby Ray rubbed his hands together, "Hotdog! We got ourselves another gig, boys!"

"Well, not quite yet...but we will!" James gave a wink!

"Now we definitely gotta find us a bass player! Who knows where this could lead us!" Nathaniel had finished his barbecue. He wiped his mouth with his napkin and tossed it on his plate.

Jessie had been quiet this entire time, content to just listen to the conversation between the boys. But when Nathaniel said that, she about dropped her spoon, accidently flicking a small amount of Jell-O at Ricky.

"Whoa, Jess! Eat much with a spoon?" he razzed her as he wiped two small beads of Jell-O from his chin.

"Sorry, RJ," she said, "it's just..." she paused and looked over at James. "It's just...haven't you told them?"

"Told us what?" Bobby Ray asked James pointedly, sensing the concern in Jessie's voice.

All eyes were on James now. Ricky, Bobby Ray, and Nathaniel sat completely still waiting for him to respond.

"Well, guys, you know last Saturday when I stopped off at that table with the army recruiter? Just after I split with you guys?" They all nodded not saying a word, no longer eating or picking at anything on their trays. They were intently captivated for the next thing James had to say.

"Well, I signed up."

"You did whaaaat?" Ricky shrieked. This time it was his turn to almost drop his spoon of Jell-O. "I knew you were stoppin' to look, but I just thought you were curious to check it out. I didn't think you were serious and that you'd really sign up. Just like that." He snapped his fingers.

"So you're leavin' the band? You're leavin' us? When?" Nathaniel said with heavy realization evident in his voice.

Jessie could feel her eyes fill up with tears again and anxious thoughts started to chip away at her. She had to be careful to harness her thoughts.

"I told you last Saturday and I'll say it again – I'm not leavin' the band. I'll just be takin' a bit of a break."

"James! Come on! Now who's the dope?" Bobby Ray sounded agitated.

"You guys just don't understand. This is…I don't know…just somethin' I gotta do right now. Well…not right now, but at the end of the year."

"So you're goin' to finish out the school year?" Ricky asked. There was a calmness in his voice again.

"Yeah, they want me to graduate first. So, I'll finish the school year with you doofs, and then I'll go. So see! We'll be able to play several more gigs…like the next poker night at Lin's. So don't go gettin' all teary-eyed on me now. Besides, I told ya, I'll probably find our bass guitar while I'm gone. And he'll probably kick all of your butts in a jam session any ol' day."

That triggered a playful scuffle at the table with James leaning across the table. He gave Bobby Ray a quick slug in the arm, messed up Nathaniel's ever-so-neatly greased hair, and tousled Ricky around the neck almost tipping him right off his seat. The guys broke into contagious laughter and resumed their usual banter back and forth, pacified for now with the answers and reassurance that James had given them.

Jessie, however, wished she could be so easily mollified. Her anxious thoughts threatened to betray her yet again. *For I know the plans I have for you declares the LORD*…yes, she would focus on such thoughts. God knew their plans. Surely she couldn't fret over what was already in God's hands.

* * *

Robert sat at the small table in the corner of the kitchen. Fully satiated, he slid his empty plate away from him which moments before had been mounded with warm bacon and eggs. He wiped his mouth one last time and then picked up his morning paper. Patty walked over to the kitchen table. She leaned in and kissed the side of his face as she grabbed for his plate. Before she could clear it away, he gently rested his hand on her small wrist, "Thanks for breakfast, Patty." His wife smiled at him. *How did she look so beautiful each mornin'?* Robert marveled. *Clearly God had blessed him.* Patty scooted over to the sink to finish cleaning up. The kids were off to school and he still sat lingering at the table. Mondays he always went in a couple hours later because the shop stayed open later on Monday evenings and it was his job to close. He had come to like the schedule, because he didn't have to rush into the beginning of each work week. He liked that he got to be a little leisurely on Monday mornings. He grabbed his newspaper and slid it over to read. He jerked his arms into extension to ease the crease from his paper.

Since President Johnson had taken office, much of the headlines were showing the intensity building in Vietnam. Robert sighed. It wasn't going to be long before U.S. troops were sent overseas. He closed his eyes and shot up a quick prayer. *Thank you, Lord, that I have daughters and don't have sons to worry about in this mess.* He opened his eyes again and glanced at a large caption in bold print, "Congress Backs President on Southeast Asia Moves; Khanh Sets State of Siege". *Yes, indeed,* he thought, *it wouldn't be long before U.S. troops were sent to South Vietnam.*

Robert outstretched his arms giving his paper a stiff jerk to straighten it out again. He scanned the headlines. In large bold print, "Beatlemania Sweeps the U.S." He shook his head; he didn't mind skimming past that girl-crazed frenzy. Patty loved the Beatles, but he thought it was just too much hype. He'd take Ray Charles any day. He skimmed the page. Another caption caught his eyes in bold black print as well, but much smaller than the Beatlemania title, "Johnson ordering raids after American ships are attacked again." What he had just been thinking was right here in print. He had almost missed it with the headline of Beatlemania taking over the page. But here it was, in small but declarative print, plain as day spelling out that President Johnson was preparing the first combat troops to be sent to Vietnam.

Robert's stomach lurched. He felt terrible for all the families who would be affected by having their boys sent over to Vietnam. He was filled with gratitude again that he had three daughters. His stomach reeled again. Suddenly he pictured James' face. He sat for a bit picturing the young man that he had met just over a week ago. And then an image of his daughter's sad expression came to mind. The look on her face that afternoon when James had told them he had enlisted. Robert realized he was holding his breath. He released a long, deep breath. He felt like someone had just punched him in the gut. It wouldn't just be other families. The pain of this war would be felt right in his own home.

***

Patty had finished the dishes and cleaning up breakfast. She went and got her sewing machine out of the hallway closet. She had a few things today that she wanted to get mended. She liked to do her sewing in the kitchen at the table since there was a window right there and the lighting was good. With one arm holding all the garments that needed mending and the other arm carrying her Singer sewing machine, she turned her backside against the push door between the kitchen and the dining room. She gave it a little bump and it swung open. She was startled to see Robert still sitting at the table. The crook between his eye brows was always a dead giveaway that something was eating at him. "What's troublin' you, my darlin'?" She set the sewing machine down and sat across from him at the table.

"Patty, this war's been goin' on since '55," he shook his head. "It's been nine years. And now Johnson is sendin' over United States combat troops." He tapped his index finger firmly on the paper to show Patty what he had read, "I used to think that it wouldn't be hard for the United States to win this war, but now I am startin' to wonder what good it will do sendin' our boys to that nightmare? *Our boys.*"

Patty's own heart stirred with an uneasy feeling. She sat quietly for a moment, carefully thinking on how to respond. She knew it would do neither of them any good to sit in idle conversation letting anxiety take root. Her husband needed something to settle his anxious thoughts. "Robert," she lifted his hand off the paper and held it in hers, "you always say if I'm not in the kitchen cookin', my nose is in a book lookin'. We've often joked that we know exactly where our Miss Lydia Ruth gets it." She paused shifting her focus and glanced down at the newspaper lying on the table. She took a breath, "You know, one of my favorite lines in *War and Peace* is 'If everyone fought for their own convictions there would be no war.'" She stopped; she wasn't sure exactly where she was going with this. She took a deep breath, "It isn't President Johnson's conviction. It is our country and its belief system that our nation was founded on that decisively affects our need to be over there. No one *wants* to go over there. But it is because of our great country and the freedoms we have that *allow* us to go over there…to make a difference in this war. And to stop the spread of communism. So we need to support our President. We need to support our leader." She looked at Robert. He was listening but the crook between his brows showed her he wasn't any more contented. "Dear, you are the leader of our family and I support you though I don't always understand your convictions. But it's your passion for our family as a whole I know so well and your strength that consistently protects our family…I just trust and have confidence in how you are leadin' our family…even if I don't always understand or agree with your choices at the time."

Robert shifted in his chair, "Hon, I think your cookin' is amazin'…but…," he paused and stammered a bit and lowered his head. Robert didn't show this vulnerable side very often. He looked back up at his wife and spoke tenderly, "But, though your food nourishes me, it's your wisdom and love that sustain me." He pushed himself away from the table and stood up. He took Patty's soft, smooth hand in his big, rough hand that was cracked and calloused from hours of physical work. He pulled her towards him and she slid off her chair. The man who could be as burly as a bear was now as gentle as a kitten. He embraced his wife, breathing in her scent, never tiring of this gift from God. "Thank you," he whispered in her ear. He lingered by her ear. She could feel his breath. Slowly he kissed her neck, moving softly up her skin until his lips came to hers. He kissed her lips. She kissed him back. As the kissing increased, so did their breathing. With a move so effortless, he picked her up off her feet and carried her to their bedroom. He'd be going in a little later than planned today.

* * *

James was sitting in the locker room on the bench changing into his gym shoes when Hank walked in, "Hank, right?"

Hank opened his locker and pulled out his gym shoes. "Yep, you're James?"

James answered with a nod as he snugged up his laces.

"So, did you sign up too?" Hank asked. They hadn't run into one another since that Saturday at the recruiter's booth.

"Yeah, I did. Had no intentions really when I went up there, but I don't know, somethin' just felt right to do it. What'd you pick for your MOS? Mine is combat correspondent. I chose journalism. How about you?"

"Infantry."

"Oh." James sat for a moment as that sank in. *Infantry.* He swallowed a lump in his throat. A restless, uneasy feeling washed over him. It was the first time he found himself emotional thinking about the magnitude of his and Hank's decisions. "Where are you goin' for your basic and AIT?"

"I'll do my boot camp and advanced trainin' both at Fort Benning, Georgia. How about you? I'm assumin' you leave right after graduation like me?"

"Yeah, I go to Fort Leonard Wood, Missouri, for basic, and then my AIT is at Fort Benjamin Harrison in Indiana at the Defense Information School."

"Did you memorize your number yet? The recruiter said to engrain it into my head. Said it'll pretty much follow us everywhere we go. So, you got yours memorized?"

James didn't get a chance to answer. The bell blared in the locker room; they were going to be late for gym.

Chapter 4
Beach Bound

"Come on! Saturday is supposed to be really hot. It's supposed to be a record breaker for October. Let's go to Disney Lake. Most of the seniors are goin'. I reckon it'll be great fun," Nathaniel pleaded around the table.

"You don't have to twist my arm any. I'm in. Well, if my parents lemme, that is!" Ricky answered.

"A chance to see chicks in a swimsuit…count me in," Bobby Ray said giving a high-five to Ricky.

Both Jessie and Betty Lou rolled their eyes. Jessie turned to James, "What do you think? Do you wanna see chicks in swimsuits too?"

"Nope, not chicks…just one chick in particular!" he winked. "It sounds fun though, Jess. And besides, I think we could use a stress reliever, don't you? I'd like to see some sparkle in your eyes again."

"Well, I'll ask my parents and see what they say," Jessie said.

Just then Gloria Sue Stonewell and Arlette Huckaby were walking by with their lunch trays giggling. They glanced at the table with flirtatious eyes at the guys and giggled some more as they strode past.

"I'd like to see those chicks in swim suits!" Bobby Ray said in a low tone.

"Bobby Ray, you're such a pig!" Betty Lou scolded.

"What?" he asked innocently. "They walked past us and flirted. So I can't help it."

"Oh, you can help it alright," Jessie joined in and used a motherly tone and a look to match it.

"Well, it's not like I'm the one with a girlfriend," said Bobby Ray. "I can look and admire…which I hope to be doin' this weekend with them in swimsuits!"

Nathaniel and Ricky started laughing, but James stifled his laughter.

"Y'all are hopeless," Jessie said trying to keep a straight face.

Bobby Ray retorted, "Correction, Jessie May, we are *hopeful*!"

This time the whole table burst into laughter.

"I think I need to go…to keep an eye on you guys!" Jessie laughed. James squeezed her hand under the table. It was good to see her laughing again.

Mr. Hagen, their superintendent, startled them all when he tapped on the table with his lunchroom megaphone. "Bell rang! Time to clear your trays. I don't wanna have to send y'all down to Mr. Bieberdorf's office for tardy slips. Let's go, kids." He rapped on the table one more time with his lunch megaphone.

"Yes, sir!" rang around the table. The group, immediately breaking up their conversation, got up and hustled to class.

As they all headed out of the lunchroom, they could hear Mr. Hagen's voice amplified through his megaphone, "Anyone missin' for class will be sent to Mr. Bieberdorf's for tardy slips. Let's go, people! No one missin'! No one missin'! Finish up your lunch!"

"Why does he say, *no one missin'*? They'd be late for class, not missin'. That sounds so stupid to say missin'," Betty Lou stated.

"Because he is stupid," Bobby Ray laughed.

"Come on, Jessie May," James grabbed her arm, "let's not be missin' for class." He winked.

Late or missing…she didn't want to be either one. Jessie nodded, grabbed James' hand and they scooted off to class. The bell was about to ring a second time.

* * *

"I'm hoooomme!" Jessie called through the house as she dropped her book bag by the front door.

"Back in the kitchen, Sugar!" she heard her mother call. She pushed herself through the swinging door into the kitchen. Lydia and Carrie were sitting at the table having a snack. She could smell that her mama had been baking fresh bread. Nothing beat the smell of fresh-baked bread. "You want a slice of bread?

Still warm from the oven," her mother said with a smile on her face.

"Mmm, do you even need to ask, Mama?"

"Well, if she didn't ask, how would she know if you wanted some?" Carrie's mouth was full and she had jelly smudged along both sides of her mouth.

"It's a rhetorical question, Carrie Grace." Lydia handed her sister a napkin, "Here, use this."

"A what?" Carrie chomped another bite of bread, neglecting to use the napkin.

"It's when you ask a question to make a point. You ask it not really for the answer, but just to make an emphatic point."

"What's emphatic?"

"Never mind," Lydia said rolling her eyes at her little sister, "just eat your bread. You should really read more to expand your vocabulary."

"I'm only eight!"

"That's obvious."

"Girls, that's enough," their mother said with gentleness. She turned back to Jessie, "So, butter or peach jelly?"

"I can get my own, Mama. You know you don't have to serve me," Jessie said.

"If I can't wait on my girls when they get home from school, then what good am I? So, don't go takin' away one of my greatest privileges." She stood waiting with her hands on her hips and then repeated her previous question, "So? Butter or peach jelly?"

"Oh gosh, tough decision. Hmm? I think just butter today. I don't know what it is about havin' just butter meltin' onto the warm bread, but I savor the taste of your homemade bread even more with butter than I do with jelly."

Jessie sat down at the kitchen table with her sisters. Her mother scooted over to the counter next to the stove where the bread still sat on a cooling rack. She picked it up and placed it on the cutting board next to the cooling rack. The cutting board was already covered in crumbs from the slices that Carrie and Lydia were devouring. She watched her mother. Jessie thought she was so beautiful. Everything about her mother was graceful and gentle. That made her think of the scripture her father often said about her mother's beauty being that of a gentle and quiet spirit. She'd have to look that up later tonight in her Bible when she went to bed. She sat quietly admiring her mother. Her mothered placed the bread on a small serving plate and smeared some butter over the top. She carried it over to the table and set it down in front of Jessie.

"You're awfully quiet. Everythin' ok?" her mother asked.

"Mmm, hmm. Just watchin' you. You amaze me, Mama. I hope I am half the wife and mother that you are."

"Land sakes, stop it now, eat your bread." Her mother was modest too. "So, tell me how your day was today. I already got to hear about Carrie's and Lydia's." She glanced over at her other two daughters, giving them affirmation of her attentive ear. Then she continued, "Lydia Ruth is pretty excited because she told me her teacher announced when their first junior high dance is…although she has yet to ask her father." She shot a loving, all-knowing look at her middle daughter. "You'll need to run that by your father first."

"I know," Lydia sighed.

Her mother went on, "And Carrie Grace tells me that her class is gettin' a class pet."

"Yes!" Carrie exclaimed. "A goldfish! And we are havin' a contest to name her. And if our name is chosen, then we get to take her home over Christmas break to take care of her! I'm thinkin' Ann!"

"Ann?" Lydia questioned.

"Yeah…Ann Chovy!"

"Oh, my goodness!" Lydia put her forehead down into her hand as her elbow rested on the table. Jessie and Patty hid their giggles.

"Well, if Daddy could vote, he'd vote for Ann! He loves anchovies!" They all laughed.

Jessie cleared her throat after laughing, "My day was good. I think I did alright on my math test. I was nervous about that, but I think I did pretty well."

"You put a lot of time into studyin' the past couple of nights, that's for sure," her mother said. "It's a good thing you know what you're doin', because you can't ask me. There's no way I can help with trigonometry!"

"It wasn't so bad," Jessie said. She took a bite of her bread, "Mmm, delicious, Mama."

"Thank you."

"And there's somethin' else I actually wanted to talk with you about. Somethin' that the guys and I were talkin' about at lunch."

"What's that?" her mother said tilting her head with curiosity.

"This Saturday is supposed to be really nice, actually hot," Jessie said. "So, several of the seniors are doin' a big beach day at Disney Lake with food and games. I was wonderin' if I could go if I make sure to get my chores done? It'll probably be the last lake hoorah before the spring."

"No fair! I wanna go!" Carrie chimed in.

"Sorry, Carrie Grace, it's just for seniors," Jessie said kindly to her sister and patted her hand. Then she turned back to face her mother, "So, what do you think, Mama?"

"I think it sounds like a lovely time, but you do know how I feel about water."

"I know, Mama, we'd be careful," Jessie responded. "There won't be any boatin'. The plan is to do games and just hang at the beach all day. We're each supposed to bring some food to share for dinner. Then I think later they all wanna eat supper together at Buckie's BBQ and cruise main afterwards. So, it'd be an all-day thing."

"Well, the other thing, I just have to voice, is that there is always a chance of alcohol bein' there," her mother said.

"Not durin' the day, Mama. I'd agree if this was a bonfire on the beach in the evenin' or somethin' like that, but I think we'll be safe for dinner and the afternoon."

"Well, I just wanted to say it. Always be aware."

"I know, Mama, and I will. But I think we'll be ok. So….is that a yes? I can go?" Jessie grinned.

"Well, you know your father gets the final say, but I think he's been pretty soft with you lately. I don't think it should be an issue. I think he'd agree that a dose of fun in the sun could be just the medicine you need."

Jessie nodded. She knew exactly what her mother meant. She needed a distraction from the thought of James enlisting and leaving in May. She was grateful for her mother's tender thoughtfulness.

"Thanks, Mama. I appreciate that."

"Can I have another slice of bread, please?" Carrie interrupted.

"May I?" Lydia corrected.

"You want another one too?" Carrie asked.

"No, it's *may* I have another slice of bread. Not *can* I. You're askin' permission if you may have another slice…not if you are capable of eatin' it."

"Well, I'm definitely capable of eatin' it!" Carrie chirped. "Twice! I'd like another slice please, Mama. So, can I?"

Lydia shook her head, "Impossible!"

"Let it go, Lydia Ruth," her mother smiled and stood up to cut Carrie another piece of bread. "What would you like on it? Jelly again?"

"Nothin'," Carrie answered.

"Nothin'?"

"Just like Jessie said, I wanna taste every bite. I don't want anythin' on it," Carrie smiled proudly.

"That's how I like mine too." Her mother set the plate down in front of Carrie with another slice of bread on it.

Carrie looked down at the plate. She smiled. She had such an innocent smile that was contagious. She started to hum. She took her index finger and poked two holes into it making eyes, then a nose, and finished by poking several little holes to make a smile in her bread. "There! It's happy bread! And I think I *can* and will eat it!"

All four broke into laughter, even Lydia, who made no effort to admonish her younger sister this time.

* * *

Jessie smiled to herself as she crawled into bed that night. Her father had said yes to Saturday's Disney Lake beach bash, and her mother was right once again…it did feel good to look forward to something. She let out a sigh. It sure felt good to smile again. She needed this. She had worn a sad and glum face too much lately. That suddenly reminded her of the scripture she wanted to read about having the beauty of a gentle and quiet spirit. She turned and picked up her Bible off her night stand. She opened to the back of her Bible to the concordance. She looked up the word *beauty*, "Ah yes, 1 Peter 3:4." She flipped to the first book of Peter. She decided to start at the first verse of chapter three. She began reading, "Wives, in the same way submit yourselves to your own husbands so that, if any of them do not believe the word, they may be won over without words by the behavior of their wives, when they see the purity and reverence of your lives. Your beauty should not come from outward adornment, such as elaborate hairstyles and the wearing of gold jewelry or fine clothes. Rather, it should be that of your inner self, the unfading beauty of a gentle and quiet spirit, which is of great worth in God's sight." She stopped after verse four. *My beauty should be of a gentle and quiet spirit. What an example my mama is of that unfadin' beauty.*

She closed her Bible and after setting it back down on her night stand, she reached over and turned her lamp off. She began to pray, *Thank you, Lord, for my mama. Thank you for her beauty and inner grace and quiet gentleness that she displays to all around her. Thank you that she is an example of Him to others. Thank you, Lord, for my daddy and the security, strength, and love he gives daily to our family. Also, my Heavenly Father, I am so thankful for my sisters who bring such happiness and comfort to my life.* Yes, she was grateful for her family. They made her feel safe, loved, and happy.

For some reason that made her picture the smiley face Carrie poked in her bread earlier that afternoon. She giggled out loud in her bed as she thought about Carrie and her happy face. She was so care-free. *Yes, Lord, thank you for my family. How blessed I am.* She closed her eyes and began to succumb to the fullness of the day. Weariness pressed upon her and the last thing she thought of was that piece of bread with a simple image – a smile. She drifted off to sleep and felt her own smile rest peacefully on her face.

* * *

Saturday morning was bright and cheery, not a cloud in the sky. It was already 85 degrees and just mid-morning. It was going to be a perfect day at the lake. Jessie was just finishing cleaning up her dishes and baking mess from making the chocolate chip cookies that she was bringing to share at the beach. She was so excited. She glanced outside. James wasn't driving today; Bobby Ray was. Bobby Ray's daddy said he could take the family car. His father was the only one who either didn't need their vehicle for the day or didn't mind if sand got in it. Bobby Ray said he'd pick up Ricky and Nathaniel first, then Betty Lou as she was riding with them too and finally James since he was on the edge of town. Then they'd head out to pick up Jessie. The car would be full when they picked her up. She hoped they had room for all their things.

Bobby Ray said they'd be out around 11:30. She glanced up at the clock on the wall. It was 10:30. She had an hour; she had better hustle. She tossed the dish rag on the side of the sink and hurried upstairs. She needed to shave her legs, do her hair, and get changed. She planned to wear her suit there with a pair of jean shorts and bring some extra clothes to change into for later when they headed back into town. She skipped up the stairs every two steps. When she got to the top, she glanced at the door closed to Carrie's room. Carrie was still in bed sick with the stomach flu. *Poor girl*, she thought. *It's such a gorgeous day to be sick in bed.* She'd have to try to bring her back something from the beach to help cheer her. She knew Carrie would like that. She was quiet as she walked past her door. Next was the bathroom door which she discovered was also shut. Mildly irritated, she wrapped lightly on the door.

"Who is it?" rang out Lydia's voice.

"I need the bathroom. I have to get ready. I'm barely goin' to have time to shave my legs and do my hair the way it is," Jessie replied.

Lydia opened the door, "Why are you doin' your hair if you're goin' to the beach? It's just goin' to get windy, wet, sandy, and messy."

"Just because," she scooted past Lydia. "Excuse me, please."

"Because why? I don't get it," Lydia shrugged.

"You will someday. Someday you'll have a boy you wanna impress and look good for just like I wanna for James."

"Ew!"

Jessie laughed, "Lydia Ruth, boys won't always be gross! Someday you'll wanna wear your hair a certain way for some boy who catches your eye."

"I don't know about that!" Lydia stated obstinately.

"Trust me, you'll wanna do your hair…even if you are goin' to the beach where it will just get messy anyway."

"Sounds like too much work. I like to just wear my hair in a ponytail. Easier that way."

"Well, if you ever change your mind and decide you wanna try somethin' new, lemme know and I'd be happy to help you," Jessie smiled. "Like maybe for your dance comin' up? I could show you how to do an up-do or put your hair in rollers and do it down with curls.”

“Yeah, maybe,” Lydia paused to give it some thought and then to Jessie’s surprise she turned to her sister and replied, “Maybe I will take you up on that.”

Jessie smiled, “With pleasure! Now….scoot!” She shoed Lydia out hastily so she could close the bathroom door and get ready.

Your beauty should not come from outward adornment, such as elaborate hairstyles. The scripture she read last night came to mind. *Lord, I do not wanna be elaborate…but I would like to look nice for James. I certainly won’t make it my focus. I think that’s the point. But, like Granny Clark used to say, ‘A little powder and paint makes a girl what she ain’t.’* She smiled to herself as she thought fondly of her daddy’s mother who had passed away when Jessie was only 14 years old. She smiled. *Granny was right too…just a little wouldn’t hurt.* She giggled. She’d better hurry up and put a snap to it. In only 45 minutes, they’d be pulling up the driveway.

* * *

“I can’t believe we fit all our stuff,” Jessie shifted slightly in the seat. She was sandwiched between James and Betty Lou with her beach bag below her feet and her Tupperware of chocolate chip cookies on top of that. Bobby Ray was driving and Ricky and Nathaniel were in the front seat with him.

“What I can’t believe is that your parents said you could go the whole day to Disney and then go to

Buckie's BBQ afterwards and drag main and be gone all day!" Bobby Ray remarked.

"I know, but I think they've really softened, especially my daddy. Ever since James told us that he enlisted, my daddy has pretty much gone out of his way to make sure I'm doin' ok."

"Man, I reckon you should've signed up a while ago, James. You could've been goin' all over the place with Jessie May," Bobby Ray said poking fun.

"Not funny, Bobby Ray," Jessie flung back.

"I think it is," Bobby Ray looked in the rearview mirror making eye contact with Jessie knowing a response would come.

"Yeah, well you definitely aren't the comic of the group," she quipped.

"Ouch!" Bobby Ray acted defeated. Then he chuckled and changed the subject, "So, can everyone go to Buckie's and drag main afterwards?"

"Yep, I got permission," said Betty Lou. "And I know Karen Norraine can too. She's meetin' us there and riding with Marshall and Jane Anne."

"My parents said we can," commented Nathaniel as he flicked his wrist back and forth pointing to Ricky and him. "RJ's spendin' the night at my house."

"Yeah, it's a good thing I'm spendin' the night at your place or I know my parents would not have lemme go all day. I'd have had to come home after the lake."

"Why do you think I asked you to spend the night," Nathaniel chuckled. "I love your parents, but swat my hind with a melon rind, they are strict!"

"I know, some day when I am a parent, I'm goin' to let my kids do whatever they want," Ricky commented.

Jessie laughed, "That just might change."

"Probably not!" Ricky turned his body to see in the back seat better.

"So if you have a girl, you'd let that daughter of yours go out all day *with a guy*? Or how about *all night*?" Jessie asked.

Ricky considered this, his eye brows furrowed while in thought, "Holy smokes, no, when you put it like that! Sweet fancy Moses on buttered toast, Jessie May, what are your parents thinkin' lettin' you go out all day *with James*?"

"Hey now!" James acted offended. "I'm . . ." he wrinkled his forehead trying to think of some clever come-back. "I'm *Gentleman James*!" he boasted emphatically. The whole car broke into laughter.

"If you say so!" Bobby Ray said laughing the hardest.

"Hey! Don't miss the turn, funny boy," James said pointing from the back seat to the sign coming up for Disney Lake.

"I see it, I see it," Bobby Ray slowed down and took a right on the gravel road. "Back seat driver!" he shook his head and laughed some more.

As they popped over the hill they could see several cars parked and several people setting up the volleyball net on the beach. Some were in the water already.

Jessie clapped, "This is goin' to be so much fun!"

"Heavens to Betsy! I see Larry Edwards and he's already got his shirt off," Betty squealed.

"Now who's bein' the pig!" Bobby Ray chuckled.

"Well, if you can't beat 'em…"

The group laughed again. The moods were light. Bobby Ray pulled his dad's car up behind another car. As soon as he stuck it into park, all four doors flung open. "Pop the back, why don't ya!" Ricky hollered. Everyone grabbed the blankets, food, and Frisbees that were loaded in the back.

"Here, lemme take your bag," James grabbed the bag flung over Jessie's shoulder.

"I don't care what the rest say…you *are* Gentleman James!" she batted her eyes flirtatiously at James as they walked holding hands down to the beach. There were two picnic tables under a shelter that were already loaded with delectable goodies. Jessie placed her Tupperware of cookies next to the other sweets. James tossed his bag of chips on the table. He grabbed her hand again.

"Let's walk down to the sand."

"Hey, you two love birds, time to split up. We each need someone to fill our teams," yelled Lyle Peterson. Lyle was quarterback and captain of the Blue Devils football team. He was athletic and competitive.

James looked at Jessie with a questioning look and then gave her hand a quick squeeze, "Well, we'll see if you still call me Gentleman James after I whip you in volleyball!" Lyle wasn't the only competitive one.

* * *

Somehow Bobby Ray finessed his way to play on the same team with Gloria Sue Stonewell and Arlette Mickelson. James was on their team too. Bobby Ray was in prime macho mode trying to impress Gloria Sue and Arlette, and Jessie couldn't quit giggling. She just couldn't help it. *He thinks the sun comes up to hear him crow*, she thought to herself. Bobby Ray was so over-the-top trying to flex his muscles and puff out his chest. And he kept walking weird. Watching him made Jessie giggle which distracted her from focusing on the game.

"Alright, this is game point," Lyle said just before serving the ball. Jessie's team would win if they were able to get this point. Lyle was a solid server. He raised his arm up and tossed the ball up in the air. His body propelled upwards leading with his left leg. His right arm planted hard against the ball. Over the net it zoomed.

92

Bobby Ray bumped it, "Oh yeah, baby! That's right!"

Jessie giggled again at Bobby Ray's air of confidence.

Off Bobby Ray's bump, Karen set the volleyball perfectly. James powered up even with the net and hammered down on the ball, spiking it over. Jessie who was still giggling over Bobby Ray's macho mannerisms didn't even see it coming. The ball came down square in her face and she stiffened. As if in slow-motion, she fell forward planting face-first into the sand. James was by her side faster than anyone. He scooped her up, "Oh Babe, I'm so sorry. I'm so sorry. Are you okay?"

Her face was full of sand. She rolled her tongue and tried to spit the sand that was in her mouth. James heard Lyle as he turned to the rest of their team, "Dang it, that means they get to serve again. They still might win."

"Game over! You guys win," James told Lyle sharply. He was more worried about Jessie than winning a stupid sand volleyball game. "Come on, Babe, let's get you over here. I'm so sorry." He helped her up and helped her walk over to sit down by the picnic table. He grabbed a couple of napkins and tried to help brush the sand from Jessie's face. All of a sudden Jessie started to giggle again. James pulled back and just sat there staring at his sand-faced girlfriend. His girlfriend who was just pelted a good one in the face by none other than himself. "Did that ball knock some screws loose?" he asked with concern.

"No!" she was still giggling. "Oh, James, what I must look like right now. Lydia Ruth was right…my hair sure did get messy and sandy! I guess I shouldn't have been worried about my hairstyle." With that, she busted out laughing some more.

James waited until Jessie's laughter subsided a bit and then helped to wipe the sand off her face, "Well, I did wanna see some sparkle to your eyes! I just didn't intend for that sparkle to be sand!" All of a sudden, they both started laughing until they were in a laughing fit with tears streaming down their faces.

Ricky walked up, looking for some food. He glanced at Jessie, whose face was covered in sand and a mixture of muddy looking tears from the laughter that still shook her body. Then he looked at James who was laughing just as hard with tears streaming down his face. "There's somethin' seriously wrong with you two!" He popped off the lid of Jessie's Tupperware and grabbed a couple chocolate chip cookies, "Hopefully there's nothin' wrong with your cookies though." They laughed harder. Ricky shook his head, popped a cookie in his mouth, sealed up her Tupperware and headed back to the beach.

As they caught their breath and finished wiping the sand from Jessie's face, a few others gathered around the table and began to pick at the array of food set around the table. James asked Jessie if she was ready to eat. He handed her a plate. Someone had brought watermelon cubed up. Looking at it made Jessie's mouth start to water. She dished up a scoopful. Someone else brought some homemade jerky. She loved jerky, so she grabbed a couple pieces. She opened a bag of chips and took a handful. She grabbed for a jar on the end of the table. Someone brought stickle pickles and she had a weakness for those. They reminded her of her Granny Clark. There were some sliced carrots on a plate. She plucked a couple out of the pile and put on her own plate. Lastly, there was a container with its lid still on. She peeled the corner back on one side and peaked inside. Someone had brought sugar cake cookies with frosting. *Oh, Carrie Grace loves those*, she thought. She pulled the lid off and picked one with pink frosting. "James, could you please grab me another plate?" He handed her a plate and she set the cookie down. Then a big grin came across her face. She thought about Carrie and her "happy bread". Suddenly she took her finger and made a smiley face in the frosting.

"Look at you, like a little kid, playin' with your food!" James teased.

"It's for Carrie Grace. She likes *happy* food!"

"Sure *she* does!" James just shook his head, "Come on, let's go sit down." He motioned over to another picnic table under the shelter that had been left open for eating.

They sat down together and began devouring the picnic food. They munched and watched another group playing volleyball. Beyond them, several were in the water having chicken fight wars. There wasn't a cloud in the sky and the sun was surprisingly intense for an early October day. The water sparkled and shimmered and the barrage of droplets splashing from the chicken fighters sent rainbows reflecting into the sky.

"It is such a gorgeous day! What a way to spend it. After we eat, do you wanna go in the water?" Jessie asked.

"I've been waitin' for those jean shorts to come off since we picked you up."

Jessie blushed, "James!"

"What?" he shrugged giving an innocent look. "Bobby Ray's not the only one who wants to see a chick in a swimsuit," he leaned in and quickly kissed her neck. He lingered for a moment. Even though it was hot and humid and she had face planted in the sand, she smelled amazing. He inhaled and exhaled with the faintest sigh.

She pushed him back playfully, her hazel eyes held his gaze with a soft and tender smile, but then her look darted over his shoulder. Something else caught her attention. She started to laugh, "Oh my goodnes, look!" James turned his body so he could see more easily as she pointed in a direction past the volleyball players. Another group of kids was getting a game of Red Rover going. "I can't believe they are playin' Red Rover. Seriously! We're seniors!"

"Says the girl who just poked her finger into her food to make a smiley face," James was humored. He wiped his mouth and crumpled his napkin, flicking it down onto his empty plate. "Wow, that watermelon really hit the spot."

"I told you, it's for Carrie! And correction…" she paused, lifted her eye brow, and with a smirk on her face continued, "I don't think the watermelon hit the spot…I think the ball did!" And with that, they each broke into a fit of laughter once again.

Chapter 5
The End to a *Sunny* Day

The day had been perfect. Now the sun had shifted in the sky to the west and a breeze had come up. The skin of almost every senior was flaming red from their day spent in the sun. Their lobster-colored skin made the breeze feel quite chilly. With most of the food mowed over, one-by-one they started packing up and heading back in to town. The plan was still to go to Buckie's BBQ for supper.

Main was buzzing when they arrived in town. "Land sakes! I think every junior is draggin' main!" Betty Lou observed with excitement.

"Yeah, they probably missed us," Bobby Ray said turning his car into the first parking spot he could find. "The word got around school that we were havin' a senior day today at the lake and that we weren't exactly lookin' to include others. So, they've probably been tryin' to find somethin' cool to do all day."

"Oh my goodness! Look at that little car next to you, Bobby Ray," Betty Lou said pointing to the car next to their parking spot.

"I think that's Mr. Hagen's new car," Ricky responded. "It's a Morris."

"What a little Cracker Box!" James laughed. "Looks light enough to pick up."

"Hmmm?" Bobby Ray said rubbing his chin.

"Bobby Ray, you just put that thought back where it came from. Don't even go there! I know what you're thinkin'!" Jessie said pointing at him with a grin on her face.

"What?" Bobby Ray put his hands up in the air like he was caught red-handed.

"Come on, you guys, or we're not goin' to get a booth," Nathaniel prodded.

* * *

Sure enough, Mr. Hagen was inside. And as luck would have it James, Jessie, Bobby Ray, Ricky, Nathaniel, and Betty Lou got seated next to his booth.

"Out of all the booths, we had to be seated next to Mr. Hagen's," Ricky rolled his eyes.

"He's out with friends. He's not even payin' attention to us," Jessie said.

"It's weird to see him in jeans," Betty Lou commented.

"And with friends!" Bobby Ray laughed. "Do you think he has his lunch megaphone?"

The group laughed. Ricky answered, "Nah, not for supper!" They all laughed again.

"I'm Sunny, I'll be yer waitress for tonight. Y'all know what you want?" the waitress interrupted. She chewed on the end of her pencil as she held her order pad in her other hand.

"I'll take the Bacon Beast with onion rings and a coke," responded Bobby Ray. He hesitated slightly, "And your number for dessert."

She rolled her eyes. "Next!" she looked over at Nathaniel.

The group laughed. "I'll take the Double Trouble Cheeseburger with French fries and a strawberry shake," Nathaniel said.

The rest of the group put in their orders and the waitress flicked her hair over her shoulder, turned her back to the group and quickly walked away.

"Smooth, Bobby Ray! Smooth!" Nathaniel laughed.

"Hey, a guy's gotta try."

"Yeah well, how about try another way!" Betty Lou commented as she made eye contact with Jessie to reaffirm with the only other female at the table that Bobby Ray had it all wrong with the ladies. Jessie squeezed James' knee under the table and they each exchanged a humored look. They loved the group they hung with. Never a dull moment.

"Hey Nathaniel, can you move?" Bobby Ray said wanting out from the booth. "I'm gonna go put some coins in the jukebox."

"What? Are you gonna ask the waitress to dance next time she comes?" Nathaniel laughed.

"Hey! That's a great idea!" Bobby Ray retorted unphased. He wasn't gone long and when he came back to the booth, the waitress was just setting their waters around the table. "Perfect timin'! I just selected a song I thought you might like," Bobby Ray said. Just then Elvis Presley's *Hard Headed Woman* came on. "Sunny, you sweet little thing, you sure won't change your mind about your number?" he raised his eye brows.

"You may lack tact, kid, but you don't lack courage. I'll give you that. But considerin' I'm at least 10 years older than you, married, and have three kids at home, I think I'll pass," she said triumphantly. She glanced around the table, "Now, if y'all need somethin', just holler." Then she turned to wait on Mr. Haugen's booth.

The table burst into laughter, all except Bobby Ray who turned several shades of red. He avoided her eye contact the rest of the evening and never said another word to her.

"It's not too often, Bobby Ray, that you're left speechless," remarked Betty Lou.

"Yeah, well I'm just thinkin' of a better pick-up line for next time."

"Like for someone your own age?" Nathaniel couldn't resist.

Again, laughter rang out from the group. "Nice one!" Bobby Ray nodded. He couldn't say much more.

The group was finishing and standing up to go pay their bills. Mr. Hagen's table next to them showed no sign of leaving any time soon. As the gang grabbed their coats and started to leave, Mr. Hagen commented, "Hey, looks like you kids were havin' fun, I was keepin' my eye on you guys. You know my job's never done. Say, Bobby Ray, you looked a little red from somethin'." The group busted into laughter.

"A day in the sun will do that to ya," Bobby Ray responded.

"Yes, a…*Sunny* day sure will," Mr. Haugen quipped. Betty Lou couldn't quit giggling. She was elbowing Jessie. "Well, you guys have a good night and stay out of trouble."

"Sure thing, Mr. Hagen," Bobby Ray tilted his head towards Mr. Hagen's table in a gesture of respect. Then as he walked out, under his breath he said, "Told ya he was watchin' us."

"I don't know, that's pretty funny! I think Sunny must have told him," Betty Lou said.

"Nah, he was eaves droppin'! Like he said, his job's never done," Bobby Ray said sounding annoyed.

"Serves you right, Bobby Ray! Maybe you've learned your lesson," Betty Lou retorted.

"Ooh, now that breeze really feels cold," Jessie snugged her sweater tighter around her shoulders.

"I think it's just because your skin is so hot. You really got sunburned," James said putting his arm around her.

As they were walking up to get into Bobby Ray's car, Bobby stepped off the curb next to Mr. Hagen's driver's side. He put his hand on his door handle and opened the door.

"Bobby Ray! What are you fixin' to do? Close that! He's right inside!" Betty Lou squeaked.

"Relax, Betty Lou! He ain't comin' out any time soon!" He poked his head inside Mr. Hagen's Morris and slid into the driver's seat. He reached for the gear shift and put it in neutral. Then hopped out and quietly closed the door. "RJ, give me a hand on this side. Nathaniel and James, get on the other side."

"You're crazy!" Betty Lou continued.

"We're just gonna roll it back and park it on the other side of the street. No harm in that."

"That would be a little funny, I have to admit!" Ricky looked over at Nathaniel and James.

"I want no part in this," Betty Lou said holding up her hands.

"I wasn't askin' you to help," Bobby Ray responded and looked at the guys.

"James?" Jessie looked at him.

"It wouldn't really hurt anythin', Jessie May," he looked at her coyly with his big brown eyes.

"Y'all are gonna get us in trouble," Jessie said glancing nervously at the front door to Buckie's.

"Nah, it's just a *little* fun with a *little* car," Bobby Ray laughed. The four boys looked cautiously if anyone was around. No one was coming out Buckie's and no one was coming down Main Street. "Jessie May, you watch Buckie's door. Tell us if anyone is comin' out," Bobby Ray gave a quick nod of his head.

"You guys, this makes me nervous," Jessie said shaking. She didn't know if she was shivering from the chilly breeze or her nerves. Her father would not be happy with her if they got caught. He may reconsider so freely telling her "yes" the next time.

"Jess, relax, it'll be funny," Bobby Ray said and grunted as they rolled Mr. Hagen's Morris into the middle of Main Street. "When my brother was a senior, they did this to Mr. Hoffered's car. It didn't hurt a thing. It sure was hilarious though."

"I remember that," Ricky laughed.

Bobby Ray reached in Mr. Hagen's driver's side and began turning the steering wheel. "There! That's enough boys. Now push it forward." Slowly the car pushed forward and they rolled it right into the parking spot across the street in front of Hank's Hardware. "There, now let's get outta here before someone does come and see us."

The group hustled back over to Bobby Ray's car and quickly got in. Bobby Ray put his father's car in reverse and backed out of the parking spot. "See, no harm done," he said with a devilish grin on his face. "Now let's cruise main!" As Bobby Ray began pulling forward, he glanced over his shoulder at Mr. Hagen's car, "It's too bad Mr. Hagen didn't have his lunch megaphone with him." He waited.

"Why's that?" Betty Lou asked.

"Because he'd probably use it to call for his *missin'* car." Bobby Ray laughed so hard at his own joke and soon the others, even Jessie and Betty Lou, couldn't help but laugh with him. "See Jessie May, I think you were wrong. I think I am the comic of the group."

Chapter 6
Hagen's Hunch

Monday morning, Jessie yawned as she opened her locker. She was tired from the weekend. Being out all-day Saturday was definitely fun but had sure exhausted her. She had really struggled Sunday to get up for church. She, of course, didn't want to miss it, but it was so hard to get out of bed. She was grateful she had gone and heard Pastor Mark's message on Philippians 4:8, another one of her favorite scriptures. *Finally, brothers and sisters, whatever is true, whatever is noble, whatever is right, whatever is pure, whatever is lovely, whatever is admirable—if anythin' is excellent or praiseworthy—think about such things.* Yes, such good food for her soul. She was determined to focus on good things, whatever is praiseworthy. She yawned again. Right now, however, she'd have to focus on perking up. Mondays sure were not her favorite day. She corrected her thought, *Thank you, Lord, for another Monday in school with James.* Another yawn.

"Well, good mornin', sleepy-head!" James greeted her, grinning.

"Goodness! You startled me. I was just thinkin' about you."

"Ohhhh, do tell!" James had a mischievous look on his face.

"You're in quite the mood! You look happier than ol' Blue layin' on the porch chewin' on a big ol' catfish head!"

"Yeah, I had a dream about you in that swimsuit of yours! Mmm! Mmm! Mmm! Woke up with good thoughts!"

"James!" she blushed.

"Hey, I like those dreams!"

Just then the intercom crackled and Mrs. Penderlyn, the school secretary, came on with the morning announcements, "Good Monday mornin', students. Mr. Hagen has asked that you please go to the gymnasium at this time before your first period class for a special school assembly in the gymnasium." She went on to give the lunch menu for the day and the usual morning messages.

"I wonder what that's about?" Karen commented as she opened her locker next to Jessie's and began pulling out her books. She shut her locker and turned to them, "See you guys in the gym, I guess."

"I can about know what that is about," Jessie said quietly to James as Karen walked away. "I bet he's on to us," Jessie said, looking over her shoulder nervously.

"Don't worry, Jess."

"What if he has a hunch it was us? James, I would be in so much hot water with my father if he knew we were prankin' Mr. Hagen with his car."

"You weren't prankin' him. We were!"

"That won't matter with my daddy, James. Guilt by association!"

James grabbed her hand and squeezed it, "Jess, it's gonna be fine. Trust me," he winked. They started walking towards the gymnasium. "Guess what else I woke up thinkin' about this mornin'?"

She cocked her head up towards him, "What?"

James broke into the tune of the Corvettes song *Mr. Sandman* and in typical James fashion, he sang his own rendition:

> *Mrs.* Sandman, I had a dream
> You are the cutest that I've ever seen
> Two eyes of hazel with sand all over
> I'd like to kiss your sweet lips like roses and clover!

Oh James! He lightened her heart, and that certainly woke her up.

* * *

With the morning classes over, the lunchroom was abuzz with students. Betty Lou set her tray of shrimp and grits down and plopped onto her seat, "Oh my goodness, the look on Mr. Hagen's face at the assembly…he was not happy."

"Yeah, but did you see Mr. Bieberdorf's face? I swear he was tryin' to hide a smile. You could almost see a smirk," James said laughing. "That was the best part, I think. Bieberdorf's face! I love that guy!"

"I don't know how Mr. Hagen didn't suspect us, but thank goodness he had no clue it was us," Jessie said with a sigh of relief.

"He has no clue! No clue most days," Bobby Ray snickered.

"Well, I am just glad we didn't get caught," Jessie said.

"Me too!" added Betty Lou.

"You girls are always the safety girls, aren't you? Always wantin' to play it safe," Ricky jumped in.

"Well, there has to be some reasonable brains in the group!" Betty Lou laughed.

The group's conversation was interrupted and drowned out by the loudness of Mr. Hagen's voice echoing through his lunch megaphone across the lunchroom, "Let's wrap up lunch, students. Anyone missin' for class, you know I send down to Mr. Bieberdorf's for tardy slips. So let's go, let's go! No one missin'! No one missin'!"

Betty Lou rolled her eyes and leaned on the table and pressed into the group, "Okay, so maybe it was a little funny!" The table roared with laughter.

Chapter 7
Giving Thanks

Robert loved when he and his kids were on holiday break. He enjoyed listening to the bustling sounds when they were all home together and loved the dynamics of everyone in the house at one time. He had always wanted a full house with lots of children, but the Lord had other plans for them. He was grateful for the blessing of his three children. He had wanted a son, yes, but with the giggling sounds of his girls coming from the kitchen as they helped their mother, his heart was content. And as the smell of turkey began to waft through the house, he felt a swelling in his heart for the many things he had to be thankful for this Thanksgiving.

* * *

They sat in the dining room at their formal table to eat their Thanksgiving feast. Robert reached over for Patty's hand and then for Jessie's. Carrie and Lydia grabbed hands with the rest too. Holding hands, they all bowed their heads to say grace.

"Dear Lord, we thank you for this food which we are about to eat and for the hands that prepared it," Robert prayed. He squeezed Patty's and Jessie's hands in thanks and continued, "And thank you, Lord, for our health and our many blessin's. For our loved ones – all our friends and family. For our home and the comfort and safety it provides. Father, I ask that your hand be upon our nation and lead us in the days that lie ahead. Be with our military and protect them as they prepare to head to Vietnam. We ask this especially with humble hearts for James as he prepares to leave for trainin' for the military and that you would carefully watch over him in your lovin' care and return him safely after his tour of duty. We lift this all up in prayer in your holy name. Amen."

"Amen!" echoed around the table. Robert gave Jessie's hand one final squeeze to comfort her heart. They talked a lot these days and he knew she needed continuous reassurance if she was going to run this race set before her.

* * *

As Jessie listened to her father's prayer, she was thankful for him. He had a way of dispelling her moments of fear. He made her feel safe and secure. He often quoted 1 Thessalonians 5:17 telling Jessie to "pray without ceasin'." Just last night, he came into her room and asked if she had said her prayers yet for the night. When Jessie told him she hadn't, he came in and sat on her bed and asked if he could pray with her.

She loved that about her father. He was always just a prayer away from the Lord. He liked to say that the Lord was his constant conversation companion. Her daddy was a true example of praying without ceasing.

He had asked Jessie if she would grab her Bible off her night stand. He told her he had a scripture that the spirit kept bringing to him lately in prayer that he wanted to read to her. He opened up her Bible and after thumbing through it briefly he found his place. He cleared his throat, "1 Corinthians 9:24-26 *Do you not know that in a race all the runners run, but only one gets the prize? Run in such a way as to get the prize. Everyone who competes in the games goes into strict trainin'. They do it to get a crown that will not last, but we do it to get a crown that will last forever. Therefore I do not run like someone runnin' aimlessly; I do not fight like a boxer beatin' the air.*" He set her Bible down. "Jessie May, do you know what that scripture means?" her father asked.

"I think so."

"You have a race set before you. You need to think of James goin' to Vietnam as a race with your faith in the Lord. The apostle Paul wrote these words and his point was not that only one Christian will win the race. It was more to draw to light the disciplined trainin' skills, effort and dedication it takes by athletes in order to persevere and win. You must pace yourself, Jess, to run this race set before you and let your focus not be on the things you cannot control, but rather set your focus on your heavenly Father, your true Comforter, who can cast away all your fears."

Her true Comforter. Jessie thought of this now at the dinner table when her father squeezed her hand. She was filled with a peace beyond herself. A peace that comes only from the Father. She closed her eyes and offered up a quick prayer. *Thank you, God, for bein' my strength when I feel weak and for fillin' my heart with a peace and security that comes only from you.* When she opened her eyes, her father was looking at her. She smiled at him to let him know she was okay.

He cleared his throat, "Let's go around the table and name three things we are thankful for now or this past year." He had started this tradition when Jessie was little and Lydia was a baby. And now, every Thanksgiving dinner they'd been doing it since. Robert said he'd go first. "I'm thankful for your mother and for her loving me even when I'm stubborn. But it's a good thing that hardly ever happens." Patty rolled her eyes and the girls each giggled at his humor. "I'm thankful for each of you, girls. Jessie May, for your sensitivity and carin' heart towards others. Lydia Ruth, for your insatiable love for readin'. And Carrie Grace, for always keepin' us on our toes. We never know what you're goin' to say next!" Jessie and Lydia laughed this time. Carrie didn't.

"What's that mean?" Carrie said with a slight whine in her voice.

"It means we love you just as you are," Patty said giving her youngest daughter a side hug from her dining chair.

"Carrie Grace, I wouldn't want you any other way. That's why I said it's one of my things I'm thankful for," Robert said smiling with great love in his eyes at his youngest daughter. "And finally…"

"Daddy, didn't you already name three things?" Carrie interrupted.

"No, your mother was my first, you girls were my second, and my third thing…hmmm, I am thankful for James…because I'm finally gettin' to see what it feels like to have a son."

Jessie couldn't believe what her father had just said. She beamed. James had been coming over more frequently, and many times she teased James that when he visited, he talked more with her daddy than with her. She thought her father seemed to be forming a mutual attachment…this was quite evident in his comment just now. That made her heart happy. She knew when James lost his daddy that there was a huge void in his life growing up. He'd told her this many times. And though her daddy never talked about it, she knew there was an empty place in his heart where he had longed for a son. So, she was grateful they had bonded. James looked up to her father and, in a short couple month, they had become close.

"Is it my turn?" Patty looked around the table.

"Yes, Mama, you can go after Daddy," Carrie answered with one nod of her head to her mama. "I don't mind goin' oldest to youngest because Daddy always says 'save the best for last'". Everyone laughed again.

"See Carrie, we never know what you're goin' to say and you make us laugh. Laughter is good for the heart." Robert said and nodded to Patty, "You're up, my dear."

"I'm thankful for my whole family. I truly don't know what I'd do without you. Well…I'd maybe get to read a little more."

"Mama!" Carrie scolded.

"I'm teasin'," Patty chuckled. She then continued with a soft tenderness in her voice, "You give meanin' to my moments and worth to each day." She paused to look each one of them in the eyes before going on. "Okay, my second thing…I'm thankful I had three good helpers in the kitchen to make this feast before us." She smiled at them, "You know me and my quotes, many hands make light work."

"I'm thankful for your quotes," Lydia interjected. She shared her mother's love of reading and couldn't help but appreciate this attribute in her mother.

"And hmmm, let's see…" both of Patty's eyes veered to the right as she gave careful consideration to her final answer. "I'm also thankful that I'll have four good helpers in the kitchen to clean up when we are finished."

"Come on, Mama, that's not fair. That's not how we're supposed to do it!" Lydia commented.

"Nope, that's fair, girls," Robert said validating Patty's answer. "The rules are you may name *any* three things you're thankful for now or this past year. So, if your mama is thankful for you girls helpin' clean up after we eat, then it counts."

"Um, Daddy? Technically the rules are for past and present. That's future. And I believe she said *four* good helpers in the kitchen helpin' with clean up," Jessie said, loving being able to point things out occasionally to her all-knowing father.

"Whaaaat? Who made up these rules anyway?" Robert bellowed. Everyone laughed. "Alright, alright! I'll help clean up in the kitchen too, especially if you want me to clean up the pie!" More laughter. The moods and hearts were light. "Jess, you're next."

"Well, I'm thankful I don't have any homework this weekend," she said and Carrie and Lydia agreed. "I'm thankful for my family and how much love we have in our family. Not everyone is this lucky. And, I'm thankful for James." Jessie turned gesturing to Lydia so she'd know it was her turn. She wouldn't elaborate on her last one. She'd save those comments for James.

"I guess we're all namin' the same thing, but I'm thankful for my family too. Nothin' in the rules said we couldn't repeat the same answer, right Daddy?"

"That's right!" Robert spoke with authority as if he was a judge at a spelling bee endorsing what was correct or not.

"What else? Hmmm?" Lydia pondered. "This is hard when you're the one listin' things."

"It is, when you're the one on the spot," said Patty, "but I like that it makes us reflect on what is important to us."

"Well, I'm also thankful for a new friend Mary Bustad who just moved here. She and I have connected and we're a lot alike. And my last thing," she hesitated slightly. "I'm thankful for James too. He's like a big brother, only better. He doesn't pick on me and he likes to read." She blushed and looked down.

Jessie felt her eyes well up with tears. For as much as Lydia had a book open in her hands, she certainly wasn't an open book herself. She didn't say things like that often. James had definitely made an impression with her whole family. Her heart soared. She couldn't wait to talk with James later.

"Okay Carrie Grace, just like you said, we 'saved the best for last'!" Robert said encouraging his youngest.

"Told ya!" Carrie was just about to stick her tongue out at her two older sisters when her mother halted her actions with a rebuking look. Carrie knew the look well and she held her tongue. "Okay, I'm thankful for our new batch of kittens that Mittens had. My favorite is little Butterscotch. So thank you, God, for tabbies. And, um….I'm thankful for Mama's pumpkin pie, sweet as the day is long."

Laughter trickled down the table.

"Where so ever do you come up with such things?" Lydia asked.

"From Mama," Carrie turned to her big sister as if Lydia hadn't been paying attention earlier when Patty was talking. "You know her and her quotes." She tried to sound so mature when she spoke.

Jessie looked across the table at both her parents. A look of amusement was written on both their faces. They were all enjoying Carrie's antics.

"And, I'm thankful for my Easy Bake oven that I want for Christmas."

"Carrie Grace! It's not even Christmas yet! How do you know you're goin' to get one?" Lydia chuckled.

"If Mama can be thankful for somethin' in the future, then I can too!"

Patty and Robert exchanged a look between them. Yes, their Carrie Grace certainly kept them on their toes. They continued the rest of the dining in merriment and joyful conversation. Carrie's answers, simple as they were, left them all feeling amused, content and immeasurably blessed. They had much to be thankful for. Maybe Robert had been right. Clearly, they had indeed saved the best for last.

* * *

Jessie lay on her bed, her eyes fixed on her ceiling. She was wide awake. She tossed and turned and fluffed her pillow hoping that would help. *If she could just get comfortable.* She looked around her bedroom. The yard light from outside cast shadows of varying shapes on her walls. She wasn't the slightest bit sleepy. The day had been wonderful, but it wasn't the thoughts of her blissful Thanksgiving spent with her family that was keeping her up. It was her anticipation for tomorrow.

She was still in disbelief that her father had agreed to let her go. Tomorrow she would be leaving with James, his mother Rita, and step-father John down to Birmingham. They were going to visit his sister Elizabeth and her husband David. Elizabeth hadn't been able to come home for Thanksgiving because of her husband's work schedule, so they were making a trip down to visit them. And, James had conjured up the thought that Jessie should come along.

Initially, James wasn't even sure if his mama would say yes, but when he asked her, he was pleasantly surprised at his mother's response. "I think that's a fine idea. It's about time your sister meets Jessie May," his mother had said.

Jessie thought it went mighty easy with Rita, but had told James that wouldn't be the case with her father. She wasn't even going to ask him because she figured there was no way her father would let her go and spend the night away with her boyfriend's family. But James had encouraged her...several times actually. And she had a hard time resisting him and that dang wink. So, she finally relented and got the nerve up to ask her father.

To her surprise and delight he had said "yes." Her father had quite a soft spot and sensitivity when it came to Jessie lately. And so it was; she was going. He had told her since they were going with James' parents, and she wouldn't miss church, that it'd be okay to go. "Just this *once*," he clarified. He barely got the last part out. Jessie flung her arms around him in a hug of immeasurable gratitude.

So, the plan was to leave tomorrow after dinner and come home sometime Saturday afternoon. It was only 32 miles away, but they wanted to go down for the day and spend time together and not feel rushed. That's why they decided it would be much easier to stay overnight at David and Elizabeth's. The thought of spending almost 24 hours straight with James! 24 hours! The thought and the excitement it stirred in her tortured her now. It was why she couldn't sleep.

James told Jessie since they would be spending the night, he wanted to take her to a drive-in movie theater. She had always wanted to go to a drive-in. James said he was going to take her to *My Fair Lady* because that was still playing. Her friend Caroline told her about it. She said it was a musical and that Jessie would love it. Of course, to Jessie, it wouldn't really matter what was playing. She was going to be sitting next to James in a parked car, alone. Her heart raced. Ricky, Nathaniel, and Bobby Ray wouldn't be there. Her father wouldn't be there so James and her daddy wouldn't be dominating the conversation. Carrie wouldn't be tagging along and pestering them with her constant jibber-jabber. It would be just James and her. No one else. Her heart pounded in her chest. She rolled over on her stomach and squealed in her pillow.

There was a light knock at the door. Jessie froze. The door opened just a little and a stream of light poured in through the small crack, "You okay, Jessie May?" her mother's voice was a whisper.

"Yeah, just can't sleep."

Her mother opened the door all the way and came in and sat down on the bed next to Jessie. "Excited for tomorrow, huh?"

"Hmm, mmm."

"I don't blame you. I would be too. I never got to do anythin' like this when I was your age."

"I know, I feel so lucky, Mama. I'm just so thankful. I still can't believe Daddy said yes!"

"That makes two of us!" They giggled quietly together knowing that even the faintest sound would echo in the quiet stillness of the night.

When they quit giggling, her mother's face took on a more serious expression. "Jessie May, I know you know this, but you will be stayin' overnight under the same roof as your boyfriend. Remember not to put yourself in a compromisin' situation that might be temptin' for you. It can be very difficult to stop…especially for James. It's more difficult for guys. They may be strong. But in this area, when tempted, they are weak."

Jessie squirmed a little, "I know, Mama. You don't have to worry."

"Well, people make mistakes all the time, sweetheart. They do things that they wish later they hadn't. And with sex, once you go too far, there is no turnin' back." Jessie turned instantly red. *Sex* – the very mention of the word elicited an uncomfortable feeling. Jessie always felt at ease visiting with her mother; her mother was very open. But despite her mother's relaxed nature, the topic of sex made Jessie squirm. It was so personal. Her mother continued in a casual tone, "You may wanna marry James, but only the good Lord knows for sure. And what I do know is that God wants you to save yourself for your husband."

"I know, Mama, thank you. It makes me uneasy to talk about, but I appreciate your openness. I admire you and Daddy." She sat up and gave her mama a hug. She laid her head back down on her pillow. She yawned; she was starting to finally feel sleepy.

"You better get some rest now. You have a big day ahead of you." Her mother stroked Jessie's hair, leaned down and kissed her forehead. And then, she did something she'd been doing with Jessie longer than either of them could remember, "Goodnight, pickle nose."

Somewhere along the memories of bedtime stories and prayers, they started saying goodnight to each other in this silly, yet endearing, little way—they'd name a food and a body part. It would continue through several exchanges while each one tried to top the other's clever response until one of them broke the streak and bid the final adieu.

"Goodnight, brussels sprout head," Jessie responded.

"Goodnight, crawfish elbow," Patty said with a smile.

"Goodnight, eggplant shoulder."

"Goodnight, cheese lips."

"Goodnight, biscuit butt." They both giggled.

"Goodnight, watermelon toes."

"Goodnight, Mama, I love you."

"Goodnight, sweetheart," her mother stood and crossed the room, "I love you too." Then she quietly closed the door and it was silent again.

Tomorrow couldn't come fast enough for Jessie. Somehow amidst her thoughts of the conversation her mother and she just had and the anticipation of seeing "My Fair Lady" and imagining the lights of "The Magic City" for the first time…Jessie drifted off to sleep.

Chapter 8
Dinner and a Show

They sat next to each other and held hands in the back seat of John's Chevrolet Impala. James rubbed her hand with his thumb as he held hers. They kept making eye contact and smiling coyly at one another.

"Do I need to do a hand check back there?" John said with humor in his voice while looking in his rearview mirror.

"John, stop that! You'll embarrass them," Rita scolded.

"Oh, come on, Rita! We were young once too!" John laughed, "I'm just teasin' a little, that's all."

"Exactly! And if you and your girlfriend were teased like that you would have blushed three shades of red! Heck, John, you blush if you sneeze too loudly in church."

"I s'pose you're right." He looked in his rearview mirror again, "Sorry, you two back there, just havin' a little fun." He readjusted his mirror and focused on the road as Rita intentionally struck up a conversation with him.

James shook his head in the back seat and rolled his eyes as he squeezed Jessie's hand. Then they both had to stifle their giggles. They slouched down together in the seat and started visiting in hushed voices.

"You were quite the talk of my family yesterday."

"Really?" James tilted his head so he could see Jessie's face better. "Tell me more."

"I don't know if I should. It may just all go to your head. I'd hate to have you get a big head. Cocky wouldn't be flatterin'."

"Come on, Jess, spill it. Or you never should have opened your mouth." He poked her playfully in the ribs. She squirmed and shot a serious look, worried that John would say something again. James was loving every minute of this. "So come on, let's have it!"

"Ok then, but you just keep your hands to yourself, mister." She was flirting with him and he liked it.

James brought both hands up in an *innocent* gesture.

"My daddy has this tradition he started on Thanksgivin' that durin' our Thanksgivin' meal we have to go around the table and each list three things that we're thankful for."

"Yeah?" James looked at her doe-eyed.

"Stop that!"

"Stop what?" he asked innocently.

"Lookin' at me like that! If you want me to finish, you have to quit lookin' at me that way."

"What way?" he was teasing and having fun with her.

"James Patterson!" she whispered so his parents wouldn't hear.

"Alright, alright, I'll stop. I'm listenin'. I'm serious now."

She paused and waited to see if he was serious about being serious. Her eyes danced, "Well, I can tell you that of the five of us, three of us listed you as one of the things we were thankful for."

"Only three?" James smirked.

She jutted her chin out a little and shot him another look. He hushed. She kept talking.

"I'll tell you about Lydia Ruth first."

"Lydia? Not Carrie?"

"I know, right! But sorry, an Easy Bake oven and kittens took precedence over you!"

"Ah, shucks!" he squeezed her hand again.

"And Lydia Ruth, she's not really an open book, ya know, with her feelin's. But she said she already thinks of you like a brother…only better, because you don't tease her and you share her love of readin'."

"Aaah, Jess, that makes me feel so good. I mean, really." James was tickled her sister Lydia thought of him this way. It was very touching to him.

"Well, wait until you hear what my daddy, MY DADDY, said."

"Your daddy was one of the three? Man, I had that pegged all wrong. I figured you, your mama, and Carrie Grace. Now you really have my attention. What did your daddy say?"

"He said he was thankful for you…because he thinks of you as a son."

"He did?!!!" James' mouth hung open.

"Shhh!" Jessie laughed quietly. "Yes. He said that he is finally gettin' to see what it feels like to have a son," she let out a gentle sigh. "James Patterson, you've made quite the impression on my family. They love you. And…well…now that brings me to the last of the three who said they were thankful for you…me." She squeezed his hand and then was quiet. She looked down, more timid now. This was the part she had saved just for James.

He reached over and touched her face. Her eyes darted to the front seat to see if John or Rita had noticed, but they were both engaged in some conversation about David and Elizabeth. James wasn't teasing anymore, not an ounce of silliness evident. He was quiet now. Waiting. "James, I want you to know how I feel about you. I mean, really feel about you. You make me laugh like no one else. Your humor can pick me up on even my lowest days. And

I know I roll my eyes a lot at all your crazy songs you come up with, but the truth is, I love your songs. I love when you sing *to me*. I feel like the only person in the room. You make me feel so important, so loved. And your voice…you are so talented, James. I could listen to you all day. And you're loyal, smart, hard-workin', and you are someone who sets your mind to somethin' and commits completely. That's how you are with me. I never have to question your feelin's about me. Ever. You make me feel so secure in our relationship. The way you look at me with your eyes, it makes my heart stop. They draw me in, melt me. And when you get close to me, I can hardly breathe. And your body," Jessie's eyes fluttered a bit as she spoke this last part. This time James squirmed. She stopped. She suddenly felt vulnerable and bashful.

James had a look of intensity on his face. His eyes penetrated hers and he didn't blink. It made her giggle a bit, but she was also a little nervous.

"Jessie May, that's not fair to stop there. Come on! You're killin' me. Please?" he implored her.

She pulled herself a little closer to James and spoke very quietly so as not to be heard by John and Rita. This was meant for James' ears only. "Your body drives me wild. I have to tell myself to stop starin' and focus. You turn me on like no one ever has. It's…it's just hard for me to catch my breath when I'm around you. Especially when you pull me close. I feel my heart rate change…like it is now. I feel things changin' in my body."

"Me too...Jessie May, we better stop this conversation now."

"Did I say somethin' I shouldn't have?" she almost looked offended.

"No! Not at all!" he quickly retorted. He took her hand in his, "It's just...now you're drivin' me wild. And I need to breathe a little. I gotta get my thoughts under control again."

"Oh, I'm sorry." She looked down shyly again.

"Don't be, I loved every word. I loved hearin' that. You've never told me all of that before. I mean, I knew it...I could feel it...I just hadn't heard you say it."

"James," she looked straight at him. "I love you."

"I love you too, Jessie May. With my whole heart." He leaned his head against hers. They were quiet for the rest of the ride. They were almost to Birmingham.

* * *

As James sat there in the back seat with Jessie, his head against hers, he could hardly believe his own feelings bursting inside himself. Never before had he been so sure of anything in his life. He loved Jessie. She loved him. And, he smiled to himself, her family loved him. He thought about what Jessie had told him. That Lydia and Robert thought of him like a brother...like a son. It made him feel part of their family.

130

Part of their family. He repeated the last part back in his head and a thought began to stir inside him. Christmas was around the corner and that would be perfect for what he was thinking.

* * *

Elizabeth made a wonderful supper for them. *When did his sister get to be such a good cook?* he thought to himself. When she lived at home, all she really made was either a bowl of cereal, Spam sandwiches or – if she got really fancy – black-eyed peas and cornbread. But her meal tonight was amazing. She made fried shrimp and okra and a sweet potato casserole plus a caramel cake for dessert. James was quite impressed with his sister. Married life sure seemed to suit her well. And her home looked great too. She was doing well for herself and James was happy for his sister.

He had talked to her about wanting to take Jessie to the drive-in and Elizabeth was more than encouraging. She teased her little brother that she and David might just come along to double! But after supper was cleaned up and everything put away, Elizabeth pulled out their Parcheesi board and told Jessie and James, "Sorry, James and Jessie, you'll just have to go without us. We play a mean game of Parcheesi and are dyin' to take on Mama and John." She winked at her brother.

* * *

Jessie caught the wink Elizabeth gave to James and almost broke out laughing. *So the wink runs in the family!*

131

James gave her an inquisitive look. He noticed her reaction and the comical look across her face was surely obvious. *I'm sure he wonders what is so funny, Jessie thought.* She raised her eyebrows at him, but enjoyed this little bit of humor for herself.

James' attention was quickly redirected from Jessie as John started to give him the run-down about driving carefully in the city and how to park his Impala. He said it shouldn't be an issue at a drive-in, but John just wanted to make sure James knew not to park too close to any other vehicles and to be careful when pulling up to the speaker post. He didn't want any scratches or door dings. "Not a scratch!" he told James emphatically poking his index finger in the air as he said it. James reassured him and said they'd be back right after the show. And then with a little reluctance, John handed over the keys and they were off.

* * *

James put the Impala in park and turned off the ignition. "Want me to go get us some popcorn and a soda?"

"Mercy, I'm full as a tick yet from supper. Elizabeth's fried shrimp was amazin' and that caramel cake was to die for."

"I know! I didn't even know my sister could cook like that." They laughed. "Well, lemme know if you change your mind. I'd hate to get called *cheap* on our first date to the drive-in. I'm pretty stuffed myself." James opened his window and picked up the speaker outside. He propped it on his window ledge and slowly started to crank the handle to roll up his window until it fit snuggly. He turned it on, but no sound came out. The big screen wasn't even on yet. He turned to Jessie and patted the seat next to him. She scooted closer. "So….can you tell me again what you told me on the way here?"

"James!"

"I'm serious. Tell me again."

"No, I told you once. You should've been payin' attention." Her voice was light.

"Oh…I was payin' attention. I just wanna hear you say it again. I stopped you earlier, but maybe I wanna hear the part about my body drivin you wild and turnin' you on." He put his right arm around her and slowly started to rub her arm. She looked up at him with her soft hazel eyes. He leaned down and paused. Then he leaned down just a little further, until he was close to her face. "What did you say happens when I get close to you?"

"James," she whispered and closed her eyes.

"Yes?"

She opened her eyes. They were looking at each other eye to eye. Slowly he turned his head slightly and brought his lips against hers. He kissed her. One small kiss. Her heart fluttered. She leaned forward and kissed him back.

They heard a crackle from James' window – the speaker. The movie was beginning, but neither of them seemed to care or notice much.

"May I touch you?" James asked.

Softly she answered, "Yes."

James brought his left arm up slowly. He brought his hand against Jessie's chest. He stayed above her blouse. The feel of his touch was wonderful and sent goose bumps down her skin. Though she had goose bumps, she felt very hot.

They kissed again. Slowly. And then the pace of their kissing increased. Their breathing changed. James brought both his hands up cradling the sides of her face.

"Jessie?" James' voice was breathy.

"Yes?"

"I need to go get some popcorn."

Her eyes popped open, "What?"

His eyes were open now too and he pulled his body back a little, "I need to go get us some popcorn….and a soda. A very large, cold soda."

"Now? Why? I thought you were full."

"So I can cool down. It's gettin' a little hot in here," he leaned forward and kissed her cheek. His comment was met with slight disappointed on Jessie's face. "Jessie May?" he tilted her chin up so she would look at him and he could have her full attention.

"I didn't always do the right thing before. You know, with a couple of the other girls I dated. I really regret that, and I've taken it to the Lord. And now, Jessie, with you it is so different. I want you so badly. But, I wanna wait. To be very careful with you. And to honor God in our relationship, in all that we do."

Jessie's heart swelled. "James, I love you." A little tear snuck out and ran down her cheek.

He slid his finger against her cheek and wiped her tear. "I love you too. Now…" he winked, "I'm goin' to get us some popcorn and that large soda. I'll be right back."

James carefully opened his door so that he didn't mess up the speaker and lightly pushed it shut. Jessie had no idea how long the movie had been playing. Audrey Hepburn was singing the song, *I could have danced all night*. She listened to the lyrics; the song resonated with her feelings now. She ran her fingers through her hair and smoothed her blouse. Jessie's thoughts took her back to her conversation with her mother last night. She recalled how her mother had warned her about not putting herself in any compromising situation. Her mother was right; it was very difficult to stop when things got heated. She would have to be more careful. But, her mother was wrong about one thing. James was not weak. He was a lot stronger than even she had realized. *Thank you, God, for James in my life and his devotion to You.* James had reminded her of her greater desire – to be pleasing to the Lord. This desire went beyond her desire for James, and she would be true to her first love…God.

The door opened again and James, returning, popped his head in. He was grinning and holding a huge bucket of popcorn and the *largest* soda Jessie had ever seen. A soda so big it would keep them both awake until they got back to Cordova if they drank the whole thing! She shook her head and laughed. He slid in and handed her the popcorn and soda. Then he carefully shut his door. The speaker rattled ever-so-slightly against the window.

"James, you better be careful!" she cautioned.

"I know!" He thrust his index finger in the air mimicking John, "Not a scratch!"

They each laughed---at John's expense---and then enjoyed their popcorn, *large* soda, and what was left of the show.

* * *

They pulled into the Clark's driveway a little after 2:00 the next day. Carrie came running out to greet them. "How was it? How was the big city? Did you see any clowns?"

"Clowns?" Jessie questioned as both she and James began to laugh. Wherever Carrie came up with such notions was beyond them, but she made them laugh. Their hearts were light. Being in love felt so good.

"Nope, no clowns. Unless you count my sister," James was quick to respond.

Jessie pushed James' shoulder, "James Theodore, you say that now when she's not here and she can't even defend herself. That's not fair teasin' her when she's not here."

"Oh, yes, it is. I had years of her teasin' me. I have to catch up any chance I get whether she's here or not."

Her father had come out on the porch now. "How was it? How was the show?"

Jessie felt her face grow hot. She hoped her father didn't notice. "It was amazin', Daddy. It was a musical. And Audrey Hepburn was fabulous in it. You should really think of takin' Mama."

"Well now, let's not go puttin' any ideas in your mother's head."

"What ideas in my head, Robert?" Jessie's mama pushed open the screen door and came and stood next to her father on the porch.

"Oh, nothin'! Jessie May was just sayin' she enjoyed the drive-in."

"Yeah, and she thinks Daddy should take you too, Mama. On a date! To the drive-in!" Carrie piped up.

Robert shot Carrie a fast look – he had been betrayed by his little tag-a-long. He smirked, "Don't you have some chores to do, like pickin' eggs or somethin'?"

"Nope, it's Jessie May's turn. Good thing she's home now!" and she skipped off.

"Well, looks like I don't get by without expectations for a future date in the makin' and, Jessie May, you don't get by without some chores you have waitin' for you."

James took the hint. "Well, thanks for lettin' her come with us. It was an amazin' time."

He turned to Jessie and gave her a quick hug. "Thanks for comin'. See you Monday." He contemplated a quick kiss on the cheek. But considering her father had just let her go on an overnight trip with him, he decided not to press his luck. He got in his step-father's car and was about to drive away when Jessie walked up to his driver-side window. She leaned down, "Thank you, James, for…you know…the large soda," she said playfully with one eyebrow raised. He knew what she meant. He nodded. "Drive home safely, James, and remember…not a scratch!" She jabbed her finger in the air just like John had done. He busted into laughter. There it was. Her humor right on cue when he least expected it. He really loved that about her. She stepped aside. He waved to her and her parents still standing on the porch. And then he drove away, still chuckling…at John's expense!

Chapter 9
A Blue Christmas

After Thanksgiving, time seemed to whiz by in a blink. Christmas was just around the corner and the halls of Cordova High School were buzzing with holiday spirit. It was Monday which meant only a few more days until school let out. All the students were antsy as ever with the upcoming long break within grasp. In three days, they'd be scot-free with no homework for almost two weeks. That itself was enough to put holiday cheer in everyone's step.

James was walking Jessie to their next class. "Can you believe Christmas break is almost here?" James asked with a twinkle in his eye. "I can't wait."

"Me too! Mama and I are gonna make fudge this weekend and old-fashioned thumb print cookies. Lydia Ruth wants to make iced sugar cookies too. We'll definitely be busy, but with no homework!"

"Don't be too busy over break, Babe! I'm worried you'll be too busy to see me!" He leaned towards her and bumped her shoulder with his as they were walking. "What am I goin' to do over this long break when I don't get to see you every day?"

James' innocent question pierced her heart. It sent an ache that radiated so fiercely in her body that she could feel it in her bones. *Every day.* That would all change in May. She wasn't able to entertain that thought long, however, because James broke into Elvis' song "Blue Christmas". It was one of his favorite Christmas songs. He was seven years old when the song was released. He had been given his first guitar that year for Christmas from his parents. It was the last Christmas his father was alive. He had come to cherish that song and the memories that came with it.

He sang the chorus to Jessie with fervor as if the song was written for her and belted out it out, not caring at all that they were amidst other students.

"James Theodore Patterson, what am I goin' to do with you?" she closed her eyes and shook her head.

"Ooh, now you're usin' my full name!" They were just coming to the door of Mr. Brink's room for their history class. James had a big grin on his face. He loved teasing her and making her smile. He loved nothing better than seeing her beautiful smile touch to the tips of her ears. He had her smile memorized and etched into his thoughts every night when he lay his head down on his pillow. He knew her face so well. Her beautiful face said so much. That's how he knew that something he had said just moments before had upset her. He didn't know exactly what it was, but he was sure it had something to do with his leaving in May. The topic hadn't really come up much lately. She rather avoided it, but he would ask her later. He didn't believe in pushing anything under the rug and not talking about it. He wanted everything open with Jessie. Even though it was hard for her to talk about him leaving, they needed to talk about it. However, now wasn't the time. So, he did what he knew best – distract her with song. He dramatically swung his arm out in front of him and offered it to Jessie so that he could escort her into the room. He curled up his lip like *the King*, gave a quick hip swing and a twist, and then without a hint of embarrassment, finished his rich baritone version of the song.

She shook her head and let out a sigh. As much as she could try and act like his singing was absurd, she had already revealed the truth to him about his silly little songs. She loved them. She adored when he sang to her. And he knew that. Self-assured, he smiled. He'd sing his heart out for her. And he'd do anything to keep that smile on her beautiful face.

* * *

When the last bell rang on Wednesday afternoon, the 23rd, everyone scrambled to their lockers to put their stuff away, grab what they needed, and tear into their long, much-anticipated Christmas break. Mr. Bieberdorf came on the intercom to wish them all a safe and happy holiday break. He finished in his usual fashion with a corny joke, "And if you're lucky this Christmas, maybe Santa Claus will grace you with his *presents*." The students could hear him snort to himself at his own joke. He always laughed at his own corny jokes – which he told on a regular basis. "All right, Blue Devils, have a good break. And we'll see you *next year*!" Again, the students could hear through the intercom – Mr. Bieberdorf amused with his own humor. Then the intercom crackled a little and went silent. James came up to Jessie at her locker and leaned against Karen's locker. She was already gone.

"That guy cracks me up. He's so corny, ya just gotta love him." He shook his head, "Ready to walk me home?"

"I am." She closed her locker.

"I kind of like this; you walkin' me home."

Jessie's parents had said it was okay if she walked James home from school their last day of school before break. She had been invited to have supper with his folks and him. Then he'd drive her home later. When they walked into James' house his mother was already home and something sweet met both of their senses.

"Mmm! My mama's bakin'! Let's go see if we can taste-test anythin'. You know, make sure it's good! I'd hate for her to set out bad cookies for Christmas and be all embarrassed. That would just be *crumby*!"

"And you said Mr. Bieberdorf has corny humor?" She cocked one eyebrow at James. "I think you're worse."

"Ouch, that hurts!" he grabbed her hand and walked her into the kitchen.

"Hi, Miss Rita," Jessie greeted James' mother.

"Oh hi, Jessie May, I'm so glad you could join us for supper. You two want a cookie?" She turned and looked at James. "I made Granny Fran's chocolate-peppermint swirl cookies."

"Oh yes, please!" Jessie answered politely as both James and she grabbed a cookie off the cooling rack. "These are amazin'! I will have to get your recipe if you're willin' to share it, of course."

"Well, we do like to keep Granny Fran's recipe in the family, but since you're *almost* family… absolutely!" Rita looked over at James, smiled, and gave a wink. "Here have another one."

"Thanks, Mama," James grabbed two, one for him and one for Jessie, "We're goin' to head up to my room for a bit, if that's okay?" He grabbed Jessie's hand again.

"Leave the door open," Rita called after them.

* * *

"Okay, so what's with this *family* wink? It's got to be a family thing?" Jessie plopped down on James' bed. "You do it all the time. I saw your sister do it when we went there over Thanksgivin'. And now I saw your mama do it also." James shrugged. She continued, "And, by the way, what did your mama mean by *almost* family when she winked and looked straight at you?"

"As far as the wink – genetic defect for sure. When we have children, our kids are doomed."

"James, you're somethin' else!"

143

"And as far as what my mother implied, she just knows how serious I am about you, that's all. She even told me the other day that she's never seen me like this before. And then she got all teary-eyed and told me how I reminded her of my father when they were datin'."

"Ooh, that's sweet, James."

"Yeah, she said I remind her more and more of him now that I'm gettin' older. You know, now that I'm a *man*." He blew on his knuckles and rubbed them on his shoulder.

"Oh goodness, here we go again!" she laughed.

He loved seeing her laugh, seeing her smile. But that reminded him and he came over and sat down on the bed next to her.

"James, are you sure we should sit on your bed together?"

"Yeah, it's fine. We're just talkin' and I got the door open."

"Mmm, I don't know, I feel uncomfortable," Jessie said with an uneasy expression.

"Jess, it's fine, as long as we leave the door open."

"Well, if you're sure," Jessie replied with some reluctance. "I just wanna be respectful in your parents' house. I know my parents would be uncomfortable with this."

"It's okay, Jess, really. Besides, I can go get a large soda here too if we need one." He winked.

"Oh my goodness!" she rolled her eyes. "James Theodore Patterson!"

"There you go using my full name again."

"Well, if you'd behave yourself!" She flirtatiously pushed him at his shoulders.

"You are so pretty when you smile."

Jessie blushed. "Thanks," she laced her fingers between his.

"Jess?"

"Yeah?"

"You remember on Monday when I sang you 'Blue Christmas'? My impressive version too I might add!" He blinked both eyes with a head nod.

"Yes, how could I forget? It was definitely impressive. I think anyone that was walkin' in the halls or into Mr. Brink's class probably won't forget!"

"I know, it was pretty good."

"Cocky!"

"Maybe," he raised his eyebrows in quick succession. "You want me to sing it again? I have my guitar here. This time I could really give you some Elvis!" James laughed but then trailed off and grew quiet. "Jess?" Silence again.

"What is it, James? What's botherin' you?" her hazel eyes were soft.

"Jess, somethin' I said before that upset you? I saw it on your face."

She sighed, "You know me well."

"I do." He squeezed her hands in his. "So, what was it? What was wrong?"

"Oh, James, do we have to talk about this now?"

"Please, Jess," he implored.

"Alright," she looked down, took a breath, and then looked up and slowly started. "I have wanted to push this out of my mind…you enlistin'. We really haven't talked about it since right after I first found out. Not since our walk home that day through Eden's Pathway. Partly because I haven't wanted to since I know I'd be a downer then to hang around. But mostly because it's easier to avoid the topic," her voice cracked. She looked down and tried to swallow. She could feel her chin start to quiver. She composed herself just enough to finish. "It's easier to avoid the topic than face the truth."

James waited. He didn't try to interject or say anything. He just let her talk.

"James, you have told me that I need to look at it as simple as it is…that you're just goin' into the military and goin' away for a bit. And that nothin' between us changes. But it does, James. In school you wanna know what upset me?"

James silently nodded his head.

"You were talkin' about Christmas break and bein' separated and said you didn't know what you were goin' to do when you wouldn't get to see me every day over Christmas break. James, it's Christmas break. For only about two weeks. Two weeks, James!" her voice raised slightly. "James, when you leave for basic trainin' and AIT and then actually get your assignment it will be for months. Months! Maybe even a year! Or…" her voice trailed off into the unthinkable. Her shoulders sunk and the tears began to flow.

"Stop, Jessie. Please." He took her into his arms in an embrace. He kissed the top of her head. He spoke softly, "You don't think I haven't thought about that? That it hasn't crossed my mind? It has, Jess." He loosened his hold on her just enough so he could look into her hazel eyes. "Right after we went to Birmin'ham to visit Elizabeth and David, I was lyin' in bed thinkin' about you and how badly I wanna be married to you and have our own place just like them. And then, like someone took the breath out of me, it occurred to me. What if I don't come home? I felt like I had a heavy weight on my chest, and I couldn't breathe. What if…" He stopped. He knew he didn't have to finish his thought. Jessie would painfully fill in the blank on her own. He moved a strand of hair off her tear-streaked face and looked at her squarely in the eyes. "But then, Jessie May, a thought hit me, a thought so powerful I knew it wasn't of me." She was staring back at him so intensely, hanging on his every word. "Just after my daddy lost his battle to cancer and my mama was left to raise my sister and me on her own, she went through some very dark days. My mama didn't know how she was goin' to go on each day without my daddy. There were days she would just sit up in her bedroom and cry – all day. Elizabeth and I would eat cereal not just for breakfast but also for supper. My sister would make sure we both got up for school and then at night she'd make sure I got my bath and a bedtime story. Maybe that's why she doesn't wanna have kids. For a while, she had to be the parent. She was forced to be at such a young age because my mama checked out for a while. I really don't know how long that lasted. I was only seven, so all the details aren't crystal clear. But one day Pastor Mark came to visit and he read in his Bible with her and that day somethin' changed. When he went home she sat for a long time in her chair in the livin' room. That day it was like somethin' hit her, much in the same way it did me that night lyin' in bed. After that, it was like my mother picked herself up, dusted herself off, and realized she still needed to be a mother. She told us Pastor Mark had shared a scripture with her and the Spirit used it to stir her from her deep mournin'. And from that day on, my mama would say that scripture over and over again to Elizabeth and me."

"What was the scripture?" Jessie was calm now, her tears abated.

"He who is in you is greater than he who is in the world." James answered and then waited to let it sink in. He repeated it. A single tear ran down Jessie's cheek. He cupped her face with his hands and gently wiped the tear away with his thumb. He leaned in and kissed her forehead. He continued, "I think she told Elizabeth and me this scripture often because she needed to hear it herself. It encouraged her and showed her that God who is in her was and is greater than anythin' she was up against. He overcomes evil. I don't understand why cancer had to take my daddy. But cancer didn't win, Jess. God has the victory over evil, always. My daddy is in heaven and my mama found a new normal. Jessie, we don't always know what lies ahead, but we can acknowledge His power and His promises through His word. God IS greater than the evil of this world – even in Vietnam – and I trust in His victory. That night lyin' in bed I chose to claim the truth of that scripture…greater is He that is IN ME than he that is of this world, of Vietnam. That promise is for you too, Jess. His promise."

They sat on his bed no longer talking, time standing still. The only words spoken were between their eyes and soft touches. After some time, Jessie opened her mouth to talk. Her voice was a little croaky. She cleared her throat, "James, that Sunday back in September – when I first found out about you enlistin' – the news was a shockin' surprise."

"I know." James hung his head, regret still heavy on his heart for how Jessie found out. He had let her down, and he knew it.

"Then that Monday when we walked home and talked about you enlistin'---actually the only time other than today that we've really talked about it--- you told me that you wanted to be strong for me and support me just like my father does. James, you've made me realize today that you don't have to go to Vietnam to accomplish that," she squeezed his hands. "You already have! Thank you for bein' strong *now*, James. For remindin' me of the strength of our Heavenly Father and that He is greater than any evil of this world. Just like when Pastor Mark brought that scripture to light for your mama and she had an eye-openin' experience, I also needed this…to have my eyes opened. I've realized I don't want the topic of you bein' enlisted to be taboo anymore. I can understand why your mama had to keep tellin' you and Elizabeth that scripture over and over. She needed to hear it…over and over. James, I realize now that we need to talk about it. I was wrong; I do need to face the truth…but His truth! And just like your mama had to keep repeatin' the scripture to be encouraged by its truth, keep remindin' me, James." She hugged him. "Thank you for lovin' me and supportin' me unconditionally just like my father…and my Heavenly Father. There couldn't be a better way for you to love me."

* * *

Christmas day had been so enjoyable. She liked when Christmas fell on a Friday. It just felt more relaxing. They had enjoyed a wonderful turkey dinner that her mother had made. Her mother was an amazing cook. She and Lydia had helped, of course, but her mother held the title of master chef. After feasting on the turkey and all the trimmings, they had exchanged gifts as a family. She had gotten a blue blouse from her mother and father that she was sure James would love on her. He told her he liked when

150

she wore green and blues because it brought out her hazel eyes. Her parents also gave her green stirrup pants that she had worn to church this morning and had gotten lots of compliments. Lydia and Carrie had given her a Beatles t-shirt too. She really didn't want school to start again, but she was pretty excited to wear all her new clothes.

Saturday morning, she and her mother had gone in to town for their annual after-Christmas-sales trek to Fancy's Mercantile. They always bought their discounted Christmas wrap and bows for the next year and just enjoyed a little mother-daughter outing. Jessie was super excited because she found some Elvis Presley Christmas wrapping paper. Leave it to Fancy to have Elvis wrapping paper! And since she hadn't wrapped James' gift yet, she just couldn't resist. It would be perfect for his gift from her.

James was coming over this afternoon for dessert and games and so that they could exchange their Christmas gifts. He had told her several times he was so excited to give her his gift that he could hardly stand it. He was also pretty proud of himself because he had used some of his gig money and bought gifts for everyone in her family. Jessie thought this was so touching. He really was becoming a part of their family.

She had put together a little something for his family too. Elizabeth and David had spent Christmas day and the weekend with David's family in Graysville, but they would come up this evening and spend the week through New Year's Day at John and Rita's. Her mother had told her that a plate of Christmas goodies would be an appreciated gift while hosting David and Elizabeth for the week. Her mother had added, "It's always nice to have a little variety to set out for the holidays. More impressive!" Jessie had to chuckle a bit to herself. Her mama always liked things "just so" when she hosted. But despite her mama's "particulars" of hosting, she did have a good point, especially considering *all* the goodies that her mother, Lydia, and she had baked. They certainly had variety, that's for sure! They had managed to get done the fudge, the old-fashioned thumb print cookies, and the iced sugar cookies, plus one of Jessie's favorites – twisted candy cane cookies. Jessie thought they always looked so festive on a plate of Christmas goodies. Rita, with her love of culinary delights and baking, would certainly appreciate this gift. And, it would definitely be a hit with everyone's palates!

Jessie was sitting on their gold oversized chair by the bay window enjoying the sun as it kissed her cheeks. Her mama loved this chair. She said she liked how it brought out the hues of her wallpaper. She also thought it was the perfect chair for reading with the light in the window. Jessie liked it also because of the light, and the sun pouring in now felt so good on her skin. It was a chilly, damp 43 degrees. She snuggled under her blanket, relishing in the warmth of the sun. Her feet were kicked up on the ottoman, and she faded in and out of sleep as she listened to her father's football game. He was pretty excited since his Cleveland Browns were playing in the championship game being televised by CBS for the first time. Her poor daddy lived in a houseful of girls who just didn't appreciate the game of football.

Her father would say, "I don't know how you girls can't love a game that has so many life lessons. Lessons about commitment and dedication, disappointments and perseverance, goals and aspirations. Lots to be learned from the game of football." Yet now as Jessie watched her father getting frustrated with the scoreless first half of the game, she didn't think it looked all that enjoyable to her. But she smiled; she loved her father's passion for the game.

Her mother was in the kitchen supervising Carrie with her new Easy Bake oven she had gotten. She was making a brownie packet, and Jessie could faintly smell it over the lingering scent of turkey that still permeated the house. It had been a couple days, but a slight hint of the feast still hung in the air. To Jessie, it was the smell of the holidays, and she loved that. Loved the peaceful feeling it gave her. Actually, she'd been feeling at peace ever since her conversation with James Wednesday. She'd been different since that talk. The Spirit had undoubtedly touched her that day with just what she needed.

She'd been reading in her Bible every night since and God's word was definitely speaking to her and equipping her for when James left. Even though she still cringed at the thought of him leaving for Vietnam---*what girlfriend wouldn't?* ---she had a calming peace deep inside her that she could only explain as being from Him and not of her. *Ah yes, greater is He that is in me, than he that is of this world.* She was overcome by how the Holy Spirit could bubble up His words at just the perfect times she needed to hear them and say them to herself. That made her think of what she had read in Luke last night, *The Holy Spirit will give you the words to say at the moment when you need them.*

"Noooo! It's third and long, Ryan, what were you thinkin'?" Her father's reprimanding snarl to his quarterback at an inopportune interception stirred her from her divine contemplating.

Just then she heard the doorbell chime, "I'll get it." She sprung to her feet, no longer drowsy. Her heart fluttered; it was James.

"Are you sure you don't want me to get it?" her father teased, obviously not moving from his front-and-center-seat to his game.

"No, no, Daddy, that's okay. You just stay comfy right there and keep scoldin' an inanimate object!" she was quick to tease back. "I'd hate to take you away from your game."

"I wasn't scoldin' an inanimate object! Frank Ryan just threw a terrible pass."

"And I'm sure he heard you, Daddy, and won't do it again!" She smiled, gave an innocent look and hustled out of the living room, not giving her father a chance to make a rebuttal. But she could hear him calling back after her, "This isn't any old game, Jess! It's the championship game!"

* * *

Robert loved to see his daughter smiling. The last few months had been hard. She tried to act normal, but her father could tell there was a heaviness weighing her down. His heart ached for her, and he and Patty would pray together often for her. But today, something in her mood seemed lighter, beyond the merriment of the holidays. There was a twinkle back in her eyes and something seemed different with her. He wasn't sure what it was, but something had changed with her recently. He closed his eyes and quickly shot up a prayer of thanks to the Lord for His hand upon his daughter and His ever-present protection. He opened his eyes again and his attention was back to the game.

"What?! Noooo!" Frank Ryan missed on a long pass to wide receiver Paul Warfield , ending the first half with a score of 0-0. "Unbelievable! We can't win if we don't score!" *Jessie was wrong, Ryan definitely had not heard him!*

* * *

Jessie flung open the door, "Merry Christmas!"

James stood there with packages in his hands. She could see his breath in the cool December air. He wore a beige sweater and some dark denim jeans, both of which must have been Christmas gifts. She hadn't seen him in either before. She stood there staring at him; he looked amazing. "Are you goin' to lemme in? Or do I have to stand out here freezin'?" His brown eyes twinkled. He too had a lighter feeling and bounce in his step since their conversation. And, the connection between them was more intense than ever.

"Get in here!" she grabbed his sleeve. "You look amazin'. And you smell good too!"

"Thanks! New cologne. I guess John picked it out. Not bad, huh? Sooooo? Is there any mistletoe hanging somewhere?"

"Maybe!" she leaned in and kissed him. Jessie was filled with a hunger she hadn't known before. James evoked feelings in her she had never experienced. She blushed.

"Mmmm, potent!" he stepped back. "Is it just me or is it hot in here?" James pulled at the collar on his sweater.

"You were just complainin' about bein' cold! Make up your mind! Come on, this way." She motioned with a side head tilt towards the livin' room, "Daddy's watchin' his Browns lose I think!"

"Oh, that's right! The big game's bein' aired on TV! I'd love to watch it with him!"

"Hey, that better not be what you came for!"

"Nope, Baby! Definitely not what I came for, but it's sure an added bonus!" he winked and she led the way into the living room.

* * *

Jessie popped her head into the kitchen. Carrie had a small tin on the table with what looked like the world's smallest brownie in it and she was just pulling a sugar cookie out of her Easy Bake oven. "James just got here. He's in the livin' room with daddy watchin' the game. He brought presents." She directed the last part towards Carrie.

"Oh goodie! More presents!" Carrie started to push herself away from the table. "Can we be done?"

"Hold your horses, not so fast, my little Betty Crocker! One of the lessons with bakin' is if you're goin' to bake in the kitchen, you clean up after yourself." She turned to Jessie, "We'll be in there in a little bit, after Carrie Grace cleans up her mess."

"Alright," Carrie said with a little disappointed but then quickly perked up again, "Jessie May, do you see what I baked all by myself? Brownies and cookies! Next year I'll prob'ly be makin' the Christmas cookies."

Jessie smiled at her sister who was so proud of her morsel of a brownie and bite-sized cookie. "Good job, Carrie Grace! That'd be great to have you helpin' Lydia Ruth and Mama and me next year. We'd get more variety with you bakin' with us!"

She walked back in to the living room where James had made himself at home with her father. Her father recapped the first half of the game for James, and James was quick to join her father in scoffing at the TV. "I agree! 0-0, that's pathetic! What a terrible first half." James tossed his hand mockingly in the direction of the TV. "That's not what we wanna see when we finally get to watch the big game on television."

She shook her head. *How men could get so into a football game!* He looked up when she walked into the room and patted the spot next to him on the couch. She went and sat down. Her arm touched against his. A shot like electricity shot up her arm. Just being close to him made her feel different. A good different. A tingling, electrifying different. James didn't put his arm around her or hold her hand. Jessie knew he was doing that out of courteous respect for her father in the room. *But oh, how she wished he would grab her hand.* The thought of her hand in his sent chills up and down her spine. And then to look into his brown eyes. She turned her head slightly to look at him. Her heart jumped. He was looking at her. *Well, maybe he wasn't as into the game as her father was!*

* * *

When her mother and Carrie came in to the room, the third quarter was just about over. "We can open gifts now!" Carrie exclaimed upon entering. "Then we can have dessert. Mama made some, but if you'd like to try my brownies or sugar cookies, we'll serve that for a little *variety*." Jessie stifled a laugh. Carrie obviously had overheard her mother and her talking, and the way she said that just now sounded so much like her mother it struck a funny bone with her. James looked at Jessie with a questioning expression. She just shook her head quietly giving him a quick tell-you-later-look.

"I'd like to try your desserts, Carrie Grace, but we'll have to wait until after the game," Robert replied. "Your brownies sound good, but my 'Brownies' are finally doin' good! They changed their offensive and defensive tactics and are finally scorin'. I do believe we are goin' to win a championship! The score is 17-0. So sweetheart, I'll have to wait for your brownies until my 'Brownies' are done!"

"Heaven to Betsy we do anythin' when the game's on," Patty said. She grabbed her husband's foot which was kicked up in his recliner and shook his stocking foot as she poked a little fun at him.

"Hey! I don't interrupt your readin' and make you play games or do stuff while you're tryin' to read. *Heaven forbid* I even talk to you while you're devourin' a good book." He smirked a little giving her own words back to her.

"Touché!" Patty laughed.

"Patty, this is so excitin' watchin' a championship game on TV! Next year, we might have to have a party to watch the game together."

"Well now, let's not get ahead of ourselves."

"Hey, you always say you want plenty of notice for hostin'. Well, a year in advance is fair notice, don't' you think! …YESSS!" he broke out in a shout. The Browns scored again.

"Where's Lydia?" Patty asked. "I thought she was in here with you guys."

"I'm sure she's up in her room, nose in a book," Robert answered.

Carrie turned to James, "Maybe you wanna go and meet Ann?"

"Ann?" James asked.

"My goldfish! Didn't Jessie May tell you about her. Her full name is Ann Chovy, but you can just call her Ann if you'd like."

James' face opened up with a big grin. He looked at Jessie as he tried to suppress his laughter. He was just about to get up off the davenport when Patty turned to Carrie, "Actually, Carrie Grace, can you sort the gifts out to each person, and when the game is over, we'll be ready to open gifts and then we can serve dessert. I'll need your help with that too since you helped with the bakin'." Patty smiled warmly at her youngest daughter. "And then maybe we can play a game or somethin'. When this game is over of course." She glanced at her husband and playfully rolled her eyes. "I'll go get Miss Lydia."

* * *

The game ended 27-0 and Robert was in a jovial mood. How he had gotten to be a Cleveland Browns fan, his family never knew. Robert's father had been a Philadelphia Eagles fan and most of the local people were Baltimore Colts fans. But Robert, who always liked to do his own thing, had embraced the Cleveland Browns. And now that his team had just won the championship, his mood was giddy as a child.

He smacked his hands together and started rubbing them, "Well, I just got the best gift ever! Third time

160

NFL Champions! Who else is ready to open *their* gifts!”

Most of the gifts had already been opened on Christmas Day so it hadn't taken Carrie long to sort them. Patty just knew she needed to detour her youngest daughter from taking James on an unending tour of her bedroom again and also knew her youngest daughter needed something to keep her occupied as she waited out the game.

“I sorted the gifts. So be careful, Daddy, when you put your recliner down or you'll squish your package.”

“Okay, thank you, sweetheart. Here, let's shut the television off.” He sat up from his recliner---being careful not to squish his gift---and went over to the TV to turn it off.

James and Jessie had made room for Lydia on the couch with them. Carrie sat on the floor, and Patty had claimed the sunny spot now by the bay window. Robert went back to his recliner. Each of them had a gift below their feet, except for Patty.

“Mama, you don't have one,” Carrie said concerned.

“No, I do, honey. Daddy and I have one to share from James.”

“Here, give this to your mama to open,” Robert handed Carrie their shared gift. “Remember, I already got a gift today!” He pumped his fist into the air, “An NFL Championship!”

Patty got up from her chair and went over to the record player console, "Let's play a little Christmas music." She picked up her new Beach Boys' Christmas album she had just gotten as a gift. "I'll play my new record from you girls." She turned her head to James, "The girls and Robert just gave this to me for Christmas."

"I love the Beach Boys!" James exclaimed acknowledging Patty's gift.

"You love all music!" Jessie patted his knee.

"I do!"

"Alright, there!" Patty got the record playing and sat down again, "Now, who's first? Youngest to oldest again?"

"Um, Miss Patty, if you don't mind, I had asked Robert if Jessie May could open hers first."

"Oh yes, I knew that. Of course," Patty responded with a smile.

Jessie was a little befuddled. What did James have up his sleeve? Her mother already knew about it? And, he had asked her father? *What on earth was he up to?*

He turned to Jessie and returned her pat on the knee, "I asked your father's permission to give your gift to you…first that is!"

Now he really had her curious. Her heart started to race. It couldn't be! *What did he mean by he "asked her father's permission"?* He wouldn't propose to her right here in front of her family. They had talked a lot more lately about getting married, but he wouldn't do it here. *Would he?* But then again, she considered how she found out he had enlisted---her father had found out the same time with her. That was a shock. *He wouldn't! Would he?* Her thoughts were racing through her head and her heart was pounding! *How could he afford an engagement ring?* She knew he had only had a couple gigs at Linny's and he wouldn't have enough to pay for a ring. *That couldn't be it. No way!* Her heart started to settle.

"Here, Jessie May!" Carrie picked up the package below Jessie's feet. "You get to be first. Then me!" Carrie wanted to open her gift. She didn't have much for patience when it came to waiting to open a present. So with Jessie just sitting there, Carrie figured she'd help her sister out and hand her the gift.

Jessie gingerly took the gift from Carrie's hand. It was a small, light-weight gift. She could feel herself starting to sweat. The wrapping paper started to feel sticky in her clammy hand.

"Go ahead," James patted her knee again. His brown eyes looked straight into her eyes, "Carrie Grace's waitin'!" He winked.

She slipped her finger under a taped down crease on one of the ends. She took a deep breath and slowly exhaled. Releasing the tape, she slowly lifted the flap up and titled her head a little to peek at the box as if it might reveal its contents before she opened it. She gently started to tug on the wrapping paper and pulled it back as she slid the box out. She held the box in her hands as they rested in her lap.

"Come on! We'll be here 'til the cows come home!" Carrie impatiently pleaded. Jessie obviously wasn't opening her gift fast enough.

"Carrie, patience, my darlin'," her mother corrected.

Jessie looked down at the box in her hands. It was a small black jewelry box, but clearly not new. It was older and weathered and part of the black was rubbed off completely on one corner where the tan color of cardboard revealed itself. Jessie felt herself relax. It couldn't be what she was thinking. He must have just needed a box this size to wrap her gift. *But what would be this small?* She started to pull the lid up and that's when she saw it. *A ring!* A ring so ornate and beautiful it took her breath away.

"James!" she let out a breathy gasp. "It's beautiful." She looked at him, confusion written all over her face.

"It's a promise ring, and I asked your father's permission if I could give it to you. And he knows I have intentions to give you somethin' else, but I wanted to give you this first."

"It's so beautiful," she paused staring down at the ring sparkling before her. "But, I don't understand…and…and, how could you afford this?" She paused again tilting the box in the light as the ring sparkled, "Oh James, it's so beautiful."

"It was my mama's ring from my daddy."

"Oh, James, I can't take this."

"No, I am *givin'* it to you. You aren't *takin'* anythin'. You're receivin' it." He gently took the box from Jessie and took the ring out. He held it in his open hand. "It's for you as a promise."

"Your mother's ring from your father…it should go to your sister."

"Elizabeth knows. She wanted you to have it," James smiled. "It's my promise to you, Jessie May, for when I get back from Vietnam. I asked permission from your father because when I get back home, l wanna give you a different ring."

Jessie looked down at James' outstretched hand. Then she looked up at him and his brown eyes met hers. He had such a soft, warm smile on his face. A smile so full of love. Slowly she reached out to James's hand. She paused for a moment and then James' smile grew bigger. She felt her heart swell. She knew she was blushing with her family all in the room, staring at her, but it was more than that. A warmth came over her body. *Greater is He that is in me than he that is of this world.* She was filled with gratitude. A thankfulness that was so full within her it resonated throughout her entire body. Tears filled her eyes. She took the ring from James. She thought of James' promise and what it meant for him to give her his mother's ring. She thought of his words *when I get back home*. Her heart was filled with the reassurance of His truth again . . . The Lord's truth. As thankful as she was for James' promise now to her, she was more humbled by *The Promise* that was from the Lord now *and forever*.

"Is it my turn to open now or what?" Carrie always seemed to pipe up at just the right times, bringing lightness and laughter to any occasion.

"Yes, Carrie Grace, it's your turn," Jessie laughed as a tear slipped out and rolled down her cheek. She grabbed James' hand and squeezed it.

"Do you like it?" he whispered.

"I love it. Thank you! It is so special, James. I hardly have the words to express what I'm feelin'. Please tell your mama and Elizabeth too how much this means to me." She was still holding the ring in between her thumb and index finger rotating it slightly in her fingers as she looked at it.

"You should try it on."

"Hey, some of us are tryin' to open our presents now," Carrie chirped.

"Carrie Grace, be patient, dear. Let's let Jessie May have this moment." Patty got up from her chair and sat down on the floor by her youngest daughter. She rubbed her back, "Remember, good things come to those who wait."

"Alright, alright already." Carrie was full of spunk and feistiness!

James took the ring back from Jessie and took her left hand in his. He slid it on her fourth finger and much to her surprise, it fit perfectly as if it had been sized just for her. She felt a catch in her throat. She thought it would be awkward in front of her family, but she was thankful she received the ring with them. She hugged James and then got up and hugged her father.

"Thank you, Daddy."

"What did I do?" Robert squeezed Jessie's hands as she stepped back and looked at him.

"For givin' your permission for James to give me this ring."

"Go on now, girl. We don't need to see a grown-man cry today, especially when his team won a national championship!" He motioned for Jessie to go back over to James to sit on the couch. "Alright, Carrie Grace, you're up!"

"Yay!" Carrie didn't have to be asked twice. She tore open the gift so fast one wouldn't have realized there was even wrapping paper on it. She squealed. James had given her a doll.

"It's from both me and my sister Elizabeth."

"I love it!" Carrie exclaimed as she hugged her doll.

"We hoped you would! When Jessie and I went to Birmin'ham to visit my sister, she gave this to me and told me she wanted you to have it. It had been very special to her; it was one of her favorites growin' up. She told me it's her *Ravin' Beauty Fashion Doll*."

"I know!" Carrie butted in enthusiastically. Patty gave her a reprimanding look to mind her manners.

James continued, "She got it when she was your age. She said since she doesn't plan on havin' children that she would like to know it went to someone that would love her!"

"Oh, I will! I will love her!" Carrie hugged her new doll, "I'll love her as much as you love Jessie May."

James laughed and looked over at Jessie and gave her---what else---a wink!

Jessie shook her head and just smiled. She didn't even worry about what her father might think this time. He already knew…and had given his permission. Her heart fluttered again.

"Okay, Lydia Ruth, you're next," Carrie directed.

Lydia picked up her gift from James on the floor. She shook it ever so gently and then opened it slowly, more methodically than her younger sister. As soon as the torn paper revealed the content beneath it, a smile broke out across her face. It was a new book – *Stormy, Misty's Foal* – by Marguerite Henry. "I love it! How'd you know I wanted this? Did Jessie May tell you?"

"No, she didn't actually. I noticed one time you were readin' her first book *Stormy* and then I happened to see that its sequel came out last year, so I figured you'd like it."

"I do, James. So thoughtful of you." She rubbed her hand across the top of the book. "Thank you!"

"Okay! Next!" Carrie ordered. "Jessie May already had her turn, so James, it's your turn now. And if you could kind of hurry, I want dessert. I'm gettin' hungry."

"Carrie child! Mind your manners! Were you born in a barn?"

"No, Mama, but I don't know why you say that like it's a bad thing. You know, we're celebratin' Christmas, and Jesus was born in a barn!"

The room burst into laughter. *Oh, Carrie Grace!* She was quite the character.

"Patty, maybe you and Robert should open your gift from me first? Carrie might appreciate it. It might tide her over."

"Oh, bless your heart, James. It appears to me you know all my daughters so well." She turned and spoke then to her husband, "Well, Robert, should I come over there and we can open it together?"

"Nah, you just open it from there, Pats. I can see it just fine from here." He was kicked back in his recliner.

"You just be careful you don't fall asleep over there, Mr. Clark. You're lookin' pretty tipped back and comfy."

"Oh no, me? I wouldn't do a thing like that," he shrugged innocently.

"Mmm, hmmm," Patty said with her southern drawl. "Carrie Grace, you keep an eye on your daddy."

"Yep, I'm your girl, Mama."

"Hey, how come you always seem to take her side?" Robert sat up slightly to look at Carrie.

"Because just like you always say, Daddy, I know where my food comes from, so I better not make Mama mad."

Carrie had everyone in stitches again. When the laughter subsided Patty opened their gift from James. "What a lovely tin." Patty complimented James. She pulled the lid off. It was filled with caramels – each individually wrapped in wax paper and neatly twisted shut.

"Those are my mama's caramels! You try to buy those at Pugsy's, especially this time of year, and they are always sold out! But I had my mama make them *special order* just for you. I hope you like them."

"We will!" Carrie shot up from the floor. "Let's try them right now."

"Yes, I think that's a good idea. And James is right; it just might tide you over, Carrie Grace! You know James has waited pretty patiently to open his gifts. So, you pass out the caramels, and let's let him finish his turn so we can get at our desserts we worked so hard to make. And maybe a game yet."

Carrie nodded proudly and picked up the tin. She surprised everyone by serving them first and then sat down and helped herself to a caramel…or maybe two!

"Okay, James, last but not least, you're up."

"Open the green one first," Jessie said. "It's from the family. The other one is from me; you can open that one last."

"I picked out your gift," Carrie said, muffled through the caramels stuffed in her mouth.

"I'm sure I'll love it then!" He winked at Carrie. James grabbed the package he was instructed to open first. He peeled off the wrapping paper almost as quick as Carrie.

"James knows how to open a gift!" she nodded her head in approval.

He turned the box so he could read it. "Yahtzee."

"It's a lot like Dutch Blitz! And Daddy said it will help me with my math," Carried explained excitedly, "and I'm gonna beat you after dessert."

"You're on!" James challenged. He turned to Jessie, "Okay, so may I open the gift from you *now*?"

"Well, it's goin' to be pretty hard to top your gift!" She glanced down at the ring on her left hand, "But yes, you may open yours now."

He looked at his last gift on the floor. It had Elvis Christmas wrap. "Nice touch!"

"I thought you'd like that!"

"Hmmm? Unusual flat-shaped package? Looks like a calendar. You got me a calendar, didn't you? So that I can keep track of my days and count down until I come home to you?"

"Nope! Just open it!" She had a mischievous grin.

He picked up the package. It was firmer and heavier than a calendar. He tilted the package and heard something slide and shift. *An album!* Jessie knew his love of music; that's what it had to be! But what would she have gotten him? He was curious now. He opened up the last savored Christmas present and, to his delight, it was Elvis' 1957 Christmas Album!

He looked up at Jessie. She had a big grin on her face and twinkle in her eyes, "I thought Elvis' Christmas album would be a perfect gift to remember our first Christmas together!"

"I could take out my Beach Boys and we could put Elvis in and play that while we have dessert," Patty interjected.

"Definitely!" He handed it to Patty and turned to Jessie, "Thanks, Jess, I love it."

Patty was switching the vinyl records in her console and Jessie called over her shoulder, a big grin across her face and her hazel eyes dancing, "Oh and Mama, James might just sing along. He really likes the song 'Blue Christmas'."

Chapter 10
A New Year, A New Question

"Happy New Year, Jessie May! Glad you could come over."

"Thanks, Miss Rita! Same to you! Thank you for invitin' me."

"You're welcome! I just can't believe the week slid by as quickly as it did and that this is the first we've seen you all break. This week has just sailed by with David and Elizabeth home. And now they leave tomorrow. I hate to see them go."

"I bet! I'm sure it's been wonderful havin' everyone under one roof again."

"It sure has been. Such a blessin'! And thank you so much for all those Christmas goodies! Very thoughtful of you, and the extras were appreciated with David in the house! He has such an insatiable sweet tooth."

Jessie laughed, "So I'm guessin' if you had any of those amazin' caramels you made us, they didn't last long here either?"

"Land sakes, no! He hunts those out with his sniffer and they are usually gone within the first couple days!"

"I can understand that! The caramels you gave my parents were almost gone before we even finished openin' gifts! We had to hide the last bit from Carrie Grace or she'd have finished them in one sittin'."

"Sounds like David!"

"Well, thank you for givin' my parent those. They were appreciated by all!"

Elizabeth came bounding into the kitchen, straight to where James and Jessie were standing against the counter. She hugged Jessie, "Lemme see your hand! I'm dyin' to see mother's ring."

Jessie felt a twinge of guilt as she held out her hand, "Are you sure, Elizabeth, that you don't want it? You're right, it is *your* mother's ring and, really, it should belong to you."

"Oh, bless your heart! Don't you even say that! Yes, it was my mama's ring. Now it's yours. It's special to me, of course, because it was from my daddy, but I am so thankful I have many other things that remind me of my daddy." She stopped and then looked at her own hand, "You see this ring on my hand?" She held her hand out for Jessie to see. "This ring is special to me, because David gave it to me. I wouldn't want any other ring on my hand, not even from my daddy. So, don't you feel badly at all. Honestly, Jess." She grabbed both of Jessie's hands and looked intently into her eyes, "And besides, I will still get to see Mama's ring when it's on *my sister's* hand!" She winked.

"Okay, it's confirmed," Jessie commented.

"What's that? What's confirmed?" Elizabeth asked slightly confused.

"The wink is a family thing!"

James and Jessie both laughed. James squeezed Jessie around her shoulder, "I told you---a genetic defect for sure!"

* * *

Robert was sitting at the kitchen table finishing his breakfast. Patty came over with the coffee pot. "Need a warmer-upper?"

"You sure do spoil me. I'm a lucky man."

"I know!" she flipped her hair and swung her hip slightly to the side as she leaned in to fill his cup.

"And we wonder where Carrie Grace gets her spunk!"

Robert picked up his newspaper. It was Monday morning, so he could relax a little and enjoy his coffee while he read his paper. The top of the *Walker County Tribune* was dated March 8th, 1965. He scanned the headlines, "First combat troops deploy into South Vietnam". He sighed and read on, "3,500 U.S. Marines arrive in Vietnam, landing at China Beach to defend the American air base at Da Nang. This first wave of U. S. combat troops deploy into South Vietnam joining 23,000 American military advisors already in Vietnam." He closed his eyes and hung his head for a moment. Then he tilted his head and, casting a look up to heaven, he raised a prayer.

Gracious Father, grant these young men and women your protection. Watch over them and keep them out of harm's way. He was just finishing his quick prayer when he heard the front door bell. He glanced at the rooster clock hanging on the wall. It was 8:10. *Now who could that be on a Monday mornin'?*

Just at the same time he was thinking it, Patty said with bewilderment, "Now who could that be on a Monday mornin'?"

"I'll get it, honey. I was just wonderin' the same thing. Probably a Hoover vacuum cleaner sales man. I heard there was one makin' his rounds again, and I'd hate for you to go gettin' any ideas in your head."

"Maybe I *should* get the door," Patty teased.

"No, no, you just keep cleanin' up in here." He got up and kissed her on the cheek. The doorbell rang again. "I'm comin'! I'm comin'!" Robert clomped down the hall.

He opened the door and, to his surprise, there stood James. He was twisting his sweatshirt in his hands like he was ringing out water. His eyes looked like a deer caught in the headlights, "Good mornin', Mr. Clark."

"Well, good mornin', James. I'm afraid Jessie May isn't here. You know, she leaves about 7:45 when she walks with Lydia and Carrie to school."

"Yes, I know that. My intention was to catch you. I knew you'd still be here this mornin'."

"Oh? Well, come on in," Robert motioned. James had him curious now. He closed the door behind James and then led them back to the kitchen.

Patty looked up in surprise, "Well, James, what on earth do we owe the pleasure of you stoppin' by? Aren't you goin' to be late for school?"

"Mornin', Miss Patty! No, first bell rings at 9:00, so I will be there by then. I wanted to stop by when Jessie May wasn't here. I have somethin' to ask Mr. Clark."

Now he had both Patty and Robert's curiosity piqued. Patty didn't want to leave but she knew James had specifically come to talk with Robert, not her, and she didn't want James to be any more uncomfortable than he already looked. She hoped everything was okay. Jessie couldn't take anymore crazy surprises.

"Oh, well, I will let you two talk then. I can give you your privacy," she tried to sound nonchalant, but inside she was dying to stay and listen in. She was hoping James would say there was no need to leave the room. However, when he didn't say anything, she stole a quick look over at Robert. "I have laundry to do anyway. Monday is my laundry day," she shrugged. "Have a good day, James, if I don't see you again before you leave," Patty scooted out of the kitchen, glancing once again at Robert.

Robert knew that look of his wife's well. He would be telling her everything later. He hadn't been married 26 years to not know her numerous nonverbal expressions and what they meant. Each look had a distinct meaning. Like when she pursed her lips together with the corners of her mouth turned down, her eyes like saucers---that meant he had better mind his words or he would be washing his own shirts. Now, her eyes were an intense hazel green, slightly raised, and she was holding her breath. Knowing this look and the anxiousness behind it, he nodded slightly at her as she left the room. A subtle understanding between them, her expression softened. Yes, he would visit with her later.

"Would you like to sit down?" Robert motioned over to the kitchen table.

"Yes sir, thanks." James sat down at the table and twisted at his sweatshirt again.

"James, what's on your mind? Is there anythin' wrong?"

"No, sir," James shook his head, "there's something I'd like to ask you."

"You wanted to ask me somethin'?"

"Yes sir, prom is comin' up."

"Okay?"

"So what I'm askin', sir, is for your permission. I'd like to take her to the prom?"

"James," Robert's furled brow lifted as his mind eased and he started to laugh, "here you had me concerned somethin' was wrong; you looked so nervous. Heck, you were less nervous to ask me if you could give your mama's ring to Jessie May. James, you know, you don't need to ask my permission for *everythin'*. I'm not sure what my daughter initially told you about me, but I'm not *that* bad." He reached across and gave James a quick pat on the shoulder.

"I know, sir, but some day I'm goin' to be a father, and I don't know how I'll be when some boy comes callin' and wants to take my daughter to her first prom. I would hope he'd be respectful with his intentions with my daughter. My father wasn't around growin' up. Prior to four years ago when John came into my mother's life, we didn't have a fatherly head of the household. My mama did a good job raisin' us though. She definitely taught me to be sensitive to women."

"Maybe I should take some notes from you," Robert chuckled but then cleared his throat, "Sorry, go on."

"Of course, there were things we missed without my father's lead. There's a reason I'm not on the football team!" Now James laughed. "I definitely missed out on throwin' balls together in the yard and just doin' guy things, but I'm so blessed with my mama. I got my love of music from her and she's the most carin' and lovin' person I know. She taught me how to be respectful to others, especially women. Mr. Clark, it comes as a privilege, not an expectation, that I would take your daughter to the prom."

"James, the privilege is mine to be able to say *yes*. Yes, you may take my daughter to the prom." He stuck his hand out to shake James'.

"Thank you, Mr. Clark," James shook Robert's hand firmly. "And if I could ask a favor of you, it would be appreciated."

"Yes?"

"Don't tell Jessie May that I asked you," James said grinning. He was no longer twisting his sweatshirt. He had relaxed.

"Deal." They each nodded and shook hands again.

James stood up from the table, "Well, I better get goin' or I will be late, and I don't want Jessie May suspicious. She'll be lookin' for me and wonderin' where I'm at. Thanks for your time."

"Thanks for stoppin' by, James. Have a good day and tell your folks hello for me."

"I sure will. Thanks again, Mr. Clark, I'll let myself out." James turned and hustled out of the kitchen.

Robert heard the front door open and shut. He sat at the table for a bit, neither sipping his coffee nor reading the paper. Just sitting. Just thinking. Patty walked in; she had a questioning look on her face. "James is gone already? What was that all about?" she asked.

"You know, I like that boy. I really like that boy."

"Ok, well…is everythin' okay with him and Jessie May?" she asked somewhat impatiently.

"You know, before Christmas he asked my permission to give Jessie May his mother's ring. He reassured me it was a promise ring and that he wouldn't do anythin' else without askin' me first. I assumed marriage. So admittedly I was a little nervous that he came over to ask for my permission to marry our daughter already."

"And?" There was no *somewhat* to her impatience now.

"Well, when he said he wouldn't do anythin' else without askin' me first, I sure didn't expect it to be for *everythin'* else." He scratched his head and shook it, "Patty, he came over here to ask my permission to take Jessie May to prom. Heaven knows I sure didn't ask *your* father for permission to take you to the prom."

"I declare! He had us all worked up for that?" Patty sighed.

"You know, maybe I should have!" He shook his head.

"Should have what?" Patty was still resolving it in her mind that everything was alright.

"Maybe I should have asked your father to take you to prom. I think I'm the one learnin' from that boy."

Patty laughed, "You still call him *that boy*. You know that used to drive Jessie crazy."

Robert laughed, "I know, still does." He sat for a moment in thought. "Patty, so many times you and I have prayed together for our girls' futures and we've prayed for their future husbands. We've prayed those young boys right now would be makin' decisions to keep them on a path accordin' to the Lord's will and that someday they would be the husbands our daughters need. We've prayed Joshua 24:15 for those young boys. We've prayed that they will become men who say, 'As for me and my house, we will serve the Lord.' Patty, I see that in James."

Patty came up behind her husband and put her hands on his shoulders and started to rub them.

"Patty, that boy…James…makes me wanna ask him permission."

"Whatsoever do you mean by that?" Patty asked.

"To ask if he'd take my daughter's hand in marriage." They both laughed. He reached up and grabbed her hand and brought her around to him. "Seriously though, we've prayed for the young men our girls will marry. Patty, he's everythin' we've prayed for."

"Robert Christopher Clark, it doesn't work like that! You can't *ask him* if he'll take your daughter's hand in marriage!" Patty laughed again. "I can't believe you of all people even said that." She couldn't help giggling some more. How her husband had changed. "I can't believe *you* wanna ask him to marry your daughter, especially when I think back to how you were when Jessie May was just tryin' to get the nerve to even tell you that she liked James." She shook her head, "My, my, how you have softened."

"Hey now, let's not go sayin' I'm soft." He grabbed his wife around her waist and brought her down on his lap and brought his nose to hers. "Okay, maybe a little bit, but you do that to me!" He paused enjoying the closeness of his wife. "I know, I never thought I would feel this way, but he's a good kid." He stopped and corrected himself, "He's a good young man. Patty, he's a Godly man, and he would be a blessed choice for our daughter."

Patty leaned her forehead against her husband's, "Robert, the Lord will decide that. They are young yet. Like you always tell me, let's leave it in God's hands. He will take care of whomever is to marry our daughter. God will decide if it is a blessed choice for *His* daughter."

Robert slid both arms around the small of his wife's back. "Woman, oh how I love you." Patty felt her heart flutter. Robert kissed her. "Have I ever shared with you the scripture I say when I am prayin' for you?"

Patty tilted her head in question at her husband's change of thought. She leaned in slightly and whispered, "No, my sweetheart, what?"

"Proverbs 31:10-11, 'A wife of noble character who can find? She is worth far more than rubies. Her husband has full confidence in her and lacks nothin' of value.' Patty, I thank God for you as my wife, for your character and who you are. With you, I lack nothin' and gain everythin'."

Chapter 11
Prom Prospects

The second half of the school year seemed to be whizzing by. With March about half gone, spring was just around the corner and so was prom, which was the buzz of conversation among the students at Cordova High.

"I'm thinkin' of askin' Donna Smith if she'd go with me to the prom," Ricky commented as he squirted ketchup onto his hotdog. The lunch room was loud. The five of them sat at one end of a table visiting.

"Yeah, I'm still scopin' my prospects," Bobby Ray rubbed his chin, "So many babes, so little time."

"You're such a putz, Bobby Ray!" Karen said.

"So, James, have you asked anyone yet?" Nathaniel asked, joining in the conversation.

Jessie shot Nathaniel a look – the exact look Nathaniel had anticipated in provoking her with his question. "What? I had to ask. I figured if Jimbo was takin' someone else, I might take you."

James retorted, "Not goin' to happen, Nathaniel. She said she'd only go with a gentleman. So…you're out."

"Hey, I can be a gentleman. Sometimes!" he laughed. "Well, Jess, if you're set on goin' with James, I might ask Charlotte Baker then."

Jessie loved how these guys always joked with each other and with her too. She enjoyed the easy feeling when they were all together. They were fun to hang around, and she liked how she fit right in with them. She turned to Nathaniel, "Well, if somethin' happens with...Jimbo," she paused, "I'll let you know."

"Hey now!" James bumped her shoulder and the gang of friends laughed. They finished eating their meal while talking more about prom, third quarter tests coming up, and their graduation on the horizon. Soon Karen, Bobby Ray, Ricky, and Nathaniel were picking up their empty trays and heading to catch a little break in the halls before classes started again. Just James and Jessie were left at the table.

"So?" James looked at Jessie. That's all he said.

"Yes?" she laughed.

"I would like to ask you somethin'."

"Yes?" he had her attention now.

"I was wonderin' if you would go to prom with me? Or if it doesn't work out, there's Nathaniel." he raised one eyebrow.

She laughed again, "Undoubtedly you, my fine *gentleman*!"

"I was hopin' that's what you'd say!" he tilted his head and gave a little wink, then wiped the corners of his mouth with his napkin, crumpled it up and tossed it on his empty tray. He slid the tray forward and leaned on the table turning slightly to see Jessie better. "I thought I'd walk you home then and ask your father's permission."

"James, I don't believe you have to ask my daddy's permission to take me to prom. That's only if you're askin' for my hand in marriage." She stifled a laugh.

"Laugh if you will. I do things differently. Just call me chivalrous. No, remember…Gentleman James." He held his chin up high and Jessie laughed at him. "Yep, I like that because it has a nice ring to it." He batted both eyelids at her.

She laughed again, flipping her hair back as the laugh came from her belly. "I love you. You are chivalrous. And, as I told you before, you are a gentleman, but…."

"Yes? Yes?" he asked again.

"Well, a *true* gentleman would have *asked* if he could walk me home rather than tell me he was walkin' me home!"

"Oh, Jessie May, you never miss a detail!" He squeezed her hands. "Yet," he drug out his words; he was having fun with this.

"Yet what?" Both were being flirtatious.

"Well, I'm a step ahead of you. I maybe just happened to already ask your father's permission to take you to prom. Soooo…I guess walkin' you home today is just a moot point." He scratched his chin, "I wonder what the boys are doin' after school."

"James Theodore Patterson!" she shoved his shoulder.

"Ooooh," James put out a pouty lip, "is *someone*—who always likes knowin'what's goin' on—just a teensy bit upset that she had no clue I already asked her father? Or maybe because she has to walk home after school by herself!"

* * *

"May I carry your bag for you, ma'am? Gentleman James at your services," James bowed down and pretended to tip his hat to the lady.

"James, you are just lucky I'm *lettin'* you walk me home today after all your shenanigans." Jessie's hazel eyes twinkled.

"Well, at least *I asked*," he winked.

"Oh, did you?" she put her hands on her hips.

"I believe I did somewhere in that conversation!" They laughed together and James took her hand in his. They walked for a little while hand-in-hand. The warmth of the afternoon sun on their faces gave a reassurance that spring was coming. And, it was evident with the trees. Spring was just starting to dress the trees in Eden's Pathway. "Let's stop here." James motioned for them to sit down on the wet, mossy ground.

"James, we're goin' to get all wet."

187

"Here, sit on my coat. I don't mind it gettin' a little wet. Bein' next to you and gettin' a little wet sounds kind of nice!" he raised his eyebrows in quick successions.

"James!"

"What?" he stopped and looked shocked. Innocent of any implications. Then he grinned and tugged her hand, taking her with him to the ground.

They sat motionless, listening to nature's symphony of winter's end. The dripping of the water off the tree branches and the clicking sound of the cicadas gave a relaxing rhythm as they snuggled next to one another.

"You know what Betty Lou told me today in English?" Jessie spoke very quietly as if speaking any louder might halt the beautiful song of nature playing around them. "James?" she repeated when he didn't answer.

"Hmm? Betty Lou…English? I don't know… maybe…why she gave up on readin' *Pride and Prejudice* …because the characters were too *Austentatious*. Get it? Jane Austen?"

"Oh mercy, James, do you and Mr. Bieberdorf attend some class together on cheesy humor?" she rolled her eyes playfully.

"No, but that's a great idea. I need a few more for the road. Vietnam might need some cheesy humor! By the way, tell your mama that joke. She'd appreciate that one."

"Okay, seriously, do you wanna know what Betty Lou told me in English class today or what?"

"Oh most definitely!" he was playing with her.

She shot him a look with her eyes. "Alright, if you don't wanna know."

"No, no, really. I do wanna know."

"Are you ready now?"

"I am, yes, what did Betty Lou tell you in English class?"

She cleared her throat, "She was tellin' me about this new musical that was just released. *The Sound of Music,* I think she said it was. It's based on a real-life story about a family just before World War II, and it's a drama and a romance! So, I was thinkin' maybe we could do another trip to Elizabeth and David's and go see it at the drive-in."

"Mmm, don't you think we should avoid drive-ins for a while?" he grabbed her waist and pulled her closer to him.

Her heart started to pound. He lowered his head so that their faces where close and then he started to kiss her. Slowly at first, but then their kissing became faster, more intense. He pulled away. He was now breathing harder and she noticed she was also. And her body was tingling. "Hmmmmm," he slightly moaned, "we both know there's no place to get a COLD soda around here, so we better find a new subject to talk about or we'll be avoidin' Eden's Pathway too!"

She took a deep breath to slow her heart beat back to some normalcy again. "James, I know we wanna wait…you know, *wait* until after we are married." James knew what she was implying.

"Yes, Jess, I wanna do things right with you."

"Well, we agreed that day in your bedroom that we wouldn't have any elephants in the room anymore. We'd talk openly about everythin' we were feelin' and any concerns weighin' on either of us with you leavin'."

"Yes?"

"James, we know we wanna get married."

"Yeah?"

"And I know you wanna wait to have *sex* until after we get married," she said the word bashfully.

"Yes, Jess, that's right. *We* wanna wait to have sex until after we are married," he emphasized the word we.

"But maybe we should get married before you leave."

"You really want this hot body of mine pretty badly!"

"James!" she giggled.

"My sweet, Jessie girl," he paused now, less joking in his voice as he rolled to his side and caressed her face, "I don't wanna rush this just to have sex with you."

"But…" Jessie started; she felt slightly rejected.

James interrupted, "We aren't rushin' into marriage just so you can take advantage of me."

"James, quit jokin' now! I'm serious!"

"So am I!" he laughed. "I mean look at me…irresistible!"

She sighed. She knew she wasn't going to be able to make her point with him. He was such a goof. She loved him—just as he was—with all her heart.

"You know though, Jess, have you thought about *where* you wanna get married once I do get back?"

She sat up surprised by his question, "Where?"

"Yeah, where we would get married."

"James, I am rather surprised. I didn't realize you gave much thought to the ceremony. I mean, I daydream about it all the time, but I didn't realize you thought about the weddin' part."

"Oh, I give it thought too…mine are just pure and not for the sex."

"James Theodore Patterson!"

"I don't think I'll ever tire of hearin' you speak my full name. I hate when my mama does it, but when you do it, it makes me laugh."

She elbowed him and asked, "Okay, so where? At First Baptist with Pastor Mark?"

"No, right here, Jess. In Eden's Pathway, but in the fall."

"Are you serious?"

"Totally! This is our spot, you know! And think of the fall colors. We wouldn't even have to decorate. Nature would do it for us."

"It starts to get chilly in the fall? Don't you think a summer weddin' might be better?"

"Nope, it'd be too hot and humid. Fall is a much safer plan, Jess."

"Yeah, but I can about imagine what my daddy and mama would say if we didn't get married in a church! And fall? I know summers can be hot and sticky, but I always pictured a summer weddin' and then havin' the reception outside the church in the courtyard." She waved her hand up and across the air like she was laying out her story as she planned it, "Gingham table clothes. Daisies. Sunflowers. Little metal buckets set on top of the tables with some of your mama's caramels in each one with little signs that say, 'How SWEET of you to come!'"

"Miss Clark, sounds like you have our weddin' about all planned! And by the sounds of it, you better start sweet-talkin' my mama if you want *buckets* of caramels! Well, I guess since the weddin' plannin' is about done, I can start plannin' the honeymoon!" He grabbed her and rolled Jessie on top of him again.

"James! Now who's the one thinkin' of *SEX!*" This time she said the word with no reserve.

"Shhh! Jessie May," ---his turn to use her middle name---"you're goin' to scare the cicadas!"

* * *

Jessie stepped inside her front door. She was just getting home from her Friday night date with James. She could see the lights of his car outside as he pulled away. She turned her back and leaned against the door and sighed. Just then her mama came down the stairs. "Well, someone looks like she had a good time tonight!"

"Very much!"

"What'd you two end up doin'?"

"We just met up with the guys and Donna Smith and Charlotte Baker—RJ and Nathaniel's prom dates. I don't know if you know them? RJ's takin' Donna to prom and Nathaniel's takin' Charlotte."

"Bobby Ray wasn't with tonight?" They walked together into the kitchen.

"No, he was with. He just doesn't have a date yet. He said if he doesn't ask someone at school, he might just take his cousin Dottie. I guess she's from Jasper. He really wants to go to his senior prom though with a date from here. But if he doesn't find someone, then she's his back-up plan."

"Want a cup of tea with me? I was just gonna put the kettle on and make myself a cup before bed."

193

"Sure," Jessie said, sitting down at the table.

Patty grabbed the kettle off the stove top and filled it with water. She flicked the top burner on, set the tea kettle down, and then took a chair at the table next to Jessie. "So was Bobby Ray kind of the odd-man-out tonight?"

"No, not at all! That's what I love about these guys! I'm usually the odd-man…or girl…out, but they never make me feel that way."

"You've got some good friends, that's for sure. I don't hear you talk about Betty Lou or Karen Norraine much anymore and I haven't really seen them since you and James made things official."

"Funny you should mention them, because I wanted to talk with you about meetin' up with 'em tomorrow. And, Mama, you don't have to worry; I'm not losin' sight of my other friends – my girlfriends – just because I have a boyfriend. I see Betty Lou and Karen Norraine every day in school. I mean, I do have a locker right next to Karen, Mama!"

 "I know, I just haven't seen them around for a while, and it's important that you nurture those other relationships too. You're goin' to need those when James leaves."

Jessie looked down, "I know, Mama. And I do appreciate your insight."

The tea kettle started to whistle. Patty got up from the table, "You want peppermint or chamomile?"

"Peppermint, please, with a splash of milk. I can get it too, Mama."

"No, you sit. I enjoy us talkin'. I'll get the tea if you keep visitin'."

"I do take time for my girlfriends…I just maybe don't talk about them like I do James," she smiled, caught in love.

"I suppose not," her mother nodded with a knowing smile on her face. Patty set a mug of tea down in front of Jessie and sat down in the chair next to her. She wrapped both her hands around her own mug. It was warm and felt good against her cold hands. She lifted her mug and took a sip, "So, what were the plans you were talkin' about with Karen Norraine and Betty Lou tomorrow?"

"Well, we thought we'd meet at Fancy's about 9:30 to pick out material together for our prom dresses and then get cokes while we are there. I was even maybe hopin' you'd help me get started on my dress tomorrow afternoon if I find material. I liked that pattern you showed me last weekend, so I just need material for it."

"Which one was that? Was it the one off the shoulders or the maxi dress? Either way, you're goin' to wanna buy some tulle as well. We'll probably only need a few yards of that though."

"I think I like the one off the shoulders. You think Daddy will be okay with that one?"

"Well, once it's made, he won't have much of a choice now, will he?" They both giggled. Patty took another sip of her tea. "I think it will be okay. It still has little sleeves; they're just off the shoulder."

"I'm hopin' to find either a pistachio green or powder blue. James loves me in greens and blues."

"You'd look lovely in either of those colors; just make sure there's enough on the ream to buy about four to five yards and that it's the wide fabric or we'll need more. You can just charge it to our account."

"Thanks, Mama." Jessie finished her cup of tea and got up to set it in the sink. She came over and gave her mama a hug, "And thanks for the tea and talk."

"The pleasure is always mine." She wrapped her arms around her daughter. "Goodnight, sweetheart."

"Goodnight, bacon ankle."

Patty smiled, "Goodnight, strawberry wrist."

"Goodnight, shrimp bellybutton," Jessie smirked.

"Goodnight, strudel knee."

"Goodnight, Mama."

"Goodnight, my darlin'."

* * *

Betty Lou giggled as she held up a garter to show it to Jessie and Karen. The girls were in the back of Fancy's Mercantile trying to find material for their prom dresses. Fancy always stayed up with the

196

current happenings around town and she had several displays of all the latest prom accents set out for purchase. On top of a glass display case there was a small metal carousel with some boxed garters for show. "I think I'll get this one. Billy would like this for sure. Maybe I'll let him take it off." Betty Lou giggled again.

"Betty Lou, shame on you!" Jessie scolded.

"What?" Betty Lou asked innocently. She put the garter back on the carousel.

"Quit messin' around, you goof ball, and get over here and grab some of these reams to look at or we'll run out of time to have our fountain sodas," Jessie laughed.

"Oh, I don't know, Jess," Karen added, "I think we need to see *everythin'* Fancy has for prom. She's always up on the latest trends." She was standing next to Betty Lou now spinning the carousel of garters to have a better look. "Ooh, I really like this black one. I wonder if Dennis will?"

"Girls, seriously! Get over here." She laughed. She was enjoying her time with her friends. "I've missed you, girls."

"Well, if you weren't so busy with James." Betty Lou gave her friend a push on the shoulder.

"I know, I know. But Betty Lou, you can't say too much. You and Billy are pretty inseparable these days."

"Yeah, I guess you're right."

"Hey, what do you two think of these?" Karen held up a box. It said, *'I'm the TRIMFLEX girl! Slim thighs, trim waist '''*.

"Maribelle was just tellin' me about those. She said it's amazin' for givin' you curves and makin' you look thin. Toss it here; I'm gettin' one," Betty Lou said.

"You want one too?" Karen turned to Jessie.

"No, they look uncomfortable…and hot."

"Suit yourself! You don't need one anyway. You got cute enough curves, girl! I'm so jealous of your figure," Karen said. "That's why you should totally get one of those garters. James would love takin' that off you!"

"I think that would be a little too temptin' for us. I told you, we are waitin' until after we get married for…you know." She cupped her hand around her mouth and whispered the last words lest anyone else was listening.

"That's so incredible, Jess. I can't imagine though; that'd be hard," Karen said.

"It is; I'm not goin' to lie. But, we're really careful to avoid things that put us in temptin' situations. So, I think I'll pass on gettin' the garter. Besides, I think that would be a little awkward to charge to my parents' account!" Jessie tossed her head back laughing.

"True, very true!" Betty Lou chuckled, "I wouldn't wanna explain that purchase to your daddy!" Their giggles were contagious.

"You do know my daddy well, don't you!" The three laughed. "Come on now, let's look some more. I really wanna find my material today. My mama said she'd help me get started this afternoon if I found material." She turned to both Karen and Betty Lou, "Girls, we're all startin' to get down to crunch time if we wanna get our dresses done for prom."

"You're right," Karen nodded. "Hey, how about this one?" She held out a ream of light blue for Jessie, "You said James likes you in blue. This is pretty, and this color is really in right now."

It was just the right shade of blue Jessie had been imagining. "Powder blue! That's it! It's perfect! That's exactly what I was picturin'! Oh my goodness! Is there enough?"

"Should be, it's full. I think it's a brand-new ream. Here." She handed it to Jessie.

Jessie rubbed her hand across the light blue material. It was beautiful. It had a hint of shimmer to it as well. Perfect for prom, a little dressier than simple cotton. Yes, James would love this. And, she thought, it would look so good with the off-the-shoulder style she had picked out. She just needed to find some tulle to go with it, and then she couldn't wait to get home and get started on her dress. She'd better help Betty Lou and Karen find their material right quick before they got sidetracked again with garters!

* * *

Betty Lou's straw gurgled as she slurped the last of her soda. "I don't know what it is about lime coke, but I just love it!"

"Not me, I'll take a regular coke any day," Karen countered.

"That's so plain," Betty Lou responded.

"Nope, not when you put peanuts in your coke!" Karen dropped a couple more peanuts in her soda which fizzed at the bottom, and then she took a sip.

"Here, ya want any more peanuts, Karen Norraine?" Jessie asked as she slid her package across the table. "My bag is still half full yet. I like my coke as is and to just eat my peanuts on the side."

"Have you tried it though? It's so good. I don't know who ever thought to put peanuts in coke, but it is so yummy. It sure makes a mess though when it foams. Fancy gets so mad when it foams and makes a mess of her booths. We better clean up after ourselves," Karen started wiping the table with a napkin.

"Yeah, my daddy always says to leave a place better than you found it," Jessie grabbed a napkin to help.

They finished cleaning up their table and then each grabbed their bags. All three had purchases successfully in hand. They headed toward the front door giggly and talking the whole way out of the store. Karen held the door open for her friends.

200

Bobby Ray was just walking up to Fancy's as they were coming out.

"Hey Bobby Ray, long time no see! What are you doin' here?" Jessie asked.

"Just runnin' an errand for my folks. Gotta get black thread for my mama and Dippity-do and tobacco for my daddy. I can buy that now that I'm 18," he said with a proud smile. Then he turned to Jessie, "So, you didn't get enough goin' out on the town last night?"

"I guess not!" Jessie smiled, "Last night was fun though, wasn't it?"

"It was! Can't go wrong with Buckie's BBQ on a Friday night. And I have to be honest, hangin' out with Nathaniel and RJ's dates wasn't as bad as I thought it was goin' to be."

"Why did you think it would be bad? Because you were the third wheel?" Jessie asked. "You know with our group that doesn't matter."

"No, that's not what I meant. I mean Nathaniel's date Charlotte Baker was more tolerable than I remember her!"

"Bobby Ray!" Jessie shook her head.

"What? I just remember her in junior high, and she was annoyin'."

"You're somethin' else, Bobby Ray," Karen piped up. "Soooo?...Mr. *Not*-annoyin', do you have a date yet? I thought there were *so many babes, so little time*?"

"I'm still workin' on it."

"Well, I wouldn't complain too much about Charlotte bein' tolerable!"

"Hey, I'm tolerable to be around!" Bobby Ray laughed.

"I'd say your prospects are dwindlin'

"What about Janet Keith? I don't think anyone has asked her yet and I think she kind of has a crush on you," Betty Lou offered.

"No way! She could eat corn through a picket fence."

"Bobby Ray, hush your mouth," Jessie used her motherly tone with him and pinched his arm lightly. "She can't help her buck teeth."

"Yeah, and besides, she can get her teeth fixed. You can't fix bein' a jerk!" Karen scoffed.

"Ouch! Okay, I'll admit, that was a little mean."

"A little?" Betty Lou razzed.

"At this rate, Bobby Ray, you better start figurin' out how you're goin' to drive your cousin Dottie over here from Jasper," Karen chortled.

"All right, all right!" Bobby Ray attempted to change the subject, "So, what are you three doin' out and about together on a Saturday mornin'?"

"We were pickin' out material for our prom dresses," Karen answered and then put both hands on her hips. "So, if your poor date—whoever she is—is goin' to make her own dress like we are you better figure out who you're takin' right quick, Bobby Ray, or she's gonna only have enough time be covered in rags!" Karen wagged her finger at him.

"Dang, I just can't get away from this topic, can I?"

"Well, you brought it up," Karen was quick to remind him.

"I did?"

"Yeah, when you started talkin' about Nathaniel's prom date Charlotte."

"Well, trust me, I won't bring up prom again," he joked.

"If that's true, Bobby Ray, then one thing's for certain," Karen said leaving him hanging.

"What's that?" he asked, his curiosity piqued. He crossed both his arms in front of him waiting for her answer.

"If you avoid the topic all together…you're definitely swingin' solo for the prom!"

Chapter 12
School Shenanigans

They were about to get up and put their lunch trays away when Ricky exclaimed, "Oh hey! I just about forgot!" he bent down and undid the strap on his book bag. "Look what I brought for us!" Ricky set four plastic squirt guns on the table.

"What in tarnation are those, RJ?" Bobby Ray asked.

"Water guns! They were left over from Tommy's birthday party," Tommy was Ricky's little brother. "They're for us!"

"What are we goin' to do with those?" Bobby Ray pressed with skepticism.

"I figured we could hide by the gym before kids head up to class and what else...squirt 'em." Ricky had a boyish grin on his face.

"That sounds so juvenile," James paused momentarily before exclaiming, "I'm in! I get the blue one!" And he hustled to grab it off the table!

The others quickly grappled for the three remaining choices on the table.

"I get the red." Ricky was quick with his fingers.

"Dang it! I wanted the red one," Bobby Ray whined. "You and those darn quick-pickin' fiddle fingers."

"Well, your piano fingers should be fast too," teased Nathaniel who had the orange one in his hand. "Looks like you get what's left…pink."

"Pink? Seriously? What kind of girly party did Tommy have anyway?" Bobby Ray retorted.

"Hey, when you buy a multi-pack at Fancy's, you get what you get," answered Ricky.

"Come on, let's go hide by the gym door in that nook by the soda machine."

Jessie didn't even have time to comment. All four boys scrambled to get their food trays picked up, put away and find the best lookout spot by the gym and staircase. Being left at the table alone, she just shook her head. *Boys will be boys!* she thought to herself. She picked up her tray and book bag and decided to head out the front of the lunch room today. The long route just might be the drier route today.

* * *

The boys were giggling worse than school girls. And the school girls…not giggling much at all. They were screaming and shrieking upon being met with a wet surprise on their way up to class. Nathaniel was giggling so hard he had tears in his eyes, "I'm goin' to go up the stairs and stop on the second floor by Mr. Brink's room. They won't expect us up there too." Nathaniel took off running.

"Hey, wait! I'll come, too, and stand on the other side of the banister." Ricky took off running.

"James, you stay here and I'll go on the other side of the gym door. We'll get 'em at different angles." Bobby Ray bolted.

James was standing tucked behind the soda machine. He could hear the shuffling of more feet. He jumped out from behind the soda machine and there was his classmate Richard and his girlfriend Myrtle. Catching them off-guard and startling Myrtle, he began squirting them with his water gun. Myrtle let out a loud, shrill scream. Richard started laughing and grabbed her hand pulling her faster towards the gymnasium doorway just as Bobby Ray jumped out and unleashed his threatening pink squirt gun at them. Myrtle squealed again. Richard tugged her hand turning her towards the stairway. The two ran up the stairs and the whole way up you could hear Myrtle still screaming as they ran unexpectedly into the ambush of Nathaniel and Ricky.

James tucked himself back into his hiding spot. Bobby Ray hid behind the gymnasium door again. They waited. James was trying not to laugh. He listened for more footsteps.

* * *

Mr. Hagen turned to Mr. Bieberdorf, "What's all the ruckus out in the hallway?"

"I was just headin' up to my office anyway. I'll go check on it," Mr. Bieberdorf nodded.

"I'll go with you." Mr. Hagen was not one to easily turn over the control of school management.

He marched in the direction towards the noise. Mr. Bieberdorf followed.

* * *

James was lurking---waiting for the next victim---trying his hardest not to laugh and give himself away. He could hear more footsteps coming. He lunged from behind the soda machine with his blue blaster ready for fire…and then froze in his spot. He looked straight in the faces of Mr. Hagen and Mr. Bieberdorf and he could tell by the look on Mr. Hagen's face, he was NOT impressed.

"Well, well, well, Mr. Patterson!" boomed Mr. Hagen.

James didn't say a word. He just handed Mr. Bieberdorf his squirt gun and said, "I'll see you after school."

"Yes, I do believe you will," answered Mr. Hagen. "Mr. Bieberdorf, it looks like we have someone who likes water. You know," he turned to Mr. Bieberdorf, "our gymnasium floors could use a scrubbin'. It will look so nice for prom after Mr. Patterson is done scrubbin' them…with a toothbrush…oh, and *water* of course." He turned and looked straight at James when he finished the last part of his sentence.

"Yes sir," James hung his head.

207

"Mr. Bieberdorf, why don't you walk James upstairs. I think he needs an escort to ensure he gets to his next class just fine. I'll head back to the lunchroom."

Mr. Bieberdorf walked James up the stairs. The stair well was quiet now other than the typical hallway noise of passing students hustling to class. Mr. Bieberdorf held the blue squirt gun in his hand, "Well, this will be a first to add to my collection of confiscated items. Maybe I can use it for cleanin' my glasses."

James didn't know if Mr. Bieberdorf was serious or if it was another one of his corny attempts at humor. He didn't dare laugh. And he wouldn't be laughing later when he got ahold of Bobby Ray, Nathaniel, and Ricky.

* * *

Nathaniel thought he had a good laugh earlier in the day with their surprise squirt gun attacks on unsuspecting victims, but that was nothing compared to the laugh he was having now. Nathaniel, Ricky, and Bobby Ray were having a hardy belly laugh at James' expense.

"You jerks! Where'd you go?" James couldn't help but chuckle himself when he finally caught up with his buddies later that afternoon.

"Oh you guys, I wish you could've seen the look on James' face when Hagen and Bieberdorf came around the corner," Bobby Ray directed his comment to Ricky and Nathaniel. "I had a great view from the crack in the gym door! Man, it was hilarious!"

"Yeah, real hilarious." James rattled off, "Why didn't you try and warn me?"

"I didn't have time and I wasn't goin' to get caught too."

Ricky jumped in, "Oh man, Nathaniel and I could hear Mr. Hagen's voice all the way up the stairwell. That's when we got the heck out of there!"

"Well, well, well, Mr. Patterson!" Nathaniel mimicked Mr. Hagen. Ricky, Bobby Ray and Nathaniel broke into a fit of laughter once more.

Nathaniel was wiping tears away. Collecting himself, he turned to James and asked, "So, what's your punishment?"

"I have to scrub the gym floor. With a toothbrush."

His cronies rolled with laughter. "Sorry, buddy!" Bobby Ray snorted.

"Yeah, you sound like you feel really bad for me."

"Sorry, James, this was the funniest day in a long time. I'm glad I brought Tommy's squirt guns to school. Good thing he doesn't want them back," Ricky howled.

"I think Bieberdorf secretly likes my blue squirt gun. He wouldn't have liked your pink one, Bobby Ray," he jabbed. Bobby Ray just rolled his eyes. James continued, "He told me he was goin' to use it to clean his glasses."

This struck the group's funny bone again. They busted out laughing once more.

"I didn't think it was *that* funny," James added.

"We do!" They were in stitches.

"Well, I won't be laughin' after school when I'm on my knees scrubbin' the gym floor."

The guys quieted.

"Yeah, probably not," Nathaniel nodded his head. His friends appeared momentarily solemn and there was a brief lull in the conversation. Then a snort was heard from Bobby Ray. Which caused Nathaniel and Ricky to erupt into hysterics again. All three doubled over in laughter, "Yep, I do believe, Jimbo, you may not be laughin' about it after school…but…we sure will be. For a long time!"

Chapter 13
The Perfect Night

James parked John's Impala at the end of the Clark's driveway. He got out of the car and kicked out each leg at the heel to smooth the creases of his flared-bottom slacks as he stood up. He straightened the light blue flower on his lapel. His mother had made him get a boutonniere. In his left hand he held a box with a corsage in it – which his mama also had something to do with. He walked up to their front door but didn't knock. He just stood there. He had never been nervous to pick Jessie up before, so why were his palms sweating now?

Tonight was a big night. It was their senior prom and he wanted it to be perfect. With their senior year winding down, they were experiencing so many "last" moments together. This was true for all of their classmates. But for James and Jessie, it was more than their high school days coming to a close. Graduation meant one thing – he'd be leaving soon. That's why tonight was so special. James wanted to make every moment count and make impacting memories that would help carry them through the next year.

He stood there staring at the door. He took a deep breath and straightened his boutonniere once more.

Then he brought his finger to the doorbell and pushed
it.

* * *

Jessie was just coming out of the bathroom after
putting on the final touches of her make-up. Her
mother was waiting for her in the hallway. "You look
beautiful."

"Thanks, you made it!" Jessie said looking down at
her powder blue shimmering dress.

"*We* made it…and it's not the dress. It's you. You're
a sight to behold." Patty laid her hand on her chest
and sighed. Her daughter was all grown up. There,
before her eyes, stood a young woman, not a little
girl. "Wait until your father sees you!"

Just then the doorbell chimed making each of them
jump.

"Why did you jump, Mama?" Jessie laughed.

"I don't know. I guess I was in such a trance lookin'
at the young woman standin' in front of me
wonderin' where my baby girl went?"

"Oh Mama, come here," she gave her mother a hug
and then looked down at her dress, "I don't know if
I'm ready?"

"You're ready, my dear. Trust me. You look
beautiful." The doorbell rang again. "Take a deep
breath and get down there. It is rude to keep your date
waitin'." She gave her daughter a quick love pat to
scoot her along.

212

Jessie walked downstairs; her father was about to open the front door. He turned when he heard Jessie coming down the stairs and his breath caught in his throat. "Oh Jessie May, you look beautiful. Now I see why you and your mama kept your dress such a secret. It is breath-takin'! And I hope you don't take this the wrong way, but you look just like your mother did at your age."

Jessie laughed, "Daddy, why would I take that the wrong way? Mama is a beautiful woman now, and I'm sure in her younger days she turned more than just *your* head."

"Right you are! I had to catch that fish and hold on tight!" He threw his fist up in the air as if he were catching something and squeezing it tight.

The doorbell rang again.

"You better answer it. I'll leave you to get the door," he stepped away from the door and kissed his daughter on the cheek. "Your mother and I will meet you there."

Jessie's heart was pounding. *Did her hair look okay? Did she have on too much make-up? Maybe she should have gone with green instead of blue? And, should she have gotten the garter?* She wondered all these things, but before she could entertain another thought the door reverberated with several loud knocks. Startled, she put her hand on the knob, turned it and pulled the door open. There stood James, handsome as ever. She could have sworn her heart stopped completely.

"Sorry if I startled you. I don't think your doorbell is workin'. And judgin' by your expression, I probably knocked a little too eagerly. I just wanted to make sure you heard me." He stared into her soft green eyes and then stopped talking. He looked at her up and down as she stood there in the doorway. She was like a fairy-tale princess standing before him in a light blue dress that shimmered in the sunlight and fit her figure perfectly. It accentuated her curves which seemed more womanly tonight.

"James?"

Jessie's voice started him out of his day-dreaming. He could feel that his mouth was hanging open and he quickly shut it. He swallowed and cleared his throat, "You look gorgeous, Jess. Stunnin' actually. I love your eyes in blue. And, your dress looks amazin' on you. I thought you said your mama and you made it?"

"We did."

"Seriously? It looks like you ordered it right out of *Montgomery Ward* or somethin'!"

"Stop it!" Jessie looked down bashfully.

"No, I'm serious, Jess. It looks amazin'…I mean…you…you look amazin'." James stared at Jessie. He was in a daze again.

"James," she spoke his name quietly. He shook his head as if coming out of a dream.

"You are the most beautiful thing I have ever laid my eyes on and I can't get over how you look right now."

"Thank you, James, that means so much to me," she blushed a little and tilted her head down. "I don't know why – we've been on numerous dates before – but I was nervous gettin' ready for this one. This is different, you know? It is somehow bigger than just another night hangin' out with friends."

"I know, I can't believe how nervous I am."

"You? Nervous?" she crooked her eyebrows at him a bit. "I find that hard to believe. You're never nervous."

"I just want everythin' tonight to be perfect…for you. We've never been to prom and I just want it to be special for you, Jess."

"It's a new experience for *both* of us, so we get to make it what we want. And with you…it would be special no matter what it was. I could be goin' to the circus for all I care, as long as I'm goin' with you, James."

James looked down. He was at a loss for words.

"James Patterson, I do believe you're blushin'!"

He looked up, slightly red in the face, "Here, I brought this for you." He held up a small box.

Jessie reached out and took the box, "James, you didn't need to get me anythin'."

"Oh, trust me, I did…my mama said." They each laughed.

Jessie opened the box and inside was a corsage. She brought her hand to her mouth, "James! It's beautiful! It's so elegant!" She stared down in the box. Whether his mama made him do it or not, it was romantic. The delicate powder blue rose blooms matched her dress. Petite little bundles of petals were adorned with a lovely combination of bitty teardrop-shaped pearls and silky, sheer organza ribbon.

"I hope you like it."

"It's perfect."

"I did at least pick it out with my mama. We got it, of course, at Pugsy's."

"James, I love it."

"Here, lemme put it on you." He took the box from her hands. "Hmm, I'm not sure how this goes. I think like this." He tied the ribbon gently around her dainty wrist.

Just then her mother and father walked in. Robert had a look on his face, "I told your mother that we were goin' to meet you both there, but she insists we get pictures here."

"Of course! Sugar, you don't think I'm goin' to get a brand-new color Polaroid camera for my birthday and not use it for my daughter's first prom, now do you?" Patty chirped. "I can take pictures here *and* there!" She smiled with satisfaction.

Robert and Jessie smiled at each other. "You're right, hon, I shouldn't have expected anything less." Robert smiled at his wife, "Where would you like them?"

"Let's go in the livin' room by the bay window. If there's too much light in front of it, they can stand by the wall in the dinin' room. And maybe we should get one outside too?"

"Whatever you'd like, dear!" Robert smiled. He knew his wife; she wasn't really asking.

* * *

At the school, Rita was seizing her opportunity for pictures. James and Jessie stood in front of the rose trellis in the transformed Cordova High gymnasium and posed for another picture. James leaned close to Jessie's face and whispered in her ear, "And I thought *your mama* took a lot of pictures." Jessie giggled. She loved the feeling of him so close and his breath tickled when he whispered in her ear. She squirmed a bit.

"Hold still, you two! If you move around, I have to turn this here thing all catawampus! I don't wanna have to take more than I need to. This film's expensive!" She turned to John who stood right next to her, "Here, hold this one, John, and wave it in the air so I see how it turns out. Maybe I'll take one by the fountain."

"Mama, I think you have enough," James cracked a grin at Jessie.

217

Just then Mr. Bieberdorf's voice came over the sound system, "We would like to start the Grand March now please, so if the couples could make their way out in the hall by the locker rooms to get lined up and all our guests please shift to the sides of the gym, we'll get started as soon as everyone is ready."

"Saved by the bell!" James rubbed Jessie's back, "Let's go get lined up." He turned and gave his mother a hug, "We'll see you later, Mama. Thanks for comin', John, and for lettin' me drive your car tonight. I'll be home after I bring Jessie May home." Then he grabbed Jessie's hand, "Come on, let's go," he said with a wink.

Jessie scanned the audience. Parents and friends and families were lining up along the sides of the gym. She was looking for her mother and father again. Her mother had already taken all the pictures she wanted of James and Jessie and had told Jessie that she and her father would make their rounds visiting with friends. Jessie spotted her mama who was waving to her so that she would see where they were standing. Her parents were next to their long-time friends, Billy and Shirley Conlin. Jessie waved back as she spotted them. Patty blew her daughter a quick kiss and mouthed to have fun. Jessie mouthed a quick *thank you*, gave one more wave and then she and James darted into the hallway.

"I see Nathaniel and Charlotte and Bobby Ray and Janet over by the trophy case. Let's go stand by them." James gently guided her with his hand.

"I still can't believe Bobby Ray asked Janet."

"I know, especially after what you told me he said to you, Karen Norraine and Betty Lou."

"Yeah, and he was so wrong. Look at her; she looks beautiful. And they actually make kind of a cute couple!"

"They do, but don't say that to Bobby Ray. You know he gets all weird with that stuff."

Jessie and James walked up to Nathaniel and Bobby Ray and their dates. "Hey guys, you look stellar. All of you! Even you Bobby Ray." James laughed and Bobby shot him a perturbed look. "You guys know where RJ is?"

"He's here. I saw him and Donna gettin' their pictures taken by the fountain," Nathaniel answered. "Oh, here he comes now." He motioned over James' shoulder.

"Hey, y'all!" Ricky had his arm around Donna. "This night is gonna be amazin'!"

"Yeah, it is!" Bobby Ray agreed. "Doesn't it look great in here? Can you believe the decorations? And especially the CLEAN floors," he shot a smart and satisfying look towards James. "They sparkle!"

Everyone laughed!

"I'm still holdin' it against you boneheads for leavin' me high and dry and lettin' me take the wrap for those squirt guns."

Again they all laughed.

Karen and her date Dennis Lee walked up. "Howdy, y'all!"

"Well I do declare, Karen Norraine, you look beautiful. I love your dress." Jessie smiled at her friend.

"Thanks, I'm so excited."

"Yeah, this night is gonna be amazin'! I heard the band is really good and can play all the latest songs, and they sound just like the records!" Ricky spoke with enthusiasm.

"I hope they play *Stardust*!" Karen commented.

"That's not a new release," Bobby Ray countered.

"No, but I love that song, and it's a good one to slow dance," she batted her eyes at her date Dennis.

"I heard Mr. Hagen is goin' to enforce 'every 5th' tonight."

"What do you mean?" Jessie asked.

"At prom you get to dance with your partner every 5th song. So, you can dance with James on the first song and then the 5th, the 10th, and so on. Otherwise, you have to dance with other guys in between. He does it to keep the dance floor from gettin' too hot…if you know what I mean," Bobby Ray explained.

"Well, that stinks," Karen answered back.

"Maybe not, you never know," Jessie said hopefully.

"Well, regardless," Ricky commented, "we're gonna cut a rug on the dance floor. Let's get this night started!" he hooted. The group energetically agreed just as their voices were drowned out by Mr. Hagen. He was making his way through the crowded hallway with his lunchroom megaphone in hand, blaring an announcement.

"Attention please, young people. Quiet down. We need you all to get in order by classes and then by the number you were assigned when you registered. For our guest students, I'd like to welcome you. We are glad you could attend Cordova High's prom. I'll do a quick run-down of our Grand March. It is very simple. Seniors are called first. We call the girls' names first and then their date whom they are escorted by. Please no visitin' back here so that you hear your names the first time they are called. Once you hear your names announced, the couple will enter the gym and walk straight to the center to the fountain. Gentlemen, remember to walk slowly. Once you are to the fountain, you will split. The gentlemen walk around the right side of the fountain and ladies on the left. When you meet again on the back side, young men, offer your arm to your date and continue to the end of the gym to the rose trellis. You may turn and stand under it and pause for the school paper photographer. Please remember that you represent your school. Inappropriate behavior will not be tolerated. Then the gentlemen will head down their respective side and ladies down their side and you will proceed around the gym. Just follow the person in front of you and do what they do. We have a lead couple, Richard and Myrtle, who are both seniors and have practiced what to do for leadin' our Grand March ceremony. So just follow them. Can I have our lead couple Richard Jackson and his date Myrtle Abrams step to the front?"

Richard and Myrtle came forward through the crowd of students who were all anxious to get things started. They took their lead spot just behind the door to enter into the gymnasium. The rest of the students managed to get in their line-order quite efficiently. Mr. Hagen gave one last set of instructions, "I will make the announcement to the audience that our Grand March 1965 is beginnin'. Then the band will begin playin' the first song and once you hear the music start, Richard and Myrtle, that's your cue to begin. Have fun tonight, young people."

Jessie's stomach fluttered with butterflies. There were lots of people out there and what if she tripped in her shoes and fell flat on her face. James squeezed her hand just then, "Hey, you okay?"

"I thought I was nervous earlier; that was nothin' compared to now," Jessie swallowed hard.

"Nothin' to be nervous about," James smiled. "This is just your chance to show off that beautiful dress you and your mama made. And for me to show off that you are *my* date," he said with a wink. Then his expression softened as he looked into her eyes and said, "*my* partner."

James had a way of making her feel so calm. And loved.

They heard Mr. Bieberdorf speaking for a short moment and then seconds later the band began to play the first song. The seniors had picked a Beatles' song, *I Want to Hold Your Hand,* to kick-off the Grand March. James turned to Jessie and grabbed her hand and started singing, matching the words of the song perfectly. However, this time, he sang quietly just for her as he whispered the lyrics in her ear.

The night for Jessie could have ended right there. James had told her earlier that he wanted the night to be perfect. What he didn't realize, it already was…just being with him.

* * *

As it turned out, Mr. Hagen did enforce the "every 5th" dance rule. But to Jessie's delight, it added to the night. She had a blast filling up her dance card as she danced with a variety of her friends. Truth be told, she probably wouldn't have danced with hardly anyone else had she been given the option to dance with James all night.

She decided to write the name of each song that she danced to next to the name of each person that she danced with. She figured it'd be fun someday to look back on the hits of her day when she was a senior in high school. Of course, she wrote "I Want to Hold Your Hand" next to where James had signed in the first slot for the first dance. She put a little heart by his name.

The band followed the first song with another song by the Beatles. Nathaniel asked her to dance, so she quickly penciled "Can't Buy Me Love" next to his name. The band was quite talented and could play a variety of the latest hits. Ricky asked her to dance the third dance which was a Beach Boys song, "I Get Around." Bobby Ray grabbed her by the arm for the fourth dance, "Doo Wah Diddy" by Manfred Mann. She couldn't help but giggle at him. He reminded her of that day out at Disney Lake when he was trying to act all macho for the girls. He was definitely in macho-mode again, but this time for one set of eyes only. He kept glancing over at Janet. He was doing a mixture of moves that looked like the Freddie and the Frug, but with gusto. Jessie giggled the whole way through the song.

When the fifth song by the Temptations came on, *The Way You Do the Things You Do*, she was out of breath from laughing so hard dancing with Bobby Ray. "Are you goin' to be okay to dance this next song, Miss Clark?" She spun around as she heard James' voice behind her.

"Landsakes! Bobby Ray cracks me up! And…I think I can laugh recklessly here…no chance of gettin' walloped in the face with an incomin' volleyball!" She gave James a smug look and then took a quick drink of punch from their table.

"Hey now! You said you forgave me for that!"

"Oh, I can forgive…I just never said I'd forget!"

"Jessie May Clark!"

She didn't give him time to add anything more, "Come on, we're wastin' our song!" She grabbed him by the arm and whisked him out on the dance floor. *The Way You Do the Things You Do* wasn't really a slow song, but as Jessie turned to face James, he brought her in tight.

"James, no one else is slow dancin'." Jessie giggled and stepped back slightly so she could look into his brown eyes.

"Well, if the band is singin' about holdin' you so tight, wouldn't I do the song a disservice if I didn't?" James winked and pulled her in closer against him again. They stayed that way for the rest of the song. It was, after all, *their* 5th song and he was certainly going to make the most of it. Jessie smiled and laid her head against his chest as she listened to James sing the lyrics with the band.

RJ was right; the band was terrific, Jessie thought to herself. *And the Bible was right too. Yes, whatever is true, whatever is noble, whatever is right, whatever is pure, whatever is lovely, whatever is admirable--if anythin' is excellent or praiseworthy--think about such things.* Ever since this fall, she had set her mind to memorizing Philippians 4:8 and focusing on being a positive thinker. It didn't matter if Mr. Hagen had enforced every 10th dance for all she cared. Tonight was perfect. James was here, still in Cordova, and she was going to savor everything that remained of their senior year.

Chapter 14
Graduation Anticipation

May came all too quickly. It was the Sunday night before the last week of school and her upcoming graduation. Jessie couldn't sleep. She had taken a long soak in the tub hoping it would relax her, but it didn't. She laid in bed and tossed and turned. She tried to read in her new book that her parents had given her for her birthday, *A Wrinkle in Time*, but she couldn't focus on any of the words. She rolled onto her side and reached for her Bible on her night stand. She opened it up hoping to read something that would calm her and bring her peace, but that didn't work either. She couldn't concentrate on anything she read. Her thoughts continued to collide and she was nowhere near settling down. She had so much on her mind.

Patty, out in the hall, was just closing the door to Carrie's bedroom. She shook her head and yawned. She had once again fallen asleep while reading bedtime stories with Carrie. She groggily tugged at the knob until she heard the door click shut. She reached for the hallway light to turn it off and was going to head down to bed herself. She flicked the hallway light off and as the top of the stairs went dim, she noticed a light coming from under Jessie's door.

She quietly opened Jessie's door and there lay her daughter wide awake, staring at her window with her Bible sitting in her lap.

"Can't sleep?"

Her mother's voice startled her. Jessie hadn't even noticed her come in; she was so deep in thought. "Oh gosh, Mama! You scared me!"

"Penny for your thoughts?"

"Oh, Mama, I'm not sure which thought I'd even give you. I just can't quit thinkin' about everythin' comin' up. I'm not tired in the least. I tried readin' my new book from you and Daddy, but that wasn't happenin'. And as you can see," she picked up her *closed* Bible, "neither is this. There's no way I can sleep with so many things goin' on in my brain."

"Get your housecoat on. I'll start warmin' some milk."

Jessie smiled as her mama's shadow followed her out the hall. Just the thought of warm milk started to relax her. She set her Bible back down on her night stand and swung her legs out of bed. The floor felt cool as her toes touched her wooden bedroom floor. She slid her feet into her slippers and grabbed her housecoat which hung on the back of her door.

Patty already had a kettle of milk on the stovetop and was twisting the cap back on the half-empty bottle of milk when Jessie walked in the kitchen.

"Go ahead and sit down, sweetheart. I'll just stir the milk and it will be ready in a jiffy."

Her mama was right. It didn't take long and Jessie had a mug of warm milk sitting in front of her. Patty joined her with her own steaming mug of milk. Patty twisted the cap off her small jar of vanilla extract and slowly allowed a few small drops to drip into Jessie's mug. She did the same to her own. Jessie stirred her milk and then took her teaspoon out and set it on her napkin. "What made you start givin' us warm vanilla milk when we couldn't sleep?"

"I don't know. It's what my mother always did. In truth, I think it was just warm because most of the time it was still sittin' on the shelf from my daddy milkin'. And my mother added vanilla so when she stirred it in, we wouldn't notice the skin that settled on top of the milk. I was a twerp. I wouldn't drink it if I saw skin on top. That was gross." Patty wrinkled up her nose and then laughed at herself.

Jessie wrapped her hands around her warm mug, "Well, I'm glad Granny Williams was one clever lady because her vanilla milk is my favorite!" she sighed holding her mug between her hands, "Thanks, Mama, it's workin' already. I'm feelin' the most relaxed I have all weekend."

"You have a big week ahead of you."

"I know! Can you believe as of this Thursday, May 27th, 1965, you will have a daughter graduatin'? Leavin' your nest?"

Patty chuckled and dabbed her mouth with her napkin, "Well, I don't think you are leavin' our nest just yet."

"Well, close. You know what I mean though."

"I do, honey, and what you're feelin' is normal. A little anxiety with change is normal. And it's not just graduation comin' up, but I can imagine your thoughts go to James leavin' right after that."

Jessie looked down and swallowed hard. Not so much her warm milk, but the lump in her throat. "Mama, as much as I try to tell myself to take all thoughts captive to the obedience of Christ, I just find the closer graduation gets, the more my thoughts are spinnin'."

"Aah, 2 Corinthians 10:5, *Bring every thought into captivity to the obedience of Christ*, You've been readin' in your Bible." Her mother smiled proudly at her daughter.

"I have been, every night now, Mama. Ever since Daddy came into my room one night before Thanksgivin' and prayed with me. He shared a scripture with me from 1 Corinthians 9 about runnin' the race set before me. He explained that just like an athlete must go through dedicated preparation to compete, it is the same with my faith in order to persevere this race before me. The scripture said our focus should not be on the things we can't control but rather focusin' on our Heavenly Father. So, if I'm not readin' in my Bible, how can I be focused on Him? I certainly wouldn't be in control and my anxiety would get the better of me."

"You are wise, my child. And so is your father. I wanna share somethin' else that I like to do when I am readin' His word. Do you ever cross-reference read?"

"No, I'm not sure what you even mean by that?"

"That is somethin', also, that I learned from Granny Williams. She would get out her old tattered Bible every Sunday after dinner and we were 'required' to have our *Daily Bread* after our meal. She told us if we didn't keep ourselves fed in His word, nothin' else mattered. And then her Sunday meal was for not. She would read us a scripture, and then she would cross it with another scripture with a similar teachin'. The scriptures when read together show how God often repeats important messages in the Bible to stress an important point. So, I learned from Granny to do that and it really brought God's word to light and gave it a richer, fuller meanin' for me." She paused, "Hang on a second."

Patty got up from the table and pushed through their swinging door leading through their dining room and out to the living room. When she came back through, she had her worn, red *Good News Bible* in her hands. She flipped to the back of her Bible to her concordance. She began scanning the words and slowly ran her finger down the page as she searched for what she was looking for. She gently tapped a spot on the page and then a little further down another spot, but spoke not a word. Then she flipped her Bible open, intent on finding something. She licked her fingers as she carefully separated the thin pages of her Bible, "Aah, here we go. Listen to 1 Corinthians 9:24-26 again that your father read to you about runnin' a race, *Do you not know that in a race all the runners run, but only one gets the prize? Run in such a way as to get the prize. Everyone who competes in the games goes into strict trainin'. They do it to get a crown that will not last, but we do it to get a crown that will last forever. Therefore I do not run like someone runnin' aimlessly; I do not fight like a boxer beatin' the air.*"

Then she started turning her pages a little further in her Bible, "Now listen to the words of Hebrews 12:1-3 about runnin' the race, *Therefore, since we are surrounded by such a great cloud of witnesses, let us throw off everythin' that hinders and the sin that so easily entangles. And let us run with perseverance the race marked out for us, fixin' our eyes on Jesus, the pioneer and perfecter of faith. For the joy set before him he endured the cross, scornin' its shame, and sat down at the right hand of the throne of God. Consider him who endured such opposition from sinners, so that you will not grow weary and lose heart.*" Patty looked back up at her daughter, "The first scripture referrin' to our faith as the race, tells us that any runner intent on winnin' a race must go into strict trainin'. The second scripture tells you basically how to train. To run this race of faith set before you, Jess, in order to persevere and have endurance to win, you must throw off everythin' that hinders and fix your eyes on Jesus. My mama used to sing an old hymn to us kids." Patty closed her eyes for just a moment and took in a deep breath. Then she began to sing with a beautiful, dulcet voice…*Turn your eyes upon Jesus, look full in His wonderful face, and the things of earth will grow strangely dim, in the light of His glory and grace.*" She opened her eyes again and looked across the table at her daughter. Jessie's eyes, though wearier than before, were captivated by her mother's singing, "So, there's your answer – Jesus."

"Mama, you said Daddy and I are wise, but I'd say you have much wisdom to share." Jessie yawned.

"Alright, I think the milk has done its magic, darlin'. Off to bed!" Patty grabbed her daughter's empty mug and her own. She stood up and walked over to the kitchen sink. She set the mugs down in the sink to be dealt with in the morning. Walking back over to the small table by the window where her daughter sat slumped in her chair, she held out both her hands. Jessie yawned again. Patty helped Jessie up from the table and gave her daughter a hug, "Good night, my sweetheart."

"Good night, Mama."

* * *

Wednesday night – the night before graduation – Jessie headed to bed an hour earlier than she normally did. She reassured her parents that she wasn't ill when they looked at her with concern as she bid them good-night so early. She explained that she just wanted plenty of time to unwind. She had a big day ahead of her. She crawled into bed just after 9:00 and was humming "Turn Your Eyes Upon Jesus" as she pulled up her quilt. She had asked her

232

mother to sing it to her a few more times during the week while helping with dishes. Now the tune was a familiar tune in her head and she found the old hymn very comforting.

She grabbed her Bible and flipped it open to the back concordance. Since Sunday night, she had been cross-reference reading like her mother had shown her. She found the word "anxiety" and ran her finger down the page just like her mama had done. She selected two scriptures that sounded like what she needed for tomorrow. She fingered her way through her Bible to Psalms 55:22, "Cast your cares on the LORD and he will sustain you; he will never let the righteous be shaken." Then she turned to the other scripture she had picked, 1 Peter 5:7, "Casting all your anxieties on him, because he cares for you." She decided to read a little further in the passage. She continued with verses 8 and 9, "Be alert and of sober mind. Your enemy the devil prowls around like a roaring lion looking for someone to devour. Resist him, standing firm in the faith." She didn't quite understand that. *Why would you have to be alert for the prowlin' of a roarin' lion? Wouldn't you know he's there if he was roarin'?* She pondered. That just didn't make sense to her. She decided to read a bit longer in 1 Peter. Maybe it would make sense if she read a little further. But, it didn't take long and she felt her eyelids grow heavy. She closed her Bible and closed her eyes. She didn't even make it through her prayers.

* * *

Jessie woke up earlier than usual the next morning. She wanted to catch her father before he left for work and ask him about the scripture she was reading last night. She hustled out of bed to get dressed. She grabbed her new sleeveless shift dress she had laid out the night before. She had gotten it for her birthday and was saving it. It was terracotta and she didn't have anything that color. She wanted to surprise James with something new for their last day of high school. She peeled off her night gown and tossed it onto her messy bed. She'd make that later. She pulled her dress over her head and then smoothed down her hair that was floating from static. She'd have to wet it a little in the bathroom. She quickly scurried across the hall to beat Lydia. There would be no catching her father if Lydia beat her to the bathroom. She ran her hand quickly under the faucet and smoothed her wispy hair down. Rather quickly, she pulled her hair into a ponytail and tied a brown ribbon around it. She thought brown nicely accented her terracotta shift dress she had on. Then out the door she flew and sailed down the stairs.

She pushed through the swinging door and bounded into the kitchen. Thankfully, her father was still sitting in his usual morning chair at their small kitchen table next to the window. With her exuberant entrance, Robert glanced up from his paper, "Well, good mornin', darlin'! You're up and at it quite punctually. Headin' to bed early last night must have been good for you. I guess Benjamin Franklin knew what he was talkin' about. Early to bed, early to rise, does make a man---or a woman," he cocked his head towards Jessie, "healthy, wealthy, and wise. You look ready for a day of success." He took a sip of his coffee, "Do you feel ready for your big day?"

"I do. I slept great, Daddy. The best I have slept in a long while. I was hustlin' to catch you this mornin'," she took a deep breath.

"Are you okay?" he asked pushing his paper aside. She had his full attention.

"Yes, nothin's wrong, but I read somethin' in my Bible last night that really confused me. I don't get it at all and I wanted to ask you about it."

"What's that? Come sit down," he patted the chair next to his.

"Do you have time?" she asked her father glancing up at the clock that hung above their sink.

"Of course, I do. If my daughter is hustlin' to talk to me before her last day of high school, it must be important."

"It is, Daddy. I feel like I need this message as I push into a new chapter. With graduation and James leavin', I am headin' into uncharted waters." Her father nodded. "It makes me anxious, which I know is normal. So last night I wanted to read about anxiety and anxious thoughts. I read in 1 Peter and it talked about castin' all my anxieties on him."

"Yep, we talked about that. You have to submit your ways to Him. Lay your concerns at His feet," her father interjected.

"I know, that part makes sense to me. The part that doesn't make sense is where it says we have to be alert and aware of the devil who will prey on us and our weaknesses and prowls around like a roarin' lion lookin' for someone to devour." She paused, her forehead wrinkled in confusion. "Daddy, that makes no sense to me. Why would you have to be alert for the prowlin' of a *roarin'* lion? Wouldn't you know he's there if he was roarin'?"

Robert patted Jessie's hand, "Yes, I can see how that is confusin'. If he was roarin', we'd know he was there, you'd think. That seems obvious. But, what if you thought about that scripture like this. You know that Pawpaw Clark worked in the coal mine, right?" Jessie nodded intently at her father. "Granny used to bring him dinner almost every day. Often, we'd go with her. I remember on one occasion while we were sittin' on a blanket eatin' dinner, I was horsin' around, like kids do. She gave me a good scoldin' and told me to sit still and eat my dinner. I can still hear her now, '*Hush, boy!*' She told me with all the minin' ruckus she was havin' a hard-enough time hearin' my father. I remember her turnin' to my father and sayin', '*How can you take all this noise all day long?*' My father just shrugged and said he was used to it. He said he really didn't even notice the noise anymore. You see, Jess, the enemy is cunnin'. He wants us to desensitize to the surroundin' noise so that we drown it all out and, in the process, we don't listen to the Lord either. That's when the enemy devours us…our strength, our courage, our faith. Because in the problems and distractions of life---the noise and chaos---you will desensitize too. If you are not alert and listenin' for the Lord and His power and His will, the devil will assert his power and agenda."

Robert squeezed his daughter's hand, "Listen, Jess. Listen. That is what it is all about. Don't let your guard down and quit listenin' to the Lord. Keep your focus on Him and He will see you through…any chaos…any noise of life. Any race."

* * *

"Can you believe it's our last day of high school?" Karen squealed.

"I know! It's crazy!" Jessie opened her locker. "We're supposed to start emptyin' our lockers out before first period assembly."

"I don't know what they want us to do with all our stuff all day. It's not like we're goin' to carry it around." Karen opened her locker.

"Mornin', gals!"

Jessie spun around and there stood James with a big smile on his face. He wore a plaid blue short-sleeved button-down shirt. Her mind suddenly flashed back to September at the beginning of the school year. She remembered him wearing that same shirt one of their first weeks of school. So many things had changed

237

since then. And yet, here he stood looking the same and making her heart flutter just like it did then.

James interrupted her thoughts, "Wow, don't you look *spicy*!" he accentuated the last word.

"You like it?"

"Mmm, hmm." He grabbed her waist and pulled her close to him. She could feel his warm breath against her ear.

"Alright, you two, get a room," Karen chided.

Jessie blushed and pulled back. Smoothing her dress, she looked up at James, "I got this for my birthday from my God-parents, Uncle Larry and Aunt Clara, and I've been savin' it. What do you think of the color? It's terracotta."

"I like it. It's somethin' different. I love you in blues and greens, but this is good for a change. Spicy!"

"Spicy, huh?" she cocked her head playfully at him. He grabbed her waist again.

"Alright, I'm out of here. James clearly can't keep his hands off you." Karen rolled her eyes with a smirk on her face and shut her locker, "I can clean my locker out later...without the love show. See ya, love-birds!" Karen waved good-bye and gave a smile over her shoulder. "I'll see you at lunch!" she called back as she headed down the hall.

Jessie and James started to giggle. She shook her head. "One thing that hasn't changed since this fall – you're still persistent."

"What? Me?" James tossed his hands up in the air and then put them down by his sides like he was sulking.

"Oh, *now* you keep your hands to yourself."

"Hey! I wasn't necessarily bein' persistent…I was bein' purposeful. Intentional, if you will. How else did you think I was goin' to get rid of Karen Norraine?"

"James Theodore Patterson!"

"Talk about things that haven't changed since the fall – you're *still* rebukin' me with my full name!" James laughed.

Her thoughts drifted back again to the beginning of their school year. ***Where had their senior year gone?*** **She turned and** looked straight ahead into her almost-empty locker like it was an endless abyss. For a moment she was motionless as if in a hypnotic trance staring into a dark cavern. Her thoughts, however, were interrupted as she felt James' hands once again on her waist. He brought his face down close against her neck.

"I do like you in this dress." He leaned in closer and whispered in her ear, "But I'd like you out of it more!"

"James!" she pulled away and turned around to face him, "I thought we were pretty clear now on the whole s-e-x thing." She quietly spelled out the word as if someone passing by might not know then what they were talking about.

"I did. I still stand firm on that. No sex until after we are married. It's a gift worth waitin' for."

She stared into his brown eyes. Charming as the fall.

"But," he continued, "doesn't mean I don't wanna sneak a peek at what's inside the package." He gave a little wink and grabbed at her again.

"Alright, you two!" This time it wasn't Karen chiding the love birds. It was Mr. Bieberdorf, "I really don't wanna carry my yard stick to measure the appropriate distance there should be between you two."

"Yes, sir," James nodded.

"I'd rather not have to drag that yard stick around with me on our last day of school, but it does seem a little *hot* in here today. Don't you two think?"

"Yes, sir." James took a couple steps back.

"So, let's keep the temperature down a bit if you know what I mean. Okay?" They each nodded. "You know, that kind of reminds me of a joke." James shot Jessie a comical look. "How do you keep warm in a cold room?" James and Jessie didn't answer. They knew Mr. Bieberdorf would quickly follow his joke with his own response, "You go to the corner, because it's always 90 degrees." He broke into a hardy laugh.

Yep, Jessie thought, *that hasn't changed either since fall.*

"Mr. Bieberdorf, I'm truly goin' to miss you," James chuckled, "I really have appreciated your jokes and humor over the years."

In a moment of shared emotions and sentimentality for all that the last day of high school held, they briefly exchanged looks. Then Mr. Bieberdorf cleared his throat and quickly sniffled, "Alright you two," his voice cracked slightly, "go on now. Time to head to first period assembly." He turned to head down the hall and then stopped and turned around, "And James, I'm goin' to miss you, too. Good luck in the army."

* * *

The evening came before they knew it. Jessie adjusted the cap on her head and dabbed the perspiration off her forehead with a crumpled facial tissue that looked like it needed to be thrown long ago. The gymnasium was packed and it was hot and sticky. Jessie thought it felt more like the beginning of the school year. She was roasting under her cap and gown and sweating profusely. She didn't know if she was sweating worse from the heat or her nerves. The audience stirred in the stuffy, crowded gymnasium. Anticipation for the commencement to begin was evident. She scanned the audience and spotted her parents near the center. Her mother was fanning herself with her graduation program. Her father had his arm around her. Lydia and Carrie sat on each side of them. Jessie smiled. Her family! Her eyes wandered through the audience some more. How grateful she was that she grew up in Cordova. She saw so many faces she knew and treasured. She liked small-town life. Hardly anyone was a stranger. There was Fanny and her husband Frank in the back. He looked crabby. But, Jessie thought, *that's nothing new*. And, Betty Lou's parents--Clifford and Florence--were sitting not far from them. Next to Clifford and Florence were Pastor Mark and his wife Arlette and behind them, she spotted James' parents, John and Rita. Her gaze stopped there.

Elizabeth and David had made it home for graduation too. Elizabeth was waving; she had noticed Jessie looking their way. A big smile was on her face. Jessie smiled and waved back. She felt so close to Elizabeth already. How blessed she'd be with another sister if she and James got married. The word *if* stung as she thought it. None of that; she pushed that thought out of her mind. Sitting next to David was James' Granny Fran, Rita's mother. His Pawpaw and Granny Patterson were there too. They were his daddy's parents, and she hadn't met them yet. They lived in Ashville. James had told her that when his father passed away, he didn't see them much after that. He was pretty excited they had come for his graduation. And he was mostly excited---he revealed to her---because he wanted to introduce them to her. Jessie smiled again thinking about the possibility of gaining another whole family.

Deep in her thoughts, she startled a bit when she heard Mr. Hagen's voice come on the sound system. He was asking the audience to stand. The ceremony was about to begin.

As the band began the slow cadence of *Pomp and Circumstance*, her heart was pounding out of her chest and her stomach was lurching. This was it! She wondered if her classmates were as nervous as she felt. *Probably not James.* She rolled her eyes. *He was probably singing right now.* This thought made her laugh a little. She took a deep breath. She adjusted her cap slightly and wiped her forehead. *Smile, walk slowly, breath* – she repeated to herself.

She didn't quite know how – as she seemed to be in some strange hypnotic trance – but somehow, she found herself standing at her designated chair. She watched Pastor Mark approach the stage. He walked up the stairs and stood behind the podium. He did a quick mic check and then gave the invocation. Next, Mr. Hagen stepped up to the podium and gave a formal welcome to distinguished guests and told everyone they could be seated. After that, it all seemed a blur through a string of graduation formalities. And the next thing Jessie knew, Mr. Bieberdorf was calling her name to come up and receive her diploma. *Smile, walk slowly, breath* – she repeated once again in her head.

She shook hands with Mr. Gill, the school board president, and then reached for Mr. Bieberdorf's hand. As she shook his hand and received her diploma with her other hand, she tilted her head down slightly so he could switch her tassel to her left side. She gave a quick nod of thanks and found her way back to her chair again.

For the first time that evening, she could feel herself start to relax. She heard the blaring of Mr. Bieberdorf's voice as he called out the names of her other classmates. The audience responded in clapping, cheers, and chants. And after announcing their final classmate – Billy Zebner – Mr. Hagen made his way back up to the podium. The microphone squealed slightly as he leaned into it, "Fellow guests, if you would please stand again." He paused briefly, allowing the audience a chance to rise, "It is my great honor…to present Cordova High School's newest graduatin' class…the class of 1965."

The audience erupted. The graduates reached for their caps. Grabbing hers exuberantly from her head---ready to toss it into the air---Jessie's thoughts suddenly shifted to her Bible reading last night about casting all her anxieties on him. She held on to her cap for just a moment. And then, as she cast her hat up, with deep conviction she cast her worries up as well…to the Lord. He would sustain her in the days ahead – through her new chapter in life. Through the chaos, the noise, Vietnam, and all.

Chapter 15
A Soldier's Armor

The moon was bright against her bedroom wall and Jessie stared straight at the beam of light that illuminated her room. Her room was still, but her thoughts bounced all over the place. It was exhausting and yet exhilarating as the events of the day unfolded in her mind. *She had graduated!* She sighed. She needed to think of something else to settle her mind. She started to think about all the things she was thankful for in her life. She thought of James, of course, which entertained her thoughts for quite a while. And then she pictured her family all sitting together at graduation. It was hot in the gymnasium and still her father had his arm lovingly around her mother. She was thankful for the way he loved her mama.

Grateful for her father, she recalled the conversation they had that morning. It already seemed days ago, but the message was etched into her mind. Her thoughts floated back to sitting at the kitchen table as her father explained 1 Peter 5:7-9. His words returned about how in the noise of life, people desensitize. Jessie's eyes switched back and forth as she quietly pondered this. *And when we desensitize, we don't **listen** any longer.*

She paused on that last thought, chewing on it awhile longer. In the quiet of her room, one word stood out tonight clear as day – listen. She said the word inside her head. *Listen.*

Under the moon beam shadows of her room, she lay utterly still. She could hear her own breath as she inhaled and exhaled. *Listen.* She heard an owl hoot his evening salutation. *Listen.* She sat up in bed and flicked on her lamp. She flung her quilt off and picked up her Bible. She grabbed the afghan which lay neatly folded at the foot of the bed that her Granny Clark had knit for her. She wrapped it around her shoulders and went over to her desk and sat down. She opened the small front drawer of her desk and took out her dictionary. She looked up the word "listen." Jessie whispered the definition into the darkness, "to hear somethin' with thoughtful attention: give consideration, to be alert to catch an expected sound." *Huh. Alert to catch an expected sound.* She thought again about the scripture she read in 1 Peter. She grabbed a notebook and a pencil. She opened her Bible to its concordance. One side of her mouth turned upward in a slight smile as she thought about her mother. Patty had shown her how to read in her Bible this way. Finding the word "listen" with ease, she penciled down related passages.

Jessie began pouring over her scriptures, writing each one down in her notebook. She could hardly write fast enough as the scriptures started to connect together in her thoughts. She underlined the word "listen" wherever she saw it. In doing so, she started to notice something. In the verses that didn't have "listen" necessarily among the words, another word consistently popped out at her – "alert." She looked back at the definition of "listen" in her dictionary. *Be alert to catch an expected sound.* She felt the Lord was trying to tell her something. She decided to underline the word "alert," as well.

Something struck a chord with her with a scripture in James. She couldn't help but smile at the coincidence that it was in the book of *James*. She put a star by the verse in her notebook and read the words out loud, "James 1:22 – Do not merely listen to the word and so deceive yourselves. Do what it says." She yawned. Having no concept of time, she pressed on. Another verse caught her eye. It was in the book of Ephesians, chapter six. *Why was this familiar? Oh, yes, Pastor Mark's sermon this past Sunday.* He had preached on Ephesians and the armor of God. Pastor Mark talked about a soldier's armor. At the time, it only made her think of the army which somberly reminded her of James leaving. But now, now she was understanding this scripture in a whole new light.

She scanned back a little further in Ephesians with a fresh set of eyes. She read about putting on the full armor of God in order to stand against the devil's schemes. Verse 14 pulled her in, "Stand firm then, with the belt of truth buckled around your waist, with the breastplate of righteousness in place, and with your feet fitted with the readiness that comes from the gospel of peace. In addition to all this, take up the shield of faith, with which you can extinguish all the flaming arrows of the evil one. Take the helmet of salvation and the sword of the Spirit, which is the word of God." Another yawn. Her eyes were now feeling heavy, and yet, the word "alert" in verse 18 grabbed her with clarity, "And pray in the Spirit on all occasions with all kinds of prayers and requests. With this in mind, be alert and always keep on praying."

She closed her eyes and thought about Pastor Mark's message. She truly did not *listen* then. She wasn't *alert* and had missed the message. She opened her eyes and glanced at the scriptures she had written. The verse in James called to her again. *Listen. And do*. She smiled a weary smile. A very clear message was revealing itself – true listening leads to action.

As she thought about the armor of God in Ephesians and the scripture in James saying not to merely listen but to do, an idea started to swell inside her. An idea for James. Another yawn. She looked at her clock. *How did it get to be 2:00 in the mornin'?* Her grand idea would have to wait. She set her pencil down and closed her Bible. She stood up and her afghan dropped to the floor. She didn't reach down to pick it up. She was too tired. She crossed the room, turned her lamp off and crawled into bed. She snuggled her quilt up close to her face and, without even realizing it, her thoughts of today entered into her sweet dreams of tomorrow.

* * *

The sun was pouring into her room when she woke the next morning. Groggily she opened her eyes and peeked at her clock next to her bed. She couldn't believe her eyes – 11:00. She had never slept in so late. Or rather, her father had never allowed her to sleep in that late. She got out of bed and stretched. She opened her dresser and pulled out a pair of sweatpants and dug through another drawer for a t-shirt.

The kitchen was empty when she walked in. The faint smell of coffee still hung in the air. She liked that smell. There was something soothing about the smell of coffee in the morning…even if it was late in the morning. She shook her head in disbelief that she had slept in so late. On the counter sat a plate with a dishtowel covering a stack of pancakes. Just as she was about to put a couple pancakes on a plate, her mother walked in, "Well, you're alive! Your father and I were startin' to get concerned we were gonna have to send a search and rescue team upstairs for you."

"Very funny!"

"So, is that breakfast…" Patty paused with playful look on her face, "or dinner?"

"You're full of it this mornin', aren't you, Mama!" Jessie laughed. "I was actually up pretty late last night."

"I know, I saw your light on still at 2:00," her mother went and sat down at the table. "I was up with Carrie. She came down to our room with leg cramps and when I went up to get her settled with half a banana and some milk and Tylenol, I saw your light on. I figured you were pretty wound up from your big day. After I got Carrie relaxed, I went to check on you. But by then, your light was off. I poked my head into your room and you were out cold."

"Gosh, I didn't even hear you up with Carrie."

"She was pretty quiet this time. We caught them early." Patty shifted in her chair to see Jessie better, "So, what were you doing up so late? Couldn't shut your mind down from your big day?"

"Yeah, pretty much. And, I had a really amazin' time with God in my Bible." Jessie turned and went to the refrigerator. She decided not to reheat her pancakes in the oven. It would take too long. She grabbed the cream and maple syrup. She drizzled some of each on her pancakes and grabbed a fork and went to join her mother at the table.

"I have to thank you, Mama. Ever since you showed me how to cross-reference read in my Bible, I am understandin' it better and it's becomin' more alive to me. And last night, I came up with a really neat idea for James. I have been tryin' to think of somethin' to give James for graduation and to send him off for the army."

"You have me curious. What's your idea?"

"Do you remember Pastor Mark's sermon this last Sunday? It was about the armor of God."

"Yes, I believe so," her mother recalled.

"After readin' in my Bible last night, I got a very clear message, Mama. I am goin' to make a picture of a soldier--a soldier of God--that illustrates to James all he needs to equip himself for what lies ahead in any battle of life. I'd like to use some of Lydia Ruth's art paper she got for Christmas if she'll lemme. And I was hopin'," she paused to take a quick bite of her pancakes, "that you would maybe lemme use your Polaroid to take a picture of me to put on the back of it. I know the film is expensive, but if I could use it just this once?"

Patty stopped her daughter. She reached across the table and put her hand on Jessie's, "I think that is a wonderful idea. And what better way to use my Polaroid than to capture an image of my beautiful daughter."

"Ah, Mama!"

"Very thoughtful! James will love it, Jess."

"Well, let's see how it turns out first. I'm no artist! Remember my 6th grade self-portrait I brought home from Mrs. Cunnin'ham's class? My nose and hair were so terrible that Daddy and Lydia thought it was a picture of a pig crossed with a lion." Jessie laughed and took another bite of her pancakes, "So yeah, we'll see how it turns out."

"True," Patty laughed. "Well, it's the thought that counts," Patty smirked a bit.

"Hey, you weren't supposed to agree with me."

"I'm sorry," she patted Jessie's hand again and started to get up from the table, "I'm sure James will love his pig soldier!"

Jessie almost spit her pancakes out of her mouth. They both began to laugh. She looked at her mama who wore a mischievous look on her face, "You *are* full of it this mornin', Mama. No doubt about it!"

* * *

James had always teased her about her doodles in class. He had even made up a game he called, *Guess the Doodle*! She chuckled a bit to herself. She had to admit it, her drawings were pathetic. Always a mystery. They never quite turned out like she originally intended. She was not good at drawing. Plain and simple. James would get a bang out of the fact that her grand idea for his gift was to *draw* for him. She shook her head and reached for her pencil. *Here goes nothing.* Like her mama had said, *it's the thought that counts.* She chuckled again and began to draw the soldier's head. *Round - that's not so hard.* She could handle round. She'd have to be careful with his facial features, especially the nose. She did not want her soldier to have a pig nose. The nice part was that soldiers didn't have hair so she wouldn't have to worry about that turning into a lion's mane.

That thought made her pause. James would have to shave his gorgeous brown hair. She liked how it sometimes hung over his eyes and he would toss his head to the side to clear his hair from his face when he was talking to her. He was so good looking. He would certainly look different without his hair. She hadn't thought about that. It was all becoming very real that he had joined the army and was leaving soon. She sighed. Back to drawing.

She added a helmet on the soldier. It turned out looking more like a mushroom, but it would have to do. James would know what it was. She wrote the word "Salvation" on his helmet. She began to add the soldier's facial features, carefully adding his nose so he didn't look like a pig. When she was done with his face, she paused briefly to critique her work. She should have skipped adding eye lashes. Her soldier looked like a girl. *Oh well!* James knew her drawing capabilities. Or lack thereof!

She drew a breastplate on the soldier's chest and added some squiggles to give it dimension. The metal armor looked like it had ruffles. She rolled her eyes. Now he really looked effeminate. Clearly, she wasn't an artist. She wrote the word "Righteousness" on the soldier's breastplate.

Next, she added a belt. That was easy enough. A rather long skinny rectangle. *Geometry had paid off after all.* She grinned and then wrote the word "Truth" on it. She drew the soldier's legs, arms, and hands. In one of the soldier's hands, she drew a sword. His hands looked like fluffy clouds, but the sword was easy. Carefully she wrote "God's Word" on the sword. She wrote each letter slowly as if she was inscribing the letters into actual metal. In the soldier's other hand, she drew a shield. *Not bad,* she thought. She added stripes hoping to make it look less feminine than her squiggles on the breastplate. On the shield, she wrote the word "Faith" which seemed to fortify it with a sense of power. An unexplainable excitement in her started to grow.

Underneath his feet she drew a book – the Bible. Her soldier took on a gallant stance. He looked ready, just like it said in Ephesians 6:15...*feet fitted with the readiness that comes from the gospel of peace*. She wrote the label "Gospel of Peace" on the binding of the Bible and added a little shading under the Bible. *Artistic flair*, she thought. She was starting to get into this! The gospel of peace, the Bible's truth – which they would stand on firmly – would get them through the days ahead.

Jessie was just about finished with her soldier, but she needed to add one last thing. She drew a flaming arrow coming towards the shield. She wrote the word "Evil" next to the arrow. A chill settled over her skin. The reality that James was going to Vietnam and would encounter evil was undeniable. But what was even more indisputable right now was the profound revelation tucked in Ephesians 6:16, "The shield of faith would extinguish all the flaming arrows of the evil one." She found great peace in this truth and knew that James would as well. *There, finished!* Satisfied with her work, she set down her pencil. She smiled. Now she just had to find the right time to give it to James before he left for boot camp.

* * *

Sunday after church she was going to James' for dinner. Rita had invited her over to eat so she could see David and Elizabeth again before they took off for Birmingham. They had decided since James was leaving early the next morning for basic, they would just leave sometime after dinner.

Jessie hustled to change out of her church clothes. Robert was letting her take their car. She couldn't believe how her father was softening. Taking the car a year ago---heck, even three months ago---would have been a hard sell. But with James leaving early tomorrow morning for basic training, her dad was pretty easy to persuade. She glanced at her clock— 11:30. She better put a snap to it. She grabbed James' package off her bed that she had wrapped. She'd wait to give it to him after David and Elizabeth left. She flung open her bedroom door and charged down the stairs. As she hit the bottom step, she called into the living room, "I'm takin' off."

Robert was sitting in his favorite Sunday spot---his tan recliner---reading his paper. He set the paper down in his lap, "Drive slowly, especially down the gravel drive."

"I know, Daddy," she yelled over her shoulder as she grabbed the keys from the entryway table at the bottom of the stairs. "See you later, Mama," she yelled into the kitchen.

Her mother was getting dinner ready. She was flinging a dish cloth over her shoulder as she pushed her way through the door. She had a somber look on her face.

"Mama?"

Patty's eyes swelled up with tears, "I know we said our good-byes to him last night when he came over, but…" her voice trailed off. Jessie could see her mother was fighting back the tears, "It's just hard."

"I know, Mama." Jessie felt her own eyes filling with tears, "One good-bye is never enough for someone you love. And I know you've come to love him too."

Patty hugged Jessie, "Tell him good-bye again and that I'll be prayin' for him."

"I will, Mama," Jessie wiped a tear that let loose down her own cheek.

"Alright, you two!" They heard her father's voice booming from the living room. "You need to let her go now, Patty, or she'll be in no condition to drive safely."

Patty pulled the dish towel off her shoulder and flung it lightly towards Jessie to shoo her off, "Alright then, you heard your father! You better get goin'! Before it's a waterworks show here!" She laughed half-heartedly.

Jessie leaned in and kissed her mother on the cheek, "I'll give James your message." And then out the front door she went.

* * *

David and Elizabeth left shortly after 4:00. Through misty eyes, they waved good-bye as they drove away. Then James turned to Jessie, "Well, now what?"

"Can we go up to your bedroom? I have somethin' I have been dyin' to give you."

James got a big grin on his face, "Ohhhh, I like the sound of that, but with my parents in the house…now? I thought we were gonna wait!"

"James Theodore! That's not what I meant."

"Dang! Here I thought you were sendin' me off with somethin' to remember!"

She just rolled her eyes and walked over to the family's Plymouth Fury.

"Hey, just because you can't have this body of mine now doesn't mean you have to leave!"

She rolled her eyes again, "I'm grabbin' your gift."

"Ooh," he rubbed his hands together, "I get a gift?"

"Yes, but only if you start behavin'." She liked being playful with him. He was being flirtatious and so was she. She pulled the package out from the front seat where she had left it. "Let's go to your bedroom and I'll give it to you there."

"Ooooh, there you go talkin' all dirty again."

"James!" she said his name with a high pitch to her voice.

"Alright, alright! I'll behave." He grabbed her hand.

They walked hand in hand into the house and through the kitchen. Rita was tidying up from their afternoon coffee. The cheesecake was still out on the counter. "Y'all comin' back for seconds?" she smiled at them.

"Your turtle cheesecake was amazin', Miss Rita, thank you," Jessie replied.

"You are more than welcome. Did y'all want more?"

"No, thanks though, Ma. We are headin' up to my room. Jessie May's considerin' givin' me this gift if I behave." He pointed to the package Jessie was carrying in her other hand.

"Good luck with that, Jess! I've been tryin' to get that boy to behave for 18 years!"

"Ma! You're not helpin' the situation!" They laughed and then he and Jessie headed up to his room. Jessie set the package down on James' bed and plopped down next to it.

"Ok, so when you open this, you need to be nice," she instructed.

"Now what's that supposed to mean? When have I ever not been nice with a gift you've given me?" He tried to look hurt as he came and sat next to her.

"You'll see when you open it. You'll know what I mean. Just remember, it was made with a great deal of love." She slid the package towards him.

James picked it up. It felt light. He shook it gently, "Anythin' breakable?"

"Nope."

"Another Elvis album?

"Nope."

"Come on, you sure? Maybe his *Blue Hawaii* album? I'd love that one, you know!" he broke into *Can't Help Falling in Love* with his deep, resonating voice.

She really wanted him to open her gift, but she loved when he sang to her. Besides, she knew that she couldn't stop him from singing even if she wanted to and she treasured this part of him. When the verse got to the part about taking his hand, he took hers in his and kept singing. He finished the verse with grand gusto going down on one knee as if beckoning her for an encore. She stared down at him, shaking her head, her eyes playfully dancing back at him. Then he leaned up and gave Jessie a kiss as he rose to sit on the bed next to her.

"Nope, I can't help it, Jessie May," he said, "I've fallin' in love with you."

"Alright, Elvis! Come on, open your gift already," she pushed him back and put the package in his lap so he could no longer delay satisfying her anticipation.

He tore into the wrapping, crumpled it and tossed it across his room to his waste basket by the door. "Score!" he put his hands up like a basketball champion. "And here I didn't think I was goin' to *score* today."

"For someone who wants to wait for sex, you sure do bring it up all the time."

"Yeah, but just because we are waitin' doesn't mean I'm not thinkin' about it. I think about it a lot." He leaned in to kiss her again.

"James, your parents," she put her hand on his chest to place some distance between them and glanced nervously out his door into the hallway. "Come on now, for real…you need to open this package or you're gonna get us both in trouble if your mama or John walk by."

"Alright! Alright!" he popped the lid off the box and stared motionlessly inside. Silence.

"Remember, be nice," she playfully warned.

"Oh, my goodness, Jess!" James started to smirk a little. He rubbed his hands together, "Do I get to play *Guess the Doodle*?" He laughed and then pointed to the soldier's mushroom-like helmet, "What's this? He kind of looks like…like…like Mushroom Man. Although," he paused, "with those eye lashes battin' at me, it might be a flirtatious girl too!" He laughed and batted his eye lashes at Jessie.

"Come on! It's a guy. And no, you don't get to play *Guess the Doodle*. For your information *he's* not 'Mushroom Man'. He's a soldier." She laughed. She had known his reaction would go like this. She had expected it and was rather enjoying his response. She took the package from him.

"Hey! Give it back, that's my gift!"

"I will, but first I wanna explain it. It's a soldier."

"I can kinda see that," James teased.

"Alright, smarty pants, hush!" Jessie took the drawing of her soldier out of the box, "It's a special soldier…a soldier of the Lord. And the important part…is the soldier's armor." She began to explain to James how her mother had recently shown her how to cross-reference read. She explained how she had sat up this week reading scriptures on listening to God and being alert and how that led her to the scripture in Ephesians on the armor of God. She told him about Pastor Mark's sermon awhile back and what it meant to her then and what it meant to her now. She went over each part of the soldier's armor and how it could help him in the army to focus on such things, "Wherever you go, He will go with you and be protectin' you."

Then Jessie turned the picture of the soldier over and there on the back was the Polaroid picture her mother had taken of her. James just stared at the picture. No impromptu melodic chorus. No singing. No words. Just speechless. Captivated by the picture. She was wearing a powder blue t-shirt that he really liked on her. It wasn't fancy; it was very simple with nothing on it. Her mother thought it was rather plain for the picture, but she had reminded Patty that James loved her in blue and that this was one of his favorite shirts on her. He had told her it was one of his favorites because he liked how the color brought out her eyes—and particularly, he had told her he liked the way it fit snuggly on her chest. She didn't tell her mother that part.

She held up the picture of herself and then said, "And wherever you go, I will go with you also. And I will be prayin' for your protection every day, my soldier."

Chapter 16
A Sweet Good-Bye

Robert stood in the quiet kitchen that was still darkened from the night's reprieve. He glanced up at the clock on the wall – 5:00. He was just about to go see if Jessie was up when she tip-toed quietly in through the swinging door. He didn't want Jessie driving in the dark tired and emotional. He had offered to drive her to James' that morning to say their final good-byes and told her he'd just stay in the car. "Ready to go?" he asked.

"As ready as I can be." She looked tired. Eyes red from lack of sleep and undoubtedly the tears that wet her pillow before she drifted off to sleep that night.

When they pulled up, she saw Rita in her housecoat standing on the driveway next to James. John stood behind them. Rita gave James a small bag and then hugged him. She didn't say anything as Jessie got out of the car. She only waved. She was crying. Rita glanced over at Robert and he gave Rita a consoling look of understanding. These moments in life were so hard as a parent. As they exchanged their somber nonverbal greetings, Rita gave a quiet head nod and then John put his arm around her and the two went inside their house.

Jessie approached James slowly as if drawing out her gait might delay his departure. James put his arms around her and locked his hands around the small of her back. It felt good. The night's chill was still hanging in the air, and she was shivering. She couldn't tell though if it was from being cold or so anxious for this moment. It had finally come. Time to say good-bye.

James leaned his forehead against hers, "I'll write you every day."

She looked at him with a knowing look. "Maybe weekly?"

"Okay, you know me too well. Daily is probably not realistic. But, know I will be thinkin' of you daily. Every day, Jess, until I come back."

A light shone on them. It was headlights from an approaching car. The recruiter was arriving to pick him up and take him to the airport. It was time.

Reading her anxious thoughts James leaned in and tilted her chin up to look at him, "Let's not say 'good-bye'. Let's just say 'I'll see you when I get back.'"

"That sounds better to me." She leaned up and kissed him; she didn't care if her father was looking. "I love you, James Theodore Patterson."

"I love you too Jessie May Soon-to-be-Patterson," he smiled. "I like the sound of that!" And with that, he kissed her one last time and then turned to grab his backpack. He reached down and also grabbed the brown paper bag his mother had just given him that was filled with one of his favorites – chocolate chip pecan cookies. His mother always said she spoke her love best through her kitchen. And there was no arguing that as he held her delectable bag of love in his hand.

He looked at Jessie one more time, then walked down the driveway and loaded his stuff in the recruiter's car. He got in and gave a final wave. She tried to smile and waved back. And then, the car rolled away from the curb. As it drove off into the lingering darkness of night, she felt a sharp pain in her heart. Like a flaming arrow had pierced her and then the tears began to come. She stood there motionless, crying and shivering in the chill of the early morning. The sun was barely creeping into the horizon and wasn't yet offering the promise of a new day.

Jessie didn't hear her father get out of their car, but the next thing she knew his arms were coming around her, embracing her safely in his hold. A comforting embrace that was strong, warm, and familiar. An embrace that comes only from the loving arms of a protective father. As she melted in her father's arms, she was reminded of the loving arms of another Protective Father. And she realized that not only would God be with James wherever he went, but that God would be with her too. God would be watching over them both lovingly and protectively. He was right now.

In addition to all this, take up the shield of faith, with which you can extinguish all the flaming arrows of the evil one...

As the sun broke through the eastern skies, the morning light began to shine on them. Her father then spoke softly to her, "The Lord turns our darkness into light." The words were balm to her soul. Not because they were her father's words, but because they were His words. Her Heavenly Father's. And there, in the light of the dawning morning, was the retreat of darkness and the promise of hope.

Chapter 17
In the Army Now

James kicked back in his bunk. He crossed one leg over the other and put both arms behind his head on his pillow. It was hard to believe that he was almost done with his advanced tech school. Some days had been long and down-right miserable. But here he was, almost done. He let his memories of the past four months surface.

His eight weeks of basic training at Fort Leonard Wood had gone by surprisingly quickly, despite his bumpy start. Unfortunately, James found out the hard way right off the bat that he had a lot to learn about military life. Hindsight is always 20/20 and, looking back now, if he would have only known the importance of Hank's question that day in the locker room, it would have saved him a lot of misery in the beginning. Hank had asked him if he had memorized his personal service number yet, but the bell rang and James never had a chance to answer. He didn't answer then and, unfortunately, didn't answer the first time his drill sergeant asked him either. He closed his eyes and recalled the incident…

"What's your number, soldier?"

Silence.

"You little flea on a maggot's ass!" he spat in James' face. "You better damn well learn your number. The next time I ask you, you have an answer or you'll be worn slap out when I get done havin' your pansy ass do push-ups. I'll be in your ugly face countin' 'til you puke your brains out…if you have any in that skull of yours."

"Yes, sir."

"Don't call me sir. I work for a livin'," he yelled in James' face. "The next time I ask you, you better have an answer, private." **There were a few more choice words in there, but James let his memory brush over the vulgarity of the incident.**

James didn't plan to make that mistake again. He memorized his number that same day saying it over and over again in his head – RA19967345. But, the next formation his drill sergeant didn't ask for his number. Instead, he asked what his first general order was and, once again, James didn't answer.

"I told you, boy, to have an answer the next time I ask you. It doesn't matter what I ask you, peabrain. You have an answer. YOU NEED TO THINK ON YOUR FEET, SOLDIER," he shouted at James, only inches from his face. Then his drill sergeant yelled at him asking what his second general order was and proceeded through all eleven – all of which James had no answer. James did the only thing he could. He stared straight forward, standing at attention, and responded, "I don't know, Drill Sergeant!"

"Do you have an answer for anythin', numbskull? You're the reason condoms have an expiration date.

Let's try an easy one for ya. What's your name, private?"

"Patterson, Drill Sergeant!"

"Ahh! Ding! Ding! Ding! We have an answer from the dummy in the front," he gave a sarcastic clap of approval to *his audience.* "Where are you from, Patterson?"

"Cordova, Alabama, Drill Sergeant."

"And are all people from Alabama this stupid? Private Patterson, you're so dumb, if you were Little Bo Peep, the sheep would have led you to school!" Then his drill sergeant turned to the rest of the recruits and yelled, "Since *your buddy* Patterson has made it quite apparent that he doesn't like to learn, you all get to be *his buddy* and help motivate him." The drill sergeant began to bark out orders for the entire platoon to do push-ups. And true to his word, James' drill sergeant was laying on the ground in his face, personally counting out each push-up for James until he was in physical agony and vomiting.

Within the first 48 hours of basic training, James came to realize that his drill sergeant had two main goals: to break the civilian out of him and to give him a crash course in military lifestyle. He had started off on the wrong foot, but from that moment on he learned to have a ready answer. At all times. No matter what was asked. *Think on your feet, soldier!* James shook his head, *how many times had he heard that?*

…And now, he was almost done with his advanced individualized training. He was coming up on the end of his eight weeks of his military journalism training at the **Defense Information School at Fort Benjamin Harrison in Indiana**. He'd be graduating the end of the week and then he'd be getting orders for his assignment. He closed his eyes again and when he opened them, he looked up at the picture of Jessie he had hanging above his bed. It was the Polaroid picture of her in her blue shirt that was on the back of the Ephesians soldier she'd given him just before he left for basic. He reached up and grabbed it. He stared at her for a bit. He sure was homesick for her. He turned it over and then couldn't help but chuckle under his breath when he looked at the soldier with the mushroom helmet. He smiled. She had put so much thought into his gift.

He should write her. He knew once he was stationed, it would probably get harder to write. So, he took out some paper and a pen and began to jot down a quick letter. He didn't have long before a sergeant would come in and order "lights out."

He put the pen to the paper and began to write.

September 27th, 1965
Dear Jessie May,

It's just about time for lights out and I thought I'd sneak in a quick letter. You know the routine, once my drill sergeant comes in telling us it's time to hit the sack, that's it. I'm done writing immediately. So, let me tell you in advance, I love you!

He did his best to draw a winking smiley face next to the word "usually." Jessie would get a kick out of that. Jessie liked his wink. She never said it, but he knew. He smiled as he thought back to a conversation they had shortly after she had met his sister Elizabeth for the first time. Elizabeth had winked after something she said---which Jessie distinctly noticed and then about a week later his mama had winked too while talking with them. He shook his head. That was the day his mother almost spoiled the surprise he was planning – to give Jessie a promise ring. It was his mother's ring from his father. After his father had passed away, his mother wore it until she met John. Then she tucked it away for Elizabeth. But Elizabeth liked wearing her ring from David, so she wanted her brother to have it. He shook his head again thinking about that day. Thankfully, Jessie missed his mother's blunder and was more fixated on the quirk of the *family wink*! He smiled while his fond memories relaxed his mind. But, he knew he better get back to his letter or he wouldn't get to finish it.

I'll be graduating from AIT the end of this week on Friday (October 1st). Easy enough day to remember, huh! I sure wish you could be here for my graduation. I will also get my orders Friday. I get the weekend off and head out on Monday. I don't know how long until I will be able to write to you again or even how long it will take for you to get a letter when I'm over there. But don't worry, as soon as I can, I will write you. Plus, I'll need to get you my new mailing address ASAP so you can write to me. Your letters are a lifeline to me.

"2200! Lights out!" he heard his sergeant bark. His letter-writing was over. He quickly scribbled an abrupt sign-off.

Gotta go,
James

* * *

Jessie sat in her bedroom at her desk and pulled out some paper and a pencil. It was hard to believe James had been gone almost four months already. She was missing him terribly, so she decided to sit down and write him again. She pulled out a brown box with a purple ribbon tied around it. She released the ribbon and let it fall off the box. She pulled the lid off. Inside were all her letters from James since he left. She pulled them out with care and counted them – just as she did every time she opened the box. Sixteen. She smiled; he had stayed true to writing her once a week.

She looked at the first envelope. She caressed his name on the return address. The initials PVT were in front of his name. She had asked her daddy what that meant. She had no clue the military had so many initials and acronyms and jargon. Her father had told her that PVT stood for Private which he explained was the lowest ranking soldier in the army. He said after basic that James would probably get promoted to Private Second Class.

She pulled out the last most current envelop and looked at it. Written behind James' name was PV2. Her daddy was right; James was a Private Second Class now. She held the envelope close to her chest and closed her eyes. She was so proud of him. She took a few deep breaths and felt a sense of peace come over her. She opened her eyes and then the envelope in her hands. She slid out the last letter he had written. It was a short one. His drill sergeant had apparently come in and called "lights out" and the letter ended way too soon. She wished there were more words to linger on. She began to re-read his letter. She laughed out loud at the part where he said she had competition with Mushroom Man. Oh, how she missed his humor! He always had a way of making her laugh. She also liked the winking smiley face he had drawn. It made her think of his brown eyes and how he was always winking at her. She loved that.

She finished reading through his letter and her eyes settled on the last sentence he had written, "Your letters are a lifeline to me." This small line tugged at her heart. She knew that would only intensify for James as time went on. It reaffirmed in her that she needed to write to James often. Besides, she found such comfort in writing to him because it made her feel not as separated. It helped her to feel like they were having a conversation together even though it was through mail. His last comment, however, made her realize that writing to him was more important for James than it was for her. She needed to keep his spirits up. She had her family around her, supporting her. But that wasn't the case for James. *Oh, how he must miss family*, she thought. She felt a small lump in her throat as her emotions started to betray her sense of peace. And then, she heard a soft voice in her head, *I will be with him wherever he goes.*

She closed her eyes and thanked God for bringing the reassurance of His truth to her mind when she needed it. Last night she had been reading in the book of Joshua and had highlighted a verse--Joshua 1:9--that stood out to her. It was just the encouragement she was needing then…and now. "Be strong and courageous. Do not be afraid; do not be discouraged, for the LORD your God will be with you wherever you go." She folded up his letter and gave it a small kiss before placing it back in its envelope. Being careful to place it at the end of the letters to keep them in order, she tucked it back in the box. And with powerful incentive and renewed zest, she began to write James back.

October 2nd, 1965
Dear James,

Nice "attempt" at drawing a winking smiley face in your last letter. And you give

273

me a hard time about my artistic abilities (or lack thereof), but I dare say, your smiley face lacks quality!

It sure feels weird not to be in school. Don't worry, I've been keeping busy though. I know you said to stay busy since I'm not going to college so that I have less time to worry. I have been doing pretty good with not worrying. My Bible reading helps greatly. I've had a lot of peace lately and have been praying you also feel His peace upon you! And yes, staying busy certainly does help!

I've been helping Mama around the house. Plus, we just got done canning. All the vegetables in the garden come due all at the same time, so we were very busy harvesting the produce. And then she taught me all her tricks-to-the-trade with canning. It was a lot of work, but so worth it. When we marry, I will be a canning-fool. I'll be a pro at preserving all kinds of yummy things for us! I'll fill our pantry with the best pickled okra you've ever tasted, James Patterson.

Oh, and you'll never guess...RJ's got a girlfriend. He's dating Landa Jane Braswell. Remember her? She's a senior this year. I always thought he flirted with her, especially in gym. He was always showing off for her--almost as much as Bobby Ray! Ha! Ha! I guess he's pretty head-over-heels. He might just enjoy her more than playin' his fiddle! But don't worry, when you get back here, you still got your fiddle player. He said as far as your band goes, he's not going anywhere! Bobby Ray and Janet are still an item too. She's good for him. Keeps him humble...well, as humble as Bobby Ray can get! Ha! And, Nathaniel's still just bein' Nathaniel.

Those three hoodlums ask about you whenever I run into them. They've all been busy with farming and busy with harvest. Bobby Ray said the pecans haven't done well this year. And I guess the cotton root rot has been bad this season. But I really don't see the guys much. They're busy and I don't go in to town very often. Maybe to bring in eggs or go to church, but otherwise I stick close to home. I just don't feel like going to town. It makes me miss you more because I know you're not there. Whereas, if I stay home, I can imagine you're just in town at your house while I'm occupied at home.

Well, that's about all I can think of for now so I should wrap it up. I'll write again soon, but I will wait for your address. I know the next time I hear from you, you'll be across the world. Strange to think about that. But no matter what, you are always close in my heart! I love you, James Theodore! So very much! I am praying for you every day! Stay you. Stay strong. Stay singing.

With all my love,
Jessie May

* * *

The flight over was long, but the sergeant kept them busy watching films about gonorrhea and syphilis. It was so appalling to James, but he knew they were trying to scare all the young soldiers into being cautious. He had heard a couple things about Vietnam…that there was lots of pot smoking…and lots of *available* women. Apparently young Vietnamese girls would come into camp and men would line up to take their turns. This was so disturbing to James. *If only they would turn to God instead.* He looked down at his helmet laying in his lap and saw Jessie's picture—the one with Mushroom Man on the back—tucked in the underside of the webbing of his helmet. Jessie was with him wherever he went and to serve as a reminder within his helmet—his armor—of his *true armor*. The Armor of God. Yes, he would turn to God before anything else. Not other women. Not even Jessie. Only God could provide for all his needs. God, his provider. God, his comforter. God, his protector. God, his savior.

He smiled and closed his eyes in a calming prayer, *Thank you, Lord, for Jessie May and how she reminds me that you, my Great Almighty, are everythin' I need. It is you who is truly with me wherever I go. Please help these other guys so that their moral compass points to you while on the foreign soil of Vietnam...and always. Amen.* He opened his eyes, but they felt heavy. *How can I be feelin' sleepy again?* He had already slept on the flight. But it helped to pass the time, so he wasn't going to fight this weary feeling. He looked down at Jessie again. Her smile--a ray of sunshine--and her soft, green eyes penetrated his soul with sustainable joy. He closed his eyes again and let Jessie's image linger before drifting off to sleep.

* * *

He awoke with the feeling of the plane's descent. The sergeant said they were landing in Guam to refuel. Another video was just starting up—one about taking their "Monday Pill" to keep them from getting malaria. James sat up, rubbing the sleep from his eyes. *Next stop – Vietnam.* He took a deep breath.

* * *

James felt exhausted from the flight as he unpacked his rucksack in his squad's tent. He looked around at the other soldiers doing the same thing. There were eight guys in his squad. The guy across from his cot looked up the same time as James was glancing his way. He had the same weary look in his eyes that James was feeling.

277

"Hey," James gave a head nod, "I'm James Patterson, from Cordova, Alabama."

"I'm Jim Beau."

"Jimbo!" James interrupted with a tension-breaking smile.

"No, it's Jim…Beau."

"Sorry, my cronies from back home call me Jimbo. You made me think of them. I miss those knuckleheads. We're in a band together."

"I play in a band too." Jim's eyes lit up. A connection had been struck. "Well, a family band. We play mostly at wedding dances and town hall dances or barn burners. I'm from Long Prairie, Minnesota. I play bass guitar. How about you?"

"I play lead guitar, but I'm also the lead singer. You know, our band is lookin' for a bass guitar player! You wouldn't per chance be interested in movin' to Alabama?" James gave a little wink. The two laughed and finished unpacking with a noticeably peppier beat than before.

* * *

Earlier in the day Sergeant Cobal had told his soldiers, "Unpack your things and get settled. Enjoy today. Hell starts tomorrow."

James had no idea what that meant for his squad and he felt uneasy. But he decided if he was going to enjoy today, he'd write to Jessie. He had promised to

get her his address. He so desperately wanted another
letter from her.

October 8ᵗʰ, 1965
Dear Jessie May,

I like how you ended your letter. "Stay you.
Stay strong. Stay singing." Yep, don't
worry, I'm still singing. However, my fellow
comrades don't seem to appreciate it as
much as you do!

It's been hot since I got here. Really hot!
It's high humidity. You know, instead of my
M-16 I have to carry every day, I could use
one of those squirt guns RJ brought to
school that we got in trouble for...well,
actually just me! I was thinking about
that the other day! Those punks! I was
totally hung out to dry! Man though, it
makes me laugh now. I miss those
knuckleheads! Speaking of...

Guess what?!!! Tell the guys that I found
us a bass guitar player! He's from Long
Prairie, Minnesota, and his name's Jim
Beau! Yeah, for real! Just like the guys call
me – Jimbo! I know, I laughed too! So tell
the boys that I'll keep working on Jim to
move to Cordova!

Pickled okra, huh? The best I've ever
tasted? Hmmm? You're just gonna have to

prove it! You know, I can think of something else I'd like to taste right now. The taste of your lips. I am missing you something fierce. I would give anything to be with you right now. Like in Eden's Pathway, our special place. That place brings me back to so many private memories with you. And then I can't help it, Jess, I start to think about the feel of your soft, smooth legs. Mmm! You never truly seemed to fight it if you were wearing a skirt and I'd rub my hand up your thigh.

Okay, I know! I need a very, VERY large cold soda right now. But Jess, it's so hard over here with all these guys who have only one thing on their mind. I better just stop now so I cool off, but I can't help thinking of when we'll finally give ourselves to each other. It makes me so excited to call you Mrs. Patterson.

And with what I'm earning now, I'll be able to buy you a real engagement ring. Not that my mama's ring isn't special. You know it means a lot to me because it was from my father. But I want to buy one that is from me. That is totally ours as a promise for our wedding. Our future. Between all my MPC's (that's military payment certificates, by the way) and the possibility of more band bookings with a new bass guitarist, heck, when I get back the first time you'll see me, Jess, I'll probably be down on one knee with a new ring in hand!

Ah crap! Sergeant Cobal just came in. Mandatory formation. Gotta go.

Love you,
James

* * *

Jessie was just coming down the stairs, when her father walked in the front door. His workday was done. He closed the door and turned with a smile on his face; he had a letter in his hand. She glanced down. It was from James! She squealed and snatched the letter, "Ohhhh, thank you, Daddy!" And giving him a big hug and quick peck on his cheek, she turned and skipped every other step back up the stairs to her bedroom and closed the door.

She flopped onto her bed, slightly breathless from her stair hurdling. She stared at the envelope. The outside border had red and blue stripes. Where normally a postage stamp would be placed, the word "Free" was written. James' return address was in the usual top-left corner and she noticed he had three new initials in front of his name – PFC. James was no longer a Private Second Class. He was now Private First Class. She rubbed her hand over his name. She was so proud of him. She sighed and turned onto her side and held his letter intimately close to her as if she was snuggling in with a teddy bear. Then, after paying homage, she began to read his letter. She giggled out loud at the part about Jim Beau. That was too funny--the coincidence of this guy's name to what Ricky, Nathaniel, and Bobby Ray call James was certainly comical. And when she read the part about James running his hand up her thigh, she started to feel parts of her body she had forgotten about. She took a deep breath and continued reading. Then she read the part about James wanting to buy her a real engagement ring. She looked down at her left hand. His mother's ring sparkled on her finger. Yes, she too couldn't wait to be called "Mrs. Patterson."

After she finished reading his letter, she closed her eyes and held the letter to her chest again and just laid there for a bit. Then as if startled, she quickly slid out of bed. She hastily wrote down his new mailing address and pinned it to her bulletin board above her desk. She had his new address and that meant one thing…it was time to replenish James with another letter.

October 19th, 1965
Dear James,

How are you? Still hot? After what you wrote in your letter, I guess that's a loaded question! Ha! But I mean about the weather! I am constantly imagining what your piece of world is like. I can't even picture it. I try to remember what we learned in history class, but I can't. You are a world away to me...but not in my thoughts.

Let' see, as for me...Hmmm? Where to start? My family is good. I think since you left, Mama has her nose in her books more now than ever. And we thought she read a lot before! Like me, the busier she stays the less time she has to worry. But why she is reading "War and Peace" again is beyond me! I wish I knew how many times she has pulled some of those old books off the shelf and reread them. And "War and Peace" of all things...such a long, boring novel. I know it is supposed to be one of the finest pieces of world literature, but I think it's an utterly tiresome read. Maybe she's reading it again now because of you being off to war. I don't know. But that's Mama for ya!

Daddy's been very busy at work. I admire how he's such a hard-working man. But you'll never believe this...he joined a bowling league. Seriously! I could hardly believe it. I think with Mama and her love of reading and seeing her go quilting every Thursday he's realized that he needs some balance to working all the time. I think you going off to war, James, has made him step back and reprioritize things. He's learning to relax and enjoy life more. He used to work so much that he really had no hobbies before this. Well, other than watching football, but that's not really a hobby. So, I'm glad he's bowling...even if he comes home grumbling about his score!

Lydia and Carrie are both doing good. Carrie Grace is super excited for Halloween. She's going trick-or-treating as a clown. Mama sewed her a cute red and white polka dot clown outfit with this ruffled hat that looks adorable on her. I think she is mostly excited because she gets to use red lipstick to rouge her cheeks! Ha! Maybe I will ask Mama if I can get a polaroid of her and send you!

And me, well, I still am not going in to town much. I just haven't really felt like being around others. Daddy told me that staying busy is a good thing, but that I need to take time to enjoy friends too. The thing of it is--staying busy is easy, but hanging out with friends is just too difficult. Being with friends is what really reminds me that you are gone. I am missing you something fierce, James Theodore. And when I'm around others, I know they mean well, but all they do is ask me about you and if I've heard from you. I'm sick of them asking. I know they are good-intentioned, but I don't want to talk about it. I'm constantly thinking about it, so I'd rather they talked about other things to get my mind off the fact that you are gone. So, we shall see! And no, I'm not being stubborn! Just realistic. It's how I feel. It's easier to stay home.

Well, I guess that's about all I have for now. I love you, James. You are forever in my heart and my prayers. I pray without ceasing the Lord will bring you back to me. Stay you. Stay strong. Stay singing.

Faithfully yours,
Jessie May Clark...Ahem, let me correct myself...soon-to-be Patterson

Chapter 18
Staying Steadfast

Another week slipped past. The first week between letters she did pretty good and kept busy enough to preoccupy her mind. But then another week went by and then another. With time stretching out again between letters, Jessie noticed something about herself. Mentally her endurance was not very good. She was trying to 'run this race' but she was starting to feel tired and overwhelmed with anxiety.

Last night she read 1 Corinthians 9 again in her Bible. Her father had shared this scripture with her back in May about running the race set before us and she had bookmarked it. In the margin scribbled next to this scripture she had written "Hebrews 12:1-3" to remind her to flip to that scripture when reading this one. The scripture in Hebrews was the one her mother had cross-referenced because it was about running the race with perseverance and fixing our eyes on Jesus. It went on to say that we should "Consider him who endured such opposition from sinners, so that you will not grow weary and lose heart." But as the days passed on without word from James, she was growing weary. And she was losing heart.

* * *

Patty's morning had been busy. She finished all the ironing as well as the dusting on the main floor. She ate an early dinner and planned to finish dusting upstairs before Lydia and Carrie got home from school. Jessie was up in her room still. She promised her mother she'd run the Kirby through the house after Patty was finished with the dusting. But before Jessie came down to vacuum, Patty hustled out to the television.

Yesterday after church--during fellowship--she was visiting with Ida Mae. Ida was the town gossip who knew just about anything. Whether it had happened or was yet to happen, Ida knew the details. For the latest news within a 30-mile radius to Cordova, Ida was the gal to talk to if you needed to know something. *She really should work for The Walker County Tribune*, Patty laughed. *Oh, Ida!* She shook her head.

Between sips of coffee and dabbing the crumbs of an icebox cookie from the corners of her mouth, Ida had told Patty to mark her calendar because tomorrow— which was today, Monday November 8th—the new soap opera "Days of our Lives" would be airing its first episode. Patty knew she probably shouldn't even flick the television on. Taking Ida's advice was like taking advice from the fox guarding the hen house, but she was all too curious. Besides…*it was only 30 minutes*, she reasoned with herself. *She deserved a 30-minute break after all. She had worked hard.*

Patty twisted the power knob of their television box on and turned the volume up slightly. "Like sands through the hour glass, so are the days of our lives," the announcer said. She was just about to get comfy in Robert's recliner when she heard the front door open. She hastily popped up and turned the television off. It was Robert. She wondered if he heard the television on when he walked in. What was he doing home for dinner? Since he went in later on Mondays, he never came home for dinner this day. She was hoping he hadn't heard the television, but as she came around the corner that concern melted away when she saw the look of worry on his face, "What's wrong? Is everythin' okay?" She was at Robert's side immediately.

"Yes, yes," he took both her hands in his. "I'm sorry, I didn't mean to startle you, but somethin' was really botherin' me at work and I just needed to come home."

"What is it, Robert? Are you feelin' okay?" Now he had Patty concerned.

"No, it's nothin' with me. I'm fine. It's Jessie May; I couldn't get her off my mind, Pats. Usually she comes down to say good-bye to me, but today she didn't. I thought maybe she wasn't feelin' well, so I went up to her room. When I poked my head into her room, she seemed very downcast. She told me she was just tired. But the more I thought about her at work, I think it's more than bein' tired. Maybe I am just over-reactin', but I think we need to be watchin' her more carefully. She is feelin' more stress than she has ever experienced," Robert sighed. "I just couldn't quit thinkin' about her at work and how vacant she looked this mornin'. It made me wanna come home and check on her…see how she is doin'…how she's handlin' things," he paused briefly. "Where is she?"

"She's still in her room. She hasn't come down yet." Patty suddenly felt horrible for not being more perceptive. She chided herself because she was so fixated on hustling to watch that blasted soap opera. Rather than being concerned with watching the drama of a soap opera, she should have been more focused on what was happening with her daughter. Real life.

"She hasn't come out of her room yet?" Robert's question was not intended with any accusation, only concern.

"No," Patty said, "she was waitin' for me to get the dustin' done so she could vacuum."

"She didn't come down and eat with you?"

"No," Patty said feeling guilty for her rush to get to the television. "We usually do eat together, but today I was just in such a rush to get everythin' done."

"I'm goin' to go and check on her." He rubbed his knuckles gently on Patty's cheek, "It'll be okay. You go ahead and finish what you were doin'."

"It wasn't important," Patty felt a piercing in her heart. "Can I go up with you?"

"Of course." Robert laced his fingers between his wife's and the two--side-by-side--headed up the stairs.

* * *

Robert knocked gently on the door.

"You ready for me to vacuum now?" Jessie asked as she looked up and saw both her parents enter her room. She sat up quickly from her bed, still in her pajamas and her hair messy. Her puffy eyes revealed she had been crying though the tears were no longer there. "Daddy, what are you doin' home now?" she asked with concern. "Is everythin' okay?"

"I don't know, is it?" Robert crossed the room and sat down on the bed next to his daughter. He put his arms on her shoulders. She felt so small to him just then…she was still his little girl. He looked straight into her eyes, "I was worried about you, Jess. I came home because I needed to know you are okay."

For a moment, she just stared back at her father. Not answering, nor hardly blinking. And then, the tears started. Robert embraced his daughter, like so many times before, and just let her cry in the comfort of his strong arms.

Patty came and sat down next to them and began to rub her daughter's back, "Oh sweetheart, I am so sorry that I did not notice how much you are hurtin'." Patty was crying now too.

"You didn't do anythin' wrong, Mama." Jessie turned slightly from her father so that she could give her mother a hug. This only made Patty cry harder.

"Oh honey, it's you who needs the consolin'. That's what I did wrong. I didn't see."

Robert embraced both Patty and Jessie and let them each feel the comfort of his love. They sat that way for a bit, and then Jessie sniffled and pointed to the box of Kleenex on her desk. Patty stood up and grabbed them each a couple.

Amidst the simultaneous blowing, Robert didn't know which one started to laugh first, but both Patty and Jessie were now giggling. He began to shake his head, "I will never understand women. One minute you're cryin' and the next minute you are laughin'."

"I know, Daddy," Jessie sniffled and half-laughed at the same time, "it's just, with us both blowin' our noses, we sounded like a couple of sick elephants in the room." She broke into laughter again which Patty echoed. After Jessie collected her composure, she scooted back against her wall so she could look at both her parents, "When James first left for Basic, it was hard. But I found comfort that he was stateside. And we were writin' to each other every week. But now it's been three weeks since I've gotten a letter from James. Three weeks! It feels like forever! And with each passin' day, I just seem to grow more impatient. And the truth is, we've only just begun. It makes me doubt and wonder how am I goin' to make it through this? I can barely stand it now, and it's been only three weeks between letters. And then worry starts to set in…what if somethin' bad has happened to James already?"

"Don't imagine things that are not." Robert advised and leaned forward to embrace his daughter once more, "James is probably gettin' acclimated to his new surroundin's. It's quite the change for him. He is busy with his responsibilities as a soldier. He's no longer a recruit, Jess. He's a soldier of the United States Army who is needed daily for the job he was trained to do. He's doin' his job there and you need to do your job back home."

"My job?" Jessie was confused.

"Yes, your job is to take care of yourself. Your health both physically and mentally are critical to *your survival* on the home front. You need to get out of bed at a decent time and…maybe comb your hair," he smiled a bit. "You need to find a purpose for each day, Jess. You need to do things that keep you busy. And, Jess," he paused for a moment, not knowing how his daughter would react to what he had to say next. He drew in a breath, "I believe if you're not goin' to college, it's time to start lookin' for a job. It doesn't have to be full-time. I know there are plenty of things your mama needs help with around the house, but I think gettin' out of the house and workin' a little would be good for you. However, I have come to realize that it's not just work that needs to always occupy one's time. I have been a slow learner with that revelation, but I have come to understand that we need other things to bring us joy. Maybe it's time you joined somethin' like I joined bowlin'. Or go quiltin' with your mother. Or just go in to town once in a while, Jess, and hang out with your friends. You know, social things to get out of your pajamas," he rubbed her leg and smiled a little, but then his features grew serious again. "Jess, it's very important you take care of yourself."

"I know, Daddy, thank you for comin' home." She hugged her daddy tightly, "I needed you."

"I know, sweetheart," he kissed the top of her head, "And I know somethin' else you need."

"What's that?" she leaned back slightly.

"A toothbrush!"

* * *

The following week—four weeks since James' last letter—Jessie couldn't help it. Her impatience grew. When she'd hear her father pull into the driveway, she'd about knock anyone over hustling out to greet him. Not so much because she was excited Robert was home from work, but because she needed to see if he had any mail for her. Now being a month since she had last heard from him, she was beside herself. And each day without a letter, her head hung a little lower with disappointment. Up until James deployed, she had gotten used to the consistency of getting a letter a week. Was this how it was going to be? She had suspected it would change once he left for Vietnam, but this was getting unbearable. She tried not to let unnecessary worry cloud her mind. She made a conscious effort to push out irrational thoughts. She recalled what her father said to her last week, "Don't imagine things that are not." Jessie knew her father was right. It did no good to worry about things that were not yct known. But being a month since she'd last heard from James, she struggled with her weariness and growing concern for his well-being. Her father's sound advice then fell on deaf ears now. *This race*, she thought, *was gettin' harder to run* with each passing day.

* * *

Since it was a Monday night—her father's late night to work at Chuck's Repair—he wasn't home from work yet. Supper had long ago been eaten and the leftovers put away. Robert's supper sat cold and untouched on a plate on the table. The rest of the dishes had been done by Jessie and Lydia who now sat together in the living room on the davenport. Lydia had her nose in a book and Jessie was intermittently watching TV. She was more preoccupied with watching out the bay window for their Plymouth Fury to come driving down the dirt road than watching TV. She glanced at the television. *The Lawrence Welk Show* was on and Jessie still wasn't used to watching it in color. Just as the Champagne Lady – Norma Zimmer – began singing a solo, she heard the gravel crunching under the tires of their car, but she didn't race off the couch like she had done all last week. She was tired; she wasn't up for another day of empty disappointment.

Lydia set her book down in her lap and said, "Daddy's home." She was staring at Jessie with a questioning look. Robert and Patty had visited privately with Lydia to be more sensitive and perceptive to Jessie. Lydia knew Jessie's reaction to

294

her father getting home had been quite predictable the last couple weeks, but now Jessie sat without moving. Lydia repeated herself, "Jessie May, Daddy's home."

"I know."

"Aren't you goin' to go see if he has a letter from James?"

"He doesn't."

"You don't know that, Jess. Go on, go see. Today might be the day!" She said, making a nudging motion with her head towards the front door.

Jessie loved the soft sparkle Lydia had in her eyes as she looked across the davenport at her sister. Lydia sure didn't say much, but her eyes always did.

"Thanks, Lydia Ruth," she got up from the sofa and patted her sister's foot that was tucked up on the cushion, "I needed that encouragement. I appreciate you, sis."

As she opened the front door, her father was parking in their driveway. Jessie stepped out on the front step and Robert glanced her way. He didn't have his tired look that was quite typical on a Monday night when he got home late from work. Instead, his eyes were dancing and a grin was splitting his face. He looked like he was hopped up on Granny Williams' strong coffee. Patty's mother always said, "Any coffee that ain't black as pitch, ain't worth drinkin'." He excitedly swung his legs out from the car and that's when Jessie saw it in his hand…a letter. He beamed as he spoke the words she'd been waiting four weeks to hear, "A letter from James."

* * *

Jessie liked to be alone when she read her letters from James. She liked to pretend that they were having their own private conversation and so she wanted complete and utter privacy. This was their only time together. Through letters.

She plopped onto her bed, her usual letter-reading spot. She sliced open the envelope with her letter opener that had sat on her night stand since the very first letter she received from James when he was in basic at Fort Leonard Wood. That seemed so long ago. She paused for a moment and, looking up to her ceiling, she offered up a quick prayer, "Thank you, Lord, that James is okay." Then, not being able to stand it a moment longer, she plunged into her long-awaited letter.

November 6th, 1965
Dear Jessie May,

In your letter you said your mama was reading *War and Peace* again. Do you think she has any tips for me over here?! For some reason, I find that humorous. Of all the books she could be reading right now to keep her mind off me being away at war, she's reading that book! It strikes a funny bone in me. But then again, I used to laugh

296

at Bieberdorf's jokes, so I guess I find humor in strange things.

Speaking of your mama, what I wouldn't do for her fried chicken right now. The food here is horrible, especially the turkey loaf in our C-rations (that just means our Combat food). It's so gross. And so is the ham and lima beans. It all comes in cans. The consolation is that we get good beer and cigarettes with our C-rations. Don't worry, Jess, I'm not smoking. I know, you wouldn't like me drinking either, but it helps to numb what's going on around here. I had no idea what I was signing up for. Seems like everyone here drinks or smokes *something* to forget. Usually with our rations, we get a four-pack of cigarettes every day. I save mine and started giving them to a papasan (that means an older Vietnamese man). You wouldn't believe how much they appreciate getting cigarettes for free. But if I don't see any papasans, I give them to my friends. Everyone here wants cigarettes. You wouldn't believe this, but cigarettes are a huge care package hit. So, I'm quite a popular guy with my C-ration giveaways! And, it's a win-win...if I give them my cigarettes, they forgive me for singing all the time! Ha! Ha!

I'm finally getting used to being over here. But I tell you, it's still hot – muggy hot. I know Cordova can be hot and humid, but there is just something about the heat and humidity here. It adds to the rest of the misery. We are just coming out of the wet monsoon season, so hopefully now it will be less humid. Maybe it's the jungle that makes it feel more unbearable because there ain't no air in there. November is supposed to be the start of their winter or drier season, so hopefully we'll start to feel some relief. I've gotten so skinny. Between the bad food and sweatin' profusely, I'm shedding weight like no body's business.

On a bright note, since getting over here I don't have to do my laundry anymore. You know I hate doing laundry. A hoochgirl here does our laundry for us (A hoochgirl is kind of like a maid or laundress). Jim said he wants to take her with him when he goes back to Long Prairie. I told him he can't because he ain't going back to Long Prairie! He'd have to bring her to Cordova! Ha! Tell the guys I'm still working on him!

So your daddy started bowling? I find that hard to believe, but good for him! I think it's great that he is doing something other than just work, work, work. You know, Jess, you need to have some fun too...go in to town and do something. See people. Interact with them. Even if it reminds you that I am gone. I AM gone and that's a fact, plain and simple. You can't just sit home the whole time I'm gone. It would be good for you to get out and about a little. Promise me, you'll get together with the guys soon. I wanna hear about what they are doing! So maybe over Thanksgiving break? That would be the perfect time. Everybody is always looking for something to do over the long holiday weekend, especially Friday after Thanksgiving. And I imagine there will be the parade and sidewalk sales in town that day to kick off the Christmas season and shopping, so there will be lots of people bustling in town that day I bet. Makes me miss Cordova! So promise me that, Jessie May! Go meet the guys for me at Buckie's! I know I sure would if I could. So do it for me! It'd be fun!

Well, I should probably get going. Please knuckle Carrie's head for me and tell her she better not get rusty playing Dutch Blitz. I owe her a butt whoopin' in that game! And tell Lydia Ruth I have a new book suggestion for her that I think she'd enjoy. It's called "Owls in the Family" by Farley Mowat. Jim got it from his mama in a care package, and when he was done readin' it, he gave it to me to read. It made me laugh; it's just some old-fashioned fun that did me good to read, especially now. I think Lydia would appreciate it because of her love of animals. It's about a couple of boys that live in Canada in Saskatoon and have quite the collection of animal pets. They bring home a couple wild baby owls with cantankerous personalities that end up giving the whole town some funny adventures. Lydia Ruth would like it. Trust me, she'd find their hilarious antics a "hoot"! Get it?! Get it?! Baby owls...a hoot! I know, I know...Mr. Bieberdorf has always had competition!

I love you, my Jessie May Clark soon-to-be Patterson! With all my heart!

Love,
James

Chapter 19
A Clever Idea

A hoochgirl? A little twinge of jealously hit her. No, she would not focus on that. She forced that ridiculous thought out of her head. Instead, she would focus on the positive. She noticed a couple things about James' letter. One, he had dated his letter November 6th. Today was November 15th, so it had taken just over a week to get to her. Two, he had mentioned care packages a couple times in his letter. That gave her an idea. She'd hurry and put together a care package for him and send off tomorrow so that he might receive it by Thanksgiving.

Another thought crept into her mind and spread a smile across her face. Recalling something he had written in one of his previous letters, suddenly a clever idea started taking shape. It was perfect actually. James would love the humor. She'd have to get up early and head in to town to see if she could get it. That one last item would be the punctuation to her package, but she'd need to hustle in the morning in order to get her package to the post office before noon. She wanted it to go out with the Tuesday mail to hopefully get to James by Thanksgiving next Thursday. This would be tight, but she knew she could do it. Without delay, she scurried downstairs to start baking some cookies. She would gather a few other items and make certain to write letter later to tuck with it. She clapped her hands together! *This was gonna be fun!*

* * *

Robert was finishing his supper and Patty sat with him at the table enjoying small talk. Jessie waltzed into the room wearing a big smile. Robert and Patty exchanged looks as the undeniable pep in her step was a welcomed sight. Jessie seemed to float over to the oven where she quickly began clanging pans together as she pulled stuff out of the drawer below.

"That smile looks good on you! It does my mother's heart good to see it, Jess. I haven't seen you wear a smile that big for quite some time. James must be well!" Patty commented.

"He is! I feel on cloud nine after gettin' his letter. And I came up with an idea I hope you both are okay with--I guess I didn't think about it--I might need help sendin' it. I have some money from my birthday still, but I'm not sure how much it will cost."

"What's that?" Robert stood to carry his plate to the sink. Patty got up to wash it for him. "No, you sit, you've done enough for today," he gave her a loving look, "I got this." Robert went to the sink and washed his own plate, "So, what is your idea?"

"I'd like to put together a care package for James."

"That's a great idea!" Patty commented. "Lydia and Carrie would add to it. They'd love to make somethin' for James also."

302

"Well, the catch is that I wanna send it by tomorrow."

"Tomorrow already?" Patty's eyes grew the size of saucers.

"Yeah, I'm hopin' for James to get it by Thanksgivin'. I think that his first holiday over there could be tough for him, so this would be a welcomed surprise. He mentioned care packages a couple times in his letter. He wasn't hintin'. He was just tellin' me about other things and just happened to mention them in his stories. So, I know this would make his day and be a total surprise for him! I'd like to bake some cookies now to put in his package. And then, if it is okay with you, Daddy, I'd like to ride in to town with you tomorrow? I wanna go to school before the rest of the kids start comin' and it gets busy."

"To school?" Robert was confused.

"Yes, there's somethin' there I'd like to get to put in his package. I don't wanna say what it is because I don't wanna jinx gettin' it. I'm hopin' it's still there. Plus, I thought maybe I would check and see if they have any part-time jobs at the school." Robert smiled at her, this made him happy. She continued, "I figure if I'm already there, I might as well ask, right?" Jessie turned both her hands up and shrugged her shoulders.

Patty stood up, "I think that's a great idea seein' if they need any help. And now, you have me all too curious what could possibly be at the school for James." She smiled and then grabbed her apron, "Here, with two of us workin', we'll whip cookies up in no time."

"Thanks, Mama!"

Robert dried his hands and then reached in his back pocket and took out his wallet. He pulled out two dollars, "I want you to take this, Jess."

"No, Daddy, that's too much!" Jessie tried to turn him down, "You don't need to do that. I wanna help pay with my birthday money, so let's wait and see how much it costs to send the cookies and…" she paused, not wantin' to give away her surprise, "*the other* item."

"No, I wanna do this. It's not just for you, it's for James. So, I want you to go to Fancy's tomorrow and pick up some things like a pack of gum, maybe a package of peanuts, some playin' cards, how about a book or magazine he'd enjoy, and some type of candy—probably somethin' that wouldn't melt so easily. This should be enough to cover that stuff and then you can use what's left to help with the postage."

"Oh Daddy, thank you! I don't even know what to say!"

"You don't' have to say anythin'. Just seein' that smile on your face says enough."

* * *

The next morning Robert dropped Jessie off at the front side of the high school at 7:30. Jessie swallowed the lump in her throat as she walked up the sidewalk towards the doors. She couldn't help but feel a little emotional. The last time she was here, she was with James. She fought back the tears. She pulled open the entrance door and was met with that familiar smell…the musty odor of old textbooks and chalkboard dust. Her eyes skimmed the trophies as she walked past the display cases on her way to the office. She smiled; it felt good to be back in the school.

As Jessie walked into the office, she could barely see the secretary, Mrs. Penderlyn, behind the counter at her desk. Mrs. Penderlyn was knee-high to a grasshopper and had been working there since her parents went to high school. All Jessie could see of her was the bright-red beehive atop her head – the same hairdo she'd been sporting since her parents' day. Though no longer her original red color, she still proved to have her same spunky, spit-fire personality as she asked "Now who's enterin' my office unannounced?"

"Hello, Mrs. Penderlyn! It's Jessie May Clark," Jessie spoke over the counter.

"Who?" the voice squawked from behind the counter. Jessie could hear the creak of Mrs. Penderlyn's chair as she scooched off to come around the counter to the opening.

"Well, if it isn't Miss Jessie May Clark! Get on over here! What, does a person have to be family to get a hug around here?"

After Jessie stooped down to give her a hug, Mrs. Penderlyn asked, "So what brings you back to school?"

"I'd like to speak with Mr. Bieberdorf if he's not busy. Do you happen to know if he still keeps the items he's confiscated from students?"

"That's not a typical question. Comin' to collect somethin' you got in trouble for, huh dearie?" Mrs. Penderlyn asked, her hands on her hips and her head cocked to one the side. With her massive beehive tilted, she looked off-balance, like she was going to tip over.

Jessie couldn't help starting to giggle. "No! No!" she answered trying to collect herself. "I just have somethin' specific I'm lookin' for, for someone else actually. Somethin' I wanna send in a care package to Vietnam."

"Well now, that's unusual. You kids never cease to surprise me. Go ahead and take a seat. I'll go check if he's in his office and has time to see you."

Mrs. Penderlyn walked behind the counter and past her desk. She went to the back of the office and disappeared in a door near the teacher's lounge. Jessie could hear Mrs. Penderlyn's voice as she spoke to Mr. Bieberdorf, "You have a student here to see you. Jessie May Clark. Yes. Okay. I'll send her back." Mrs. Penderlyn returned, "You can go on back. He's waitin' for you."

Jessie had never gone to the principal's office, so it felt strange now walking back to his office. She approached Mr. Bieberdorf's door and knocked lightly. "Well I declare, Jessie May!" he said getting out of his chair while enthusiastically waving her in, "What a nice surprise! Come on in, sit down! How are you? What brings you back here?"

"I'm doin' good. Thank you for seein' me without callin' ahead. I have kind of an unusual request. Do you by chance keep the items you confiscate from students? I'm really hopin' you do."

"Hmm?" he folded his hands in front of his face. "I do. You have my curiosity quite piqued, Miss Clark. No one has ever come and actually asked to get an item back. But, what has me even more baffled is that I don't remember ever confiscatin' anythin' from you."

"It wasn't me. It was from James, and I was hopin' to send it to him as a joke in a care package."

"Aaah, yes! I believe I know what you are lookin' for," Mr. Bieberdorf opened the drawer on the right side of his desk and there amidst an array of other confiscated paraphernalia was a blue plastic squirt gun. "Is this what you are after?" he asked with a big grin.

Jessie smiled. He still had it!

"I'll give it to you, on one condition."

"What's that?"

"You deliver it with a note from his ol' principal."

"Deal!" Jessie reached for the squirt gun that Mr. Bieberdorf was handing over his desk.

Mr. Bieberdorf grabbed for his pad of paper on top of his desk that said *From the Desk of Mr. Bieberdorf* and tore off a piece. He reached for a pencil in a coffee mug that had a Blue Devil on it. She never did like their mascot. He lightly tapped the end of the pencil against his mouth as he thought for a moment. Then with a nod and a grin he began to write something. He quickly scribbled out his message and then folded it over. He opened up his middle desk drawer and grabbed an envelope with the Cordova High emblem on it. He slid the note into the envelope and licked it shut. "There ya go!" he handed it over to Jessie.

"I can't thank you enough, Mr. Bieberdorf. Really!" Jessie stood up to leave and Mr. Bieberdorf stood at the same time.

"Jessie May, it was good to see you. Don't stay away so long now. Maybe see you at a ball game or two? You need to come back sooner next time!"

"Oh, my goodness, that reminds me, I almost forgot! Is the school perchance in need of any part-time help? Like someone to help with any extra secretarial things or maybe help cleanin' classrooms after school? I'm a hard worker."

"I remember that very well about you, Miss Clark," Mr. Bieberdorf's smile was warm and genuine. "This must just be your lucky day! Mrs. Penderlyn was just tellin' me she'd like to cut back a little so that she could have a couple afternoons open for her new grand-babies. You know, her daughter Clara Sue just gave birth to twins and could use a little extra help. So, I'd say this is divine timin' on your part, Jessie May. Let's take you back out to Mrs. Penderlyn and she can get you set up with the details for which afternoons to come in. Can you start this week?"

"I sure can!" Jessie was beaming, a sense of accomplishment and purpose welling up inside her.

The conversation was brief with Mrs. Penderlyn. It was all arranged; Jessie would come in every Tuesday and Thursday afternoon. Mrs. Penderlyn wanted her to start this Thursday for training. She would continue training next Tuesday and Thursday with Mrs. Penderlyn, but then the following week she'd be on her own. Jessie felt excited. As she headed out of the school, she knew one thing – her parents were right. It did feel good to be out and to have a purpose. It felt good to be doing things again. That made her think of something she should do quickly before heading to Fancy's. If she hurried, she could probably still catch him.

* * *

Someone was knocking on the front door. "I'll get it!" he called over his shoulder. As Nathaniel opened the door, his jaw about dropped to the floor.

"You're home. I wasn't sure if you'd be here or out in the cotton fields already. Long time no see," Jessie said a little sheepishly.

But no sheepishness about Nathaniel, who scooped Jessie up and gave her a big hug. "Jessie May! What are you doin' here, stranger?" he set her back down. "You know, I have a notion to be right done mad at you."

"Me? Why? What did I do?" she asked a little defensively.

"It's not what you've done. It's what you haven't done. You've totally ditched me and the guys."

"I know," Jessie looked down. She couldn't deny it. "It's just, it hasn't been easy."

"I'm sorry, Jess. I know it hasn't. I just like to give you a bad time." He gave her an awkward, light punch on the arm like he would have done with one of the guys, only harder. "But it hasn't been easy for us either. We miss him too."

"I know. I'm sorry. Can I make it up to you?" her tone shifted as the mood lightened with her peculiar proposition.

"How's that?" Nathaniel tilted his head like a dog questioning his master.

“Would you like to go out next Friday? To Buckie’s?”

“Well, I do declare! James is gone six months and you’re hittin’ on me!” he said and gave her a shove again.

Jessie blushed, “I’m not askin’ you out on a date. I’m fulfillin’ a promise to James.”

“James wants you to date me?” The more Nathaniel teased Jessie, the redder her face grew. And the redder her face grew, the more he was enjoying himself.

“No! I mean with all you doofs. RJ and Bobby Ray too.”

“You’re sure you want Bobby Ray?”

“Nathaniel!” she laughed. “Yes, Bobby Ray too! And he can bring Janet if he wants and I’d love if RJ brought Landa Jane.”

“Well, there you go pairin’ us two up again.”

“Stop that now!” they laughed, “You and I will just be the odd ones out.”

“Yeah, I have always thought you an odd one.”

Jessie rolled her eyes and put her hands on her hips, “Are you goin’ to stand there until the cows come home or do you want to answer if you wanna or not? And, can you get ahold of the guys?”

"Yeah, I'd like to go. I'll make sure it's fine with my parents first, but it should be. Then, leave the rest of it to me."

* * *

Jessie slowly pulled into a parking spot in front of Buckie's BBQ. It felt strange to be driving somewhere by herself and she was still a little uncomfortable behind the wheel, but she was thankful her parents had allowed her to take their family vehicle in to town. They were elated to hear she found herself a job, and to top that off, they were quite thrilled she chose to go out with her friends of her own accord.

She slid out of their Plymouth Fury and gave the door a bump with her hip as she stuck the keys in her purse. When she walked in and scanned the room, she saw Ricky waving in the back booth. As she walked up, he was the first to speak, "Hey Jess!" He jumped up and gave her a quick hug. "We've missed you. How have you been?"

"You dope, how do you think she's been? James is in a war zone. What a dumb question to ask," Bobby Ray blurted.

Still blunt as ever, Jessie thought to herself. She smiled, "You haven't changed, Bobby Ray. Thanks for not changin'. I've missed y'all." She turned to Ricky, "And really, RJ, I don't mind you askin'. I think it's sweet of you to ask, so thank you."

Ricky shot Bobby Ray a look like he was a little kid ready to stick out his tongue as if to say *I told you so.*

Jessie started to laugh. She had missed this. These guys. The playful banter. The easy way they had with each other.

"Jessie May, this is my girlfriend Landa Jane."

"Yep, I remember you from gym class. Nice to see you again. And good to see you again too, Janet."

The table buzzed with conversation and laughter as the group of six sat cozy in the back booth of Buckie's. The jukebox could barely be heard over the hum of chatter at the table. And before they knew it, the waitress was bringing a heavy tray with their food orders. She passed the plates around the table. Nathaniel and Jessie--each sitting at the end of the table across from one another--reached for the ketchup bottle at same time. Their fingers touched. Jessie pulled her hand away quickly, "Go ahead."

"No, ladies first."

Jessie hastily grabbed the bottle and twisted the lid off. She tipped the bottle of ketchup upside down to shake some ketchup next to her fries. She felt a little light headed. *What had just happened?* The touch of Nathaniel's hand against hers made her feel funny. It wasn't like the intense spark she'd feel when James touched her--that always made her heart skip a beat--but Jessie couldn't ignore that she felt something just now. Suddenly she was filled with guilt and remorse.

"Whoa, girl! Are you goin' to leave any ketchup for the rest of us?" Bobby Ray laughed. A huge ketchup blob was spilling over her plate and down onto the table. Jessie felt her face turn as red as the ketchup.

"Well, there's a first time for everythin', Bobby Ray!" Nathaniel retorted, "Usually you're the one makin' the mess at the table."

The table erupted with laughter and Jessie was thankful for the shift of attention. And just as quickly as the conversation had died, it picked right back up. Jessie tried to act normal. She didn't want anyone to think anything was wrong, especially Nathaniel. But she couldn't quit thinking about what just happened. She felt like her thoughts were betraying her. Worse yet, she felt like she had just betrayed James. She was glad to be with her friends now, but that's just what they were. Friends. She didn't like that touching Nathaniel's hand made her feel different. She loved James and her heart ached for him now more than ever.

* * *

When Jessie got home later that evening, she felt emotionally drained. She turned the car off and pulled the key from the ignition and just sat there, not moving. She wondered if both her parents would be sitting in the living room or if she could slip in unnoticed. Usually when she'd get home from being out, her mama would put the kettle on and they'd sit and visit about her evening over a cup of tea. But tonight, she'd didn't feel like talking. She replayed in her mind the hand-touching incident and how it

314

made her feel. She cringed and guilt came over her again. She started to cry.

No, she didn't feel like talking right now. She could see the lights on in the living room shining through the front bay window. She'd have to be quiet and quick. She knew her parents would want to know she was home. She thought it through a moment longer. She'd just yell as she came in that she was home, but not feeling well and then hustle upstairs. She just wanted to go to her room and go to bed.

She opened the car door and quietly tried to close it. As she approached the front door, she took a deep breath and then slowly turned the knob. She could hear the TV on. She closed the door.

"Is that you, Jess?" Robert said from the living room.

She took another breath, hoping that her voice wouldn't sound different from crying. "Yes, it is. I'm home, but I'm not feelin' well so I'm just goin' straight up to bed. Love you! Tell Mama goodnight!" And with that, she scooted up the stairs to avoid any further interaction.

* * *

That was strange, thought Robert. He was sitting in his chair and had been watching TV when his daughter got home. Patty was lying on the davenport, totally out cold, with her book in her lap. A slight whistle came from her mouth with each exhale. *Should he wake her?* No, he'd let Patty sleep. No need to worry his wife when he wasn't even sure there was anything of concern. Nonetheless, his radar

315

detected something. It was unusual that Jessie didn't pop her head in when she got home. *And further*--he thought--*she always said goodnight to him.* He hoped her avoidance had nothing to do with alcohol. It was not like Jessie or any of her friends to be drinking. She hung with a pretty good crowd that he absolutely trusted. Yet, he also recalled what it was like when he was her age with the pressures to explore alcohol. He was no fool. Still, if he had to guess, it had more to do with James not being there. He put down the foot-feet of his recliner. Yes, he'd better check on her.

Quietly Robert made his way up the stairs. At the landing, he looked at Carrie's closed door. It was dark underneath. She had been in bed a couple of hours already and was no doubt sawing logs. He looked at Lydia's door and could see a muted light on under her door. He smiled and shook his head; she was probably still reading. As he approached Jessie's door, he was surprised to see it was already dark underneath just like Carrie's. He paused to listen for a moment. Nothing. He knocked lightly and waited. No answer. He tapped his knuckles against the door again and heard a muffled *come in.*

He opened Jessie's bedroom door and the light from the hallway crept into her room. The column of light revealed his daughter was in bed already, lying on her stomach with her face buried in her pillow. Muffled sobs were certainly soaking the pillow beneath her hidden face. He sat down on the bed next to her and placed his hand gently on her shoulder, "Oh, honey," he began, "what's wrong?"

Jessie sat up and curled into his huge chest and arms. "Oh, Daddy!" she sobbed.

Robert just stroked her hair and said nothing. He sat and waited patiently. He knew Jessie would answer when she was ready. After a couple minutes, she reached for a Kleenex next to her bed. Her sobbing had somewhat subsided, so she dabbed her eyes. She looked at her father. His eyes were so full of love. He was a presence of reassuring comfort. When she got home, she hadn't felt one bit like talking. But now, she found herself wanting…needing…to share. And so, for the next five minutes, she poured out everything. She told Robert what had happened when she and Nathaniel reached for the ketchup at the same time and how it made her feel. She explained how it was so confusing and how it had made her feel like she had betrayed James. She told him that it felt good to be with her friends until that happened. She expressed in no uncertain terms that they were just friends. Period. She needed it to be convincing to herself as well. She did not like how it had mixed up all her feelings and made her feel confused. Jessie paused and her eyes began to fill up with tears again. She looked at her father and waited now for him to respond.

Robert sat for a moment. He chose his words carefully, "You know, your mama's always got her nose in book. The other night I picked up her tattered old copy of *War and Peace* that she had sittin' in the livin' room. I think she goes back to those same old books and rereads them when she needs them most." Jessie looked slightly confused while trying to follow where her father was going with this, but she was fully attentive and hung on his every word. Robert continued, "I began flickin' through the book because I noticed she had ear-tagged several pages. On one page your mother had underlined a sentence – *The two most powerful warriors are patience and time.*" Robert took a deep breath, "Honey, you cannot be so hard on yourself for what you felt when your hands accidentally touched. God created us as bein's of feelin's and emotions. Praise God for that! It has been six months since James left. That's a long time. And yet, your feelin's for him have not waivered. What you felt tonight when Nathaniel touched your hand was merely a reminder of what God created you to be…a young woman with feelin's, but not necessarily for Nathaniel. You merely felt what you felt, acknowledged it, and then the crucial part…you didn't entertain it. That's the most important element – that you didn't act on the temptation." Robert paused for a moment, "Jessie May, even Jesus was tempted." Then he turned on the lamp and grabbed Jessie's Bible off her nightstand, "I can't quite remember where the scripture is, so give me a moment."

Jessie watched her father as he paged through her Bible.

"Ah, yes. Luke. Chapter 4, verses 1 through 4." Robert cleared his throat, and began to read, "Jesus, full of the Holy Spirit, returned from the Jordan and was led by the Spirit in the desert, where for forty days he was tempted by the devil. He ate nothin' durin' those days, and at the end of them he was hungry. The devil said to him, 'If you are the Son of God, tell this stone to become bread.' Jesus answered, 'It is written: Man does not live on bread alone.'"

Robert lowered the Bible down onto his lap, "You see, Jesus – the very Son of God – was tempted. But the key, Jess, is that he didn't act on it. It is so important, my darlin', that you understand that temptation itself isn't the sin. Everyone is tempted. It's when you succumb to it. That's why I think this scripture is so powerful. It shows that temptation doesn't need to end in failure. For Jesus to accomplish God's will, he had to face Satan and prevail. So Jess, don't be dismayed by tonight. Celebrate it! You faced a temptation and you prevailed!" Her father picked her Bible back up and flicked through it again, "I also like Mathew's account of this story and what he adds to this. Listen to what the last verse says, 'Man does not live on bread alone, *but on every word that comes from the mouth of God.*' That ties in with the sentence your mother underlined in her book…*the two most powerful warriors are patience and time.*" Robert paused for a moment and then he cupped his daughter's face gently in his hands and said, "Jessie, with patience and time, you have come to rely not on your own strength, but on God's sovereignty. And that, my dear, is how you will prevail through any of life's battles."

* * *

Jessie was beyond thrilled. It had only been two and a half weeks since she sent her package off and she was already getting a letter from James. She hugged his letter tightly. He must have received her package in time for Thanksgiving. That made her smile. She had hoped it would get there in time and that it would bring him a touch of home for the holiday. Like usual when she received a letter from James, she scurried up to her room and shut the door.

There was a chill in her room, so she grabbed her afghan at the end of her bed and snuggled in like she was hunkering in with a good book. She couldn't believe that a letter from James had already come. She opened his letter and let her eyes dance across the words. She imagined hearing James' voice as she read his words.

Friday, November 26th, 1965
Dear Jessie May,

Oh my gosh, where do I start with my thanks for all the things in my care package. It made my day. And what perfect timing – I got it a day before Thanksgiving. Knowing you, that's just what you had planned! It made me feel like I had a part of you with me for the holiday. Thank you so much! All the stuff was so thoughtful. I've been enjoying my comic strip "Sparky". It's a good distraction. And God knows in this place, we need those. Jim said he'd like to be next in line to read it. I guess he loves Sparky. The chocolate chip pecan cookies are out-of-this-world good. You know those are my favorite! And, mmm, a taste of home. The chocolate chips were melting in them a little which made me imagine they were pulled right out of the oven. Oh man, are they good. I shared them with the rest of the guys in my squad. They were begging for more. I saved a stash for me though and had some for dessert after my Thanksgiving meal.

If you can believe this, our Thanksgiving meal wasn't half bad. Some choppers dropped in Mermite cans and we got hot turkey and mashed potatoes and gravy. We got some cornbread stuffing which was really pretty tasty. Plus, there were some sweet potatoes, peas and cranberry sauce. Not bad, huh? No warm pie though, but not to worry because your cookies hit the spot for dessert. The meal was not as good as my mama's, but it tasted pretty dang good. And even though there was no family gathered around a table for a traditional Thanksgiving meal, I felt pretty blessed to be eating such a feast with my combat "brothers".

And Jess, my favorite...FAVORITE part of my care package was the squirt gun! Did you hear me laughing all the way back to Cordova? I busted a gut with that surprise. How did you ever think to go ask Bieberdorf for that? You are amazing! And what else is amazing is the fact that he still had it! When I opened it, I got a chuckle out of his note too. Since it was sealed in an envelope, I imagine you don't know what he wrote, but I bet you could take a wild guess! A joke! True to his nature...he sent me a corny joke! He wrote: "Dear James, I hope you know that as I return this squirt gun, I wonder *WATER* you up to!" Ha! Ha! Oh my gosh, Jess, I laughed. I've missed that guy and his humor. That was by far the best part of the package!

I should correct myself. The squirt gun was a close second...next to your letter. I always, ALWAYS love getting your letters. There is nothing better than hearing from you. In your letter you thanked me for always explaining the military acronyms and Vietnamese lingo. You are welcome. I'll keep doing that. It took me awhile to understand all the jargon so I figured I'd explain it to you as I write. And no, you don't have to be jealous of a hoochgirl. I know it sounds kind of bad, but trust me...you're the only one I have eyes for. Well....I guess I'm lying to you a little...there's still mushroom man. Your contender.

So, should I give you a lesson? There's a lot of things to learn over here, lots of military acronyms and terms. Some of them are so derogative though. I'm called a FNG and I won't even write what that means. And to top off being a new guy I further stand out because I enlisted. Most guys here were drafted and they can't believe I signed up for this "stuff"...except they say a different "S word". It adds a little stress between us soldiers if you can imagine. And since I'm a journalist, they also call me a REMF...which I cannot bring myself to tell you what that means either.

You know what, scratch the military lesson. That's boring stuff and most of it is stuff I'd rather get my mind off anyways. But what I have appreciated though is learning about another way of life, so I will enlighten you with what I've learned about the Vietnamese culture. And since the sound of a hoochgirl made you jealous...although I kinda like that... let me start by explaining a hoochgirl to you. I know it sounds bad, but a hooch is what they call a hut or a simple dwelling here, either military or civilian. So see, it's really not as bad as it sounds. It's a hut girl who does my stinky socks...and let me tell you, in this hot and rainy weather, that's not a fun job.

Hmm, what else can I tell you? They don't use ketchup over here. Their popular condiment is nuoc-mam which is a fermented fish sauce. I think it's disgusting, but Jim think's it's the cat's meow. Maybe your daddy would like it. He really likes his fish. Oh, and here's a fun fact for your mama. Tell her she is a "mama san" which is an older Vietnamese woman and your father is a "papa san" for an older man.

Oh, and remember that papa san I told you about that I always give my cigarettes to? He gave me Ho Chi Minh slippers which are basically sandals made from tires. They're surprisingly really comfy. I know the guys back home would make fun of me, especially Bobby Ray. But if they tried them on, they'd be wishing they had a pair.

Oh dang it, I hate to cut your lesson short, but one of the guys just came in and asked if I want to play a game of sand volleyball. That's one of the things we do to keep occupied when we aren't out on a mission. Thank you again for your care package and letter. I always love hearing from you. Oh! I almost forgot - CONGRATULATIONS on getting a job! That's great, Jess! Just don't start wearing your hair like Mrs.

Penderlyn! If I come home and you have a resemblance to her, I'm going to be creeped out! Ha! Ha! But, I am glad you are getting out of the house and I was so happy to hear you're getting together with the guys like I asked. Hey, come to think of it, that's actually today! You said in your letter that you were getting together with them on Friday after Thanksgiving! So, that's today! Wow, as I write this, maybe even this very moment, you're hanging with the gang! I miss them all so much. Tell them that. Well, I'll be thinking of you today with the guys and will be so excited to hear all about it. I love you, Jessie May!

Love,
James

* * *

After reading James' letter, Jessie felt a twinge of guilt come upon her again. About the time James was writing her and thinking about her being with the guys, she was groping his best friend's hand.

No Jess, you're not goin' to think like that any longer. Bring every thought into captivity to the obedience of Christ. She was grateful for the Spirit rebuking her thoughts now. She had memorized that scripture--2 Corinthians 10:5--and the Spirit was bringing that truth to light now.

325

"Take all thoughts captive to the obedience of Christ," she spoke the words out loud firmly and with authority.

Her father had shared another scripture with her recently, John 14:26-27, "The Holy Spirit, whom the Father will send in my name, will teach you all things *and will remind you of everything I have said to you.* Peace I leave with you; my peace I give you. I do not give to you as the world gives. Do not let your hearts be troubled and do not be afraid."

Yes, the Holy Spirit was reminding her now to take her thoughts captive to His obedience. There was no reason to have a troubled heart. Like her father had said, she was a woman with feelings, and she did nothing wrong. She knew what she was feeling – she missed James terribly and her heart belonged to him and him alone. She was not going to self-condemn with her thoughts anymore. And the one other thing she wasn't going to do any more…go in to town any more than she *had* to. It was just easier being at home. It may not be the best for her, but it was the easiest. She knew her father would not agree with her logic, but that's why she decided to quietly make this decision without him. But, that night over supper Jessie did enjoy sharing with her family what James had to say in his letter. She told them about James' lesson on the Vietnamese culture. She shared with them about the *nuoc-man* instead of ketchup to which Carrie wrinkled her nose quite emphatically. Jessie explained what *mama san* and *papa san* meant and told her parents how James had related to Patty as a mama san and Robert as a papa san.

Patty interrupted, "Mama san is an *older* Vietnamese woman? What does he think? That I'm *old*? You'd better correct that boy!"

"Now who's the one callin' him *that boy*?" her father snorted as he laughed, which never happened. Everyone busted out laughing at the table.

It was good to eat together and, maybe even more importantly, talk together. Conversation was always feasted upon gathering as a family at the supper table.

Chapter 20
Time Marches On

The days went by and turned into weeks which soon became a month. Now it was hard to believe it was almost Christmas. Jessie hadn't received another letter from James since the one he'd written right after Thanksgiving. She had written him twice since then, but received no response. With the time stretching out between his letters, she tried to remain positive. She forced herself to keep reciting 2 Corinthians 10:5 in her head when worrisome thoughts would creep into her mind, *Bring every thought into captivity to the obedience of Christ.*

She also remained consistent with her vow of not going in to town any more than she had to. She went in Tuesday and Thursday afternoons to work at the school, Saturday mornings to bring in the eggs, and Sundays for church. Nothing much beyond that. Precisely when she *had* to…and now, tonight, she had to. She suspected her parents had figured out her self-proclaimed vow of solitude since they insisted that she go pick Carrie up from a birthday party. "If the Lord's willin' and the creek don't rise, you're goin' in to town to get Carrie Grace," her father had said. The party was supposed to be a sleepover, but Carrie did not want to spend the night. So, her parents had asked Jessie—or rather told her—to go and get her sister. "It's a beautiful evenin', so the half-mile walk and fresh air will do you some good," her father had said to her as she walked out the front door.

As she and Carrie returned home down River Road, the winter air was crisp and the smell of moisture was in the air. It was fresh and renewing, appeasing all of her senses. She sighed and shook her head, nodding with reluctant resolve – her father was right. Again. It did feel good to be out. The moon was full tonight and its brightness illuminated the streets as they walked. The moon's light stretched down and seemed to shine the spotlight on Carrie as she talked about the party. Carrie slid her cold little hand into Jessie's. Her little sister had hardly taken a breath since stepping off her friend Jenny's porch, chatting non-stop about the party the entire stroll home.

"After we had cake, Jenny opened her presents and, Jess, I know what else I want for Christmas. Everythin' Jenny got for her birthday!" Carrie laughed. "Definitely the *Barbie* board game and *Bewitched* board game, maybe a Chatty Cathy doll, but mostly I want Barbie's little sister Skipper. I really want that. I'm gonna tell Santa I want that now instead of my picture story camera. Then after Jenny opened all her gifts, we played games. Pin the tail on Rudolph was fun, but kind of…you know, kiddish." Carrie tossed her hand in the air like she was beyond that. Jessie stifled a giggle. "But I liked the Freeze game her mama had us play. We danced to music and when the music stopped, we had to freeze. She played the Elvis Christmas album like you gave James. Isn't he the one who sang that song *Blue Christmas* like James?"

The way Carrie said the last part like Elvis was singing a song like James—instead of James singing a song like Elvis—struck a funny bone in Jessie which she could no longer contain. She began to laugh. And then her laughter grew and wouldn't stop.

"What's so funny?" Carrie asked through her own laughter. She wasn't sure why she was laughing with her big sister. She just was.

Between fits of tears and cackles Jessie uttered, "You, Carrie Grace, you. You make me laugh. I needed this. I was havin' a *blue Christmas* mood, but you have a way of changin' that." Jessie laughed some more.

Once she had caught her breath, she explained that *Blue Christmas* was by the King of Rock 'n' Roll…not James. Jessie laughed at Carrie's sweet innocence. "James likes to sing music by Elvis because he can belt out the songs with his deep, baritone voice."

Jessie cleared her throat and attempted to break into *Blue Christmas* with a deep voice. Carrie stared at Jessie with wide eyes, her mouth pinched tightly shut. She was speechless for the first time their entire walk home.

"Okay, okay," Jessie held her hands up as if guilty as charged with Carrie's quiet accusation. "I'll leave the singin' to James." And they busted out laughing again.

* * *

The girls were still giggling when they walked through the front door.

"Well, look at you two giggle boxes." Patty set her book down in her lap. She had been sitting on the davenport devouring Jane Austen's *Mansfield Park.*

Robert cleared his throat and tried to look perky. The girls' laughter had just woken him from a snooze, "You know your mother…if she's not nourishin' our family with her cookin', she's feastin' herself on a good book. And me, well, I was makin' sure she had … well … company."

Patty rolled her eyes and shook her head at her husband. A little smirk tugged at the corner of her mouth. She turned her attention back to the girls, "So, how was the party, Carrie Grace?"

Carrie took a deep breath. Jessie shot both her parents a quick look. As her eye brows lifted, Robert and Patty could read her quiet expression, *Are you ready for this?*

Carrie proceeded for the next 30 minutes to give them the entire rundown, from the gingham dress Jenny wore to the color of the paper napkins and not forgetting to mention her complete updated Christmas gift list and addendum to her wish list from Santa.

Her father glanced at the presents lying wrapped under the tree. "Well, looks like we will have to take those presents back then." He clicked his tongue a few times and shook his head. Then he looked at his youngest daughter playfully, "What a shame! What a shame! But if you are changin' your list, I guess we'll need to just change those presents too." He turned to Jessie. "Jess, could you scoop up any presents with Carrie Grace's name on them and take them to our room? We'll need to get rid of them."

"Oh wait!" Carrie interrupted, "I think I could just leave my list as it is. You know…I could save some of Jenny's *new* ideas for my birthday."

Robert winked at Jessie, "Okay, Jessie May, I guess just leave those presents there. We'll cross our fingers that Carrie likes them." Then he turned to Carrie, "Alright darlin', I think it's time you go get your bath done, don't you think?"

"Yes, Daddy! Can I do bubbles? Mr. Bubble! Mr. Bubble! Pleeeeaaase!"

"I don't know," Robert drawled, "what do you think, Patty?"

"It's a Friday night, why not!"

"Yay!" squealed Carrie.

"Just keep them in the tub this time," Patty called after Carrie, but she was pretty sure her daughter didn't hear her as she scampered off. Patty shook her head, quite certain she'd be wiping bubbles off the bathroom floor again later. Then she patted the sofa next to her, "Come sit down." She jerked her head in a beckoning motion.

Jessie sat down on the davenport next to her mother and curled her feet under her. She propped a pillow in her lap and reached down to grab a basket that was on the floor next to the davenport. She hadn't totally ignored the things her father and James had said about finding a pastime. She found cross-stitching. She had hoped it would take her mind off James, but it didn't seem to work. Her latest project was a dishtowel she was cross-stitching and she couldn't help but imagine it hung on her own stove as Mrs. James Patterson. She was hopeless, hopelessly in love. And aching to hear from James.

"How was your walk?" her father asked.

"As usual, you were right, Daddy. It did me good to get out. Thanks for givin' me the nudge I needed."

"It isn't good to shell yourself up here at home, Jess."

"I know, but I've just been strugglin' again and I really don't wanna go in to town any more than I have to."

"Yes, but sometimes what you want and need are two different things," her father interjected.

"I know. Even though bein' here is what I think makes me most happy, it's probably not what's best for me. Or for others…I realize I'm not all that joyful to be around."

"Honey, that's not our point at all in gettin' you out of the house," Patty reached to rub her daughter's foot.

"I know, but I've been kind of a scrooge lately. Admittedly, I haven't really been lookin' forward to

Christmas. But, I'm so thankful for Carrie Grace; she inspired me tonight." Jessie sat pensive for a moment. "It's hard to think that James was here last Christmas."

"I know, sweetheart, I was thinkin' the same thing just today," her mother spoke tenderly.

"It feels so long ago," Jessie glanced down at the ring on her hand. It didn't feel like a whole year had passed since James had given her his mother's weddin' ring as a promise ring for their future together. And now they weren't together. Physically anyway. "I'm just really missin' him this Christmas season. But, Carrie helped put me in the Christmas spirit tonight. Gotta love that girl! And her gift of gab!" The three of them started to laugh.

"She doesn't get that from me, you know." Robert raised his eyebrows with his chest puffed up thinking he was pretty funny.

Patty just rolled her eyes and attempted to ignore him.

"Mama, I was thinkin' tomorrow maybe we could make some old-fashioned thumb print cookies since we haven't done those yet. And I thought maybe we could bake some different ones for James. I'd like to send him another care package so he'd have it for Christmas, and I don't think the thumb print ones would be very good to send with the heat."

"That's a great idea. Time spent with my daughter and doin' somethin' for James…that's a win-win for me. How about we make some pecan tassies to send over for James?"

"You ladies makin' one of my favorites – pecan tassies – sounds like a win-win for me too!"

"Who said we were makin' any of those for you, darlin'? Those are for James," said Patty who raised her eyebrows while looking at her husband smugly.

Jessie enjoyed this about her parents. They teased each other often and always had a playful look in their eyes. That made her think of James and his brown eyes. What she'd give to look into his dreamy brown eyes. And to touch him. And smell him. And kiss him. And hear him singing in his deep Elvis voice. But right now, she'd settle for just hearing from him. She longed for a letter. He was probably too busy to write. She wouldn't worry. He was busy. That's all.

And tomorrow she'd be busy too, baking cookies for him and enjoying time with her mama. Then Sunday after church she'd work on another letter for James to stick in with his care package. As much as she needed a letter from him, she knew he needed one from her more.

* * *

James knew he should be writing, but he just couldn't bring himself to. He lit his Marlboro and drew in a deep breath. He had lost his interest in writing somehow. He didn't have anything new to tell Jessie, and he didn't want to write about what he was doing over here anymore. Or what he was seeing. It made

335

him sick. If she knew the missions that he went on in order to write his stories for military papers, she wouldn't sleep at night. He hardly slept at night. He couldn't do that do her.

He took another draw on his cigarette. He knew this wasn't fair to Jessie. He exhaled allowing the smoke to exit his nose and slowly drift past his head. It was just easier not to write her. That made him sick too. And Jessie would be sick if she knew he was smoking right now. However, it hadn't taken James long before he found out that cigarettes and war are inseparable. He shook his head and tilted it back while he blew smoke into the air. No, he'd write Jessie later. Not now.

* * *

How could January be half gone already? And, he still hadn't written Jessie. He inhaled deeply. He knew he couldn't put off writing any longer. He felt like a jerk. He hadn't even thanked her yet for the care package she had sent him for Christmas. He crushed his cigarette into the side of his boot and grabbed hastily for some paper and a pen.

January 16th, 1966
Dear Jessie May,

I'm sorry, Jess. I know it has been awhile since I wrote you last. Things here have been...well...busy. The days all just seem to blend together and not much new to write about. Your Christmas sounded nice

336

though. And no, I don't think you are a fuddy-dud for being in bed before midnight on New Year's Eve. Being in bed with you before midnight sounds like the best New Year's Eve I could imagine. I better not let my mind go there. I think these guys have been wearing off on me. Their minds are on only one thought. They all need a large cold soda if you know what I mean? So, I better change the subject.

I wanted to say a great big THANK YOU for your thoughtful care package you sent for Christmas. Once again, the timing was perfect. I bet you didn't know this...but my mama sent me old-fashioned tea cakes too. No joke! So, once again I was quite popular with the guys because I had LOTS to share. They started calling me the "Cookie San"! So, thanks, Jess, the cookies were awesome. And so are you!

I know this is short, but I gotta go. Sorry! Sergeant Cobal is calling a formation. We leave at 1800. I love you with all my heart. I ache for you.

Love,
James

* * *

She set his letter down. How could she be disappointed? Afterall, she had finally gotten a letter from James. That's all she had wanted for Christmas and that came and went. She had hoped to celebrate the new year with a letter, but that didn't happen. So, when her daddy finally brought home the mail and handed her a letter from James, she could hardly wait to devour it. However, this was barely a morsel to satiate her hunger for James.

She picked James' letter up and read it again. What did he mean *these guys have been wearin' off on me*? She had never thought herself the jealous-insecure-type, but somehow doubt seemed to creep into her mind and flood her with paranoia and unsettling thoughts.

No, she thought, *I will not do this to myself.* She picked up her Bible and flipped to Philippians 4:8, "Whatever is true, whatever is noble, whatever is right, whatever is pure, whatever is lovely, whatever is admirable—if anything is excellent or praiseworthy—think about such things."

She set her Bible back down and picked up James' letter and read it again. When she was finished, she closed her eyes and one single tear slid down her cheek. She tilted her head up and offered up a prayer, *Thank you, Lord, for lettin' me hear from James. Thank you for his love for me. Continue to strengthen our love for each other and protect Him in your lovin' care. Amen.*

She felt a sense of peace come upon her. A peace that was not of her own, but a peace that transcends all understanding. A peace that was guarding her heart and her mind. She opened her eyes and glanced at her Bible still lying open to scripture in Philippians. She decided to read a couple verses that preceded verse eight, "Do not be anxious about anything, but in every situation, by prayer and petition, with thanksgiving, present your requests to God. And the peace of God, which transcends all understanding, will guard your hearts and your minds in Christ Jesus."

She took a deep breath in and then let it out slowly. No, she did not have to worry or doubt James' purity. He was aching for her. He said so himself. And, oh how she was aching for him. She wished he had written more, but she would be thankful she had gotten a letter. That meant he was okay. That is what she would focus on—that he wrote a letter meant he was okay – which was indeed excellent and praiseworthy.

* * *

It was February 3rd. Robert reached for his paper and slid it across the table, "Well Pats, let's see if the groundhog saw his shadow yesterday."

"I hope not," Patty was wiping up the counter by the sink and still cleaning up the supper dishes. "I'm ready for spring. I think we all could use the promise of *new* right now."

"Well, my darlin', you are in luck because looks like Punxsutawney Phil did not see his shadow."

Patty let out a sigh, "See! The winter is past; the rains are over and gone. Flowers appear on the earth; the season of singin' has come, the cooing of doves is heard in our land."

"Beautiful. Lemme guess…Jane Austen?"

"No, Solomon," Patty batted her eyelashes at Robert and tossed her dishcloth up over her shoulder. "But like with Jane Austen, I do think *Song of Songs* is a poetically romantic read." She winked at Robert. Her eyes had a playful twinkle about them.

Robert just shook his head and began scanning the rest of the paper. Ten minutes passed by while he read the paper and Patty finished cleaning up the remnants of supper. She glanced over at her husband. He was quiet and his eye brows were pulled down tight over his eyes as he read. Often as Patty worked in the kitchen, he would give her an abridged version of what he was reading, but tonight he sat quietly as he read his paper.

"Anythin' good to catch me up on?" Patty asked as she flicked the light off over the kitchen sink.

"It's not good in Vietnam, Pats. I'm just glad Jessie got a letter from James. With everythin' I keep readin' and hearin', I admit I was startin' to get a little concerned myself. I knew Rita hadn't gotten any notices and sometimes no news is good news, but I just started to have a sick feelin' in my stomach."

Patty came and sat next to her husband, "Robert, do you know why I memorized that scripture from *Song of Songs*?" She didn't wait for his answer, "It's not because it's so poetically beautiful. Sure, it is, but it is more about the promise of the verse. Winter ends and spring brings with it new life, new promises. I like how the verse says the time of singin' has come, and the cooin' of the dove is heard in our land. Remember when Noah first sent out a bird to see if there was any sign of dry land?" This time she waited for Robert to respond.

"Yes, he sent the dove and it came back with nothin'."

"Well, he first sent a raven. Then he sent a dove. Three times actually. I think that part often gets overlooked and we don't consider how wearin' and tryin' this time must have been for Noah and his family. When Noah first sent the dove out--just like the raven--the dove found no signs of dry land and returned to the ark. The second time Noah sent the dove out, they waited. How that season of waitin' must have been agonizin'. Stretchin' them to wait and persevere with trust and hope. When the dove did return, it had an olive branch in its beak. What a sign – a promise – that must have been for them that surely there would be dry lands. The third time he sent the dove out, it never returned. They had to have been overcome with peace knowin' that the waters had receded from the land. I like how Solomon says that the cooin' of the dove, the voice, is heard in our land. The voice of peace. We can be filled with that same peace as spring brings forth its newness. And, like the voice of that turtledove, it delivers a promise."

Robert took his wife's hands in his own, "You are right, Patty. This season too shall pass. I need to keep my faith strong, especially for Jessie May, and wait with patience and trust that James will come back. Yes, the voice of the dove is heard in our land…and Vietnam's too."

Chapter 21
Guitar Ghost

Despite the United States increasing air assaults, the North Vietnamese always seemed to find a way to get close. They typically had the upper hand on the time and location of battle. They were skillfully trained in warfare, especially with bayonets. James' platoon leader had given the orders that it was time to shift locations again. Their company would move out early evening and their platoon would lead. For now, they would hunker down and rest.

James was sitting next to his buddy Jim. His rucksack was packed and he leaned against it. His squad all sat together, but no one was talking. Each of them had their helmets on. They were ready to go. Jim pulled a cigarette from his pocket.

"I'll take one," James said. His voice was raspy like he had a frog in his throat. He coughed to clear his throat.

"Sounds like you don't need another."

"Hand one over," James retorted.

Jim tossed him a cigarette and fumbled in his pocket for a lighter. "I can't find my lighter."

"Here," another soldier tossed one over to James.

James caught it with both hands before it hit the dirt. It was a Zippo. He didn't remember a lot about his father, but he remembered his daddy always having a lighter in his pocket. He rubbed it in his left hand as he sat transfixed by the memory of his father. His daddy had a 1936 prototype Zippo that he proudly carried around every day in the breast pocket of his shirt, despite the fact that his mother loathed his smoking habit. He cringed. That thought made him think of Jessie. She would loath *his* smoking habit too. He sighed. Her letters had stopped. But, what did he expect? He hadn't been writing her either. He had stopped writing back in January. It was just too complicated with having to relocate more often. And frankly, it was just too hard mentally. He never knew it would be like this.

Oh God, watch over her. I miss her so much.

"You gonna light that cigarette or just sit there caressing that lighter like it's your girlfriend." His thoughts were interrupted by Randy Dawson who sat on the other side of Jim impatiently waiting his turn for the lighter. There was a little laughter from his squad which faded off as James lit his cigarette. James pitched the Zippo to Randy. Jim gave James a questioning look of concern. He knew that James had quit writing Jessie. He also knew that Jessie had quit writing James. So, though Randy's comment was just in fun, Jim knew it would leave a sting.

And yes, it certainly did leave a sting. More than a sting. A harsh blow to reality really. James was here in this hellhole, and the girl he loved was a world away. And he had chosen this. His stomach turned in knots. There was nothing he could do now but to keep on keepin' on.

Jim lowered his voice, "You okay?"

James nodded at Jim and gave him quick wink. He sat in silence smoking his cigarette. When he was finished, he leaned his helmet back against his rucksack and managed to doze off a bit as he clenched his M16 against his side. The next thing he knew, he was waking to Sergeant Cobal stirring his squad with orders. His first platoon would lead. Second, third, and fourth platoons would follow. It was time to move out.

* * *

Jessie sat next to her mother. Her father and sisters were on the other side of her mama. The choir was just finishing with the closing hymn. Her mama held a hymnal in her arms as she belted out the words. But Jessie sat quietly, her mouth not even moving to the words of the lyrics. She didn't even know what song they were singing. Her thoughts were elsewhere. She couldn't quit thinking about Pastor Mark's sermon on anger. Pastor Mark had read Ephesians 4:26-27. The same scripture her mama had shared with her the night she found out James had enlisted. Pastor Mark had preached a message on not letting the sun go down while you are still angry so as not to give the devil a foothold. Jessie almost scoffed at the irony in the scripture coming back to her now full circle.

I've let many suns go down in my anger, she thought to herself. *But, it's not my fault.* Too many nights had passed without a letter. No word. Nothing. She had somehow quit writing James too. A twinge of guilt pulsed in her chest. *What am I supposed to write? Small talk? Buckie's finally added a new item to their menu, "sweet chips," made out of sweet potatoes. Our neighbors got a new car that my daddy is obsessed with – a Studebaker Daytona Wanonaire. Blah! Blah! Blah! And oh, by the way, how are you? I don't know because you stopped writing to me. If you wanna know, I'm the same. Missin' you terribly. My heart is breakin'.*

Jessie's thoughts were tormenting her intensely. She teared up. How could people just go on as if everything was normal when things for her were torn apart? A tear let loose and snuck down her cheek. She quickly wiped it away before her mama noticed and sniffed back any remaining tears. Jessie could feel anger well up within her.

She thought of Pastor Mark's sermon and let out a huge sigh. *She had given the devil a foothold.*

* * *

> In the jungle, the mighty jungle
> The VC sleeps tonight
> In the jungle, the quiet jungle
> The VC sleeps tonight

Sergeant Cobal barked at James, "Patterson, you're gonna get us all killed with that nonsense singing."

"I'm buildin' moral, Sergeant."

Sergeant Cobal shook his head. He liked James. "Well, quiet it down and sing *pianissimo*." He shot

James a look, "Yeah, that's right, Specialist, you're not the only musical one here."

The guys laughed quietly as they continued walking. But suddenly, the point man, Rodriguez, froze. He slowly raised one fist, indicating they all stop. A couple of the men moved up to see what was going on. The others crouched and faced outwards as they had done so many times before. James watched Rodriguez; this time it was different. Rodriguez slowly turned and his face was without expression. He looked pale. Just then the spot where Rodriguez had stood a moment before erupted in a flash of smoke and debris. The men running up to Rodriguez were mowed down in a spray of shrapnel. The landmine had detonated and the loud explosion sent James' platoon frantically running. They retreated to a shallow ditch and dense area with brush. The area, however, would not provide much cover from the assault that was now upon them.

Sergeant Cobal's left ear was lacerated. He had the radio up to his right side and was trying to call to the other platoons in their company.

Think on your feet, soldier. James began scanning the area. They had to move or this place would soon become the entire platoon's grave. Just to the left, positioned at about 10:00, James spotted a sheltered ravine around 200 yards away. They had to make it to that area. There they could seek some cover from the raining terror of bullets ripping through the tall grass and trees above them. From that spot they'd be able to defend themselves better until help could arrive. They had to move. And quickly. They were sitting ducks where they were.

How could they mobilize their platoon safely with this barrage of firing coming at them? James doubted.

Faith, my son. He heard the voice plain as day. *Take up the shield of faith to extinguish all flaming arrows of the evil one.* He pictured Mushroom Man, the soldier he had affectionately nicknamed, that Jessie drew for him which was tucked in his helmet. And then he pictured her on the other side.

Yes, faith! He could do this. He had to. For her.

He nudged Jim next to him, "Hey, battle buddy, can you be my back-up bass?" He eyed the area he intended to make a run for. "We need to move this platoon or this is goin' to be our mass grave if we don't get the hell out of here. If I get over there, I'll cover for you and then we can cover for the rest."

Jim nodded. He propped his M16 up on the crest of the ditch and began revengefully emptying his 30-round magazine as he swept the opposing area. James' heart was racing. He nodded to his sergeant who was still relaying coordinates to their relief efforts. He quickly popped up so he was even with the surface of the ditch. Exposed. Then he ran. The hum of bullets whizzed by his ears. He braced his own thoughts with a focus he didn't know he had. He let the rhythm of the bullets humming by his ears be the music that carried his feet swiftly to his destination. Before he knew it, he was down in the ravine. He waved to his platoon, motioning for the next to come as he got his rifle positioned. However, there was no movement. No comrades followed him.

Where was Jim? What were they doing? Were they just gonna sit there and get themselves shot up?

He yelled at Jim. *Had Jim misunderstood him? Why wasn't he following?* He couldn't believe he was going to do this again. He was going back. Going back to get his platoon. One by one if he had to. He shot out of the ravine. Jim Beau continued firing as James made his way back across. He dove down into the small bump below.

"What the hell? Let's go, Jim," he yelled.

Jim shook his head, "It ain't gonna work that way. If I'm gonna be your bass guitar, I gotta always be back up. You get the others going. I'll cover you."

"Morris!" James yelled above the deafening nose. "Let's go, Morris!" he yelled again to a stark-eyed young private who sat shaking, paralyzed in fear. "Morris, now! We are takin' a new spot. Follow me." He put his arm around Morris and before Morris had much time to think – or fear – what was about to happen, James popped up again from the minimal cover offered from the small dip of earth. He and Morris were channeling their way to the ravine. And by the grace of God, they were quickly down in the cover of the narrow ravine.

"How'd you do that?" Morris said in disbelief.

"I don't know. I just focus on those whizzin' bullets bein' my rhythm to drive me. And my feet just move.

It's like when I'm playin' guitar. My fingers move with the rhythm. It just happens."

"Well, that wasn't possible how fast we just got from there to here. It's like you are a ghost."

"Call me…the Guitar Ghost!" he sputtered with a quick laugh and threw himself out into the open once more and put all his energy and focus into making it to his platoon again. Alive.

* * *

7, 8, 9…one by one he kept going back. He brought soldier by soldier to the protection of the ravine. A few, after seeing what James was doing, joined his efforts and began helping those that were injured or frozen in fear.

14, 15, 16…

As his fellow comrades lay protected in the ravine, they coordinated a rotation of gunners.

20, 21, 22…

Nervous cackles were quickly exchanged between the men as Morris repeated what James had called himself---Guitar Ghost! They didn't care what he called himself if he could keep bringing soldiers over safely the way he was somehow miraculously doing.

29, 30, 31…

Five soldiers had been fatally shot. James' heart sank with them as they sank into the ravine and he released their lifeless bodies from his grip. But he had to keep going. He now had two soldiers left. Sergeant Cobal, who was still on the radio, and Jim, his bass. His battle buddy.

James dove into the ditch and Sergeant Cobal motioned for James to take Jim next.

"No!" Jim insisted. "What we've been doing has worked." James looked at his buddy with questioning concern. "You don't rewrite a masterpiece, do ya James, when you've nailed the song? Take Sarge. I got your back again. I'll go last and you can cover me like you originally said."

"No, we all three go," barked their Sergeant.

No defying orders from above. They nodded in unison.

"Okay, you two lead," Jim said almost out of breath. He had been firing relentlessly for 20 minutes now, "I will follow with my see-ya-later-assholes-M16-salute!"

James loved the humor that Jim could bring to less-than humorous situations. "Ready?" he yelled.

Nods of confirmation, and without any more hesitation, up they jumped.

* * *

He hadn't kept track of how many times he had made that 200-yard trek. He should be tired. Dragging. Yet he ran swiftly with his feet just like his fingers plucking away at his guitar. He could hear Jim's M16 behind him. Their target was close. Moments away.

He felt an odd burning in his right shoulder and some warmth that felt wet. He kept moving. Just as he pushed Sergeant Cobal in, he heard Jim's firing stop. He dove in. They had made it.

* * *

He closed his eyes for a moment. Breathless. They had made it. It was quiet next to him. Suddenly his eyes popped open. Instant panic. He didn't see Jim. "Where's Beau?" he yelled. Sergeant Cobal's eyes were closed too, but they instantly flashed open. James scrambled to his feet and stretched up the ravine. There, at the top just a foot from dropping into the cover of the natural bunker lay his friend motionless. He grabbed his flank with both his fists and yanked him in, "Jim?! Jim?!" he pleaded, his heart pounding.

"I always knew I couldn't play bass forever, Patterson," he said through a gurgling sound. James could see blood pulsing from the side of his neck. "But, I played one heck of a last song," his eyes closed…he was gone.

"No, Jim! Noooo! Hang on, buddy! It's gonna be okay!" James was trying to put pressure on Jim's wound but his right arm just wouldn't work.

"Patterson, let him be. He's gone now. You gotta let him go."

"Noooooo! He can't be number six! He's my bass guitar."

352

"You did all you could. It's not your fault. You gotta let him go. We're gonna get Striker to take a look at your shoulder. You've been hit. We need to see how bad it is."

The burning, the warmth that had felt wet…now he knew what that was. In his adrenaline he hadn't even known--he had been shot. But the only pain he felt now was in his heart as he stared down at his battle buddy. His closest friend.

He sank to ground. Suddenly he started to feel sick. He vomited. And then, everything went black.

* * *

His eyes fluttered open and closed again. The lights were bright and he felt very groggy. He could hear someone saying his name. He tried hard to open his eyes again.

"Patterson? Patterson? Can you hear me?"

James opened his eyes and tried to clear his throat. No words came out. The face in front of him was out of focus, but he thought he could make out Sergeant Cobal's voice.

"I was just getting my ear stitched up and wanted to come by and check on you. Son, you are one brave soldier. And, you will be one very decorated specialist. I am putting you in for a Silver Star. You deserve recognition for what you did for those men…for what you did for me."

James just stared blankly up at the ceiling. Tears slid down his cheeks. No other reaction. No words.

"Patterson, did you just hear me? The Silver Star Medal."

"I didn't save enough. Six men I didn't save."

"I know, and we mourn those six, but you saved 31." Cobal repeated himself, "31, James, of your platoon." Sergeant Cobal had never called James by his first name. James looked at Sergeant Cobal and noticed a tear sliding down his cheek, "Be thankful for those 31."

"But six men!" James said, cringing as he shifted in bed. The pain in his shoulder reminded him of what he had been through. "You know, Sarge, there's six strings on a guitar. A guitar!" he said in disgust. "That was somethin' that was worth so much to me before the army. My guitar meant everythin' to me. But now, I'd trade my guitar and everythin' I own for those six lives I couldn't save." He laid his head back on his pillow and began to sob. The thought of his friend that he didn't save brought an agony so deep he could feel it pierce his heart. "Oh, Jim, I'm so sorry!"

"Patterson," Sergeant Cobal reached out to touch James' hand, "you're going to write one last piece. And you honor those fallen soldiers, Specialist. But you make certain in your final story, you write yourself a hero. Because that's what you are," Sergeant Cobal paused for a moment and then let a small grin lift the corners of his mouth, "Guitar Ghost."

Robert sat at the kitchen table scanning over the mail. Nothing again from James. He dreaded Jessie coming in from picking the eggs and seeing the stack of mail on the table. She didn't ask anymore, but he knew it was still on her mind. She would just quietly try to hide the unbearable disappointment that was no doubt plaguing her thoughts.

He pushed the stack of mail aside and looked over at Patty. "Supper is smellin' good, hon."

"Country ham with red-eye gravy and grits, buttermilk biscuits and creamed collard greens," Patty responded as she stood stirring the bowl of biscuit batter.

He looked back down at the stack of mail and shook his head somberly with a disgruntled expression across his face. His wife glanced up and noticed. She interpreted his disgruntled look as disapproval to the supper menu. "Lemme guess, you didn't want creamed collards?"

"Huh?...Oh, no…no, that's not it at all, Pats. I like your creamed collard greens. I wouldn't say *love* them, but I like them." He turned up his hands and offered a guilty smile to his wife.

Patty put her hands on her hips, "Well, then what was that look of displeasure for?"

"This stack of mail here. No letter from James again, and you and I both know that Jessie May will be walkin' in any minute now from pickin' eggs and she'll glance at that pile of mail. Lookin'. Hopin'. And then knowin' there is nothin' there for her, she'll walk away heart-broken once again." He sighed and shook his head. Then slid the newspaper over and picked it up to scan the headlines.

What news worth reading was there for him on this sunny day in July? On the front cover a headline and picture caught his attention and made his breath catch in his throat.

Guitar Ghost saves 31!
A Vietnam Honky-Tonk Hero

Robert squinted as he looked at the picture underneath the headline. The picture looked somewhat like it was James, but a lot thinner than he remembered. *It couldn't be?* He quickly perused the article and there he read it…

> Specialist James Patterson of the 2nd squad, first platoon, 5th infantry heroically saved 31 of the 37 in his platoon.

The article had accounts from several fellow comrades. They all testified and shared in disbelief how James had risked his life to save theirs as he helped relocate the entire platoon to a safer area until rescue efforts came. James' platoon had encountered difficulties when his first platoon was ambushed and the other platoons in his company had gotten cut off. He made trip after trip amidst enemy fire back and forth to get to an unprotected location where the platoon had been forced to retreat.

Robert was almost in a hypnotic trance as he read. He had to stop for a moment and take a deep breath before continuing.

> Private First-Class Eric Morris said he didn't know how Patterson dodged the bullets. "It was like he was a ghost, nothing touched him." Morris said he asked Specialist Patterson how he did it, "he just told me he sailed through the constant rhythm of bullets that were shooting past him and let that be the rhythm to his feet, like the beat of music when he plays guitar." Then Morris said Patterson laughed and called himself *The Guitar Ghost* just before going back for more. Patterson suffered a bullet wound to his shoulder and lost a significant amount of blood. He is recovering in a mobile army surgical unit and is expected to make a full recovery. He earned a Purple Heart and, additionally, because of his numerous heroic sacrifices, will be receiving the Silver Star for valor. He saved 31 of his 37 platoon members. We honor and pay our respects to the six fallen soldiers: SPC James Beau, SPC Michael Coleman, Jr., PFC Gerald F. Hall, SPC Arlan T. Muller, PFC Ricky C. Randall, and PFC Jerome Smith.

"Pats, you're never goin' to believe this?"

"What?" she paused from her supper prep and glanced over at Robert.

"James is in the paper."

She set her bowl of batter down in haste and her wooden spoon flicked out, splattering batter all over the countertop. She ignored it. She ran to the table and practically ripped the paper from her husband's hands.

As she read, she began to shake and cry, overcome by sobs of joy.

* * *

They heard the back-screen door and knew Jessie would be walking in with the hen's count for the day. Jessie walked in the kitchen and set the pail of eggs in the refrigerator being careful to switch the older pail to the front. When she stood up, she saw both her parents were sitting at the table. Her mother looked like she had been crying.

"Ma, what it is?" Jessie hustled over to the table where they each sat holding hands. "What's wrong?"

"Sweetheart, why don't you sit down?" her mother's words were soft, but she smiled.

"You're scarin' me. What is it?" Jessie paused and then glanced at the stack of mail still on the table and all of a sudden her eyes became the size of jar lids, "It's James, isn't it? Somethin's wrong?"

"No, honey, everythin' is okay. Here, I want you to read this." Robert slid the paper over to Jessie. The crease in her brows revealed her confusion. "Look closely at the picture, Jess."

"Oh my gosh!" Jessie let out a shriek. "It's James." She began to sob just as her mother had done moments before her. She pulled the paper close to her and with tears streaming down her face, she began to pore over the words.

When she was finished, she set the paper down and began to cry unabated. Both her parents stood and comforted her. They rubbed her back and soothed her just as they did when she was a little girl. They held her and let her weep tears of joy. Weep tears for days lost worrying. Weep tears for past anger. Weep tears of relief. And weep tears of humble gratitude.

Carrie walked in, "What's wrong with Jessie May?" Both her parents just gave her a head nod to leave the kitchen.

"She's okay, Carrie Grace, just give us a little privacy," her mother spoke lovingly to her youngest daughter. "Why don't you go make sure your room is all cleaned up. That way after supper we can play *Bewitched* before bath time. I know you've been wantin' to play your new game." Pacified with this distraction, Carrie gave one last look at Jessie and then walked out of the kitchen.

Jessie sat sniffling at the table, "Can you grab me a Kleenex, please?"

Her father grabbed her a tissue from the counter. "Here you go, honey." He rubbed her tear-soaked hair from her face.

"Thank you," she said blowing her nose and sniffling back some straggling tears. "All this time, I've been waitin' for news. It feels so strange. I'm so relieved. And yet, I'm worried if he is okay."

"The article said he's expected to make a full recovery," Robert reassured her.

"No, Daddy, I mean mentally okay, not physically. Jenny Mae told me after church that Isabelle Jenkin's brother Larry came back and he is not the same." She looked somberly as a tear rolled down her cheek, "She said he's messed up."

"That Jenny Mae, she's just like her mother Ida Mae! Always gossipin' and doesn't know when to keep her mouth shut," Patty scoffed.

"But mama, this isn't gossip. It's the truth. She said Isabelle's brother can't sleep. He has nightmares and has no interest in anythin' but drinkin' and smokin'. He's removed...." the tears began to double down her cheeks again. "What if that's James when he comes home? Removed. Different. I couldn't bare it. The article says nothin' about how he is mentally. What if..." She choked up. Her words were thick in her throat and she couldn't say anymore.

"Darlin', you have to trust that he is in God's care now just as he has been this entire time. He is goin' to be different. But, so are you, and that isn't a bad thing. I have seen some amazin' things change in you, Jess, so trust in the good. You need to keep your faith. The Lord hasn't failed us this far." And with those words, Robert took both Patty's and Jessie's hands in his own and bowed his head and began to pray, *Heavenly Father, thank you for your mercy to us and unendin' grace. We come before you now with thanksgivin' for this article today in the paper that has brought us news that we can rejoice over. We put our faith in you, Father, that James is okay. In your lovin' care, make him well. God, in your word you say in Romans 8:28 that we can know and trust that in all things you are workin' for the good of those who love you. We love you, Lord, with our whole hearts. There is no greater love than you. And, we beseech you now to heal James completely and bring him home safely to us. And if I might be so bold to ask, SOON! In your lovin' name we pray, Amen.*

Chapter 22
A Ghost at the Door

"Are you sure you don't wanna go into town with Carrie Grace and take her Trick-or-Treatin'?" Patty said to Jessie. "It'd be good for you to get out of the house?"

"No, you know I've always liked passin' out the candy…a piece for them…and a piece for me!" Jessie raised her eyebrows and smiled at her mama. "Plus, you got Charleston Chews this year. My favorite! So, you and Daddy go on. Trust me, little Miss Carrie will relish in the attention of both of you and not havin' to walk since you'd take the car," she chuckled a little. "Besides, then you can pick up Lydia Ruth after her party at Robbi Jo's. So, go now, I got it covered here." She picked up her mama's ceramic pumpkin bowl full of candy and snitched a Charleston Chew as if to reassure her mama that she was really okay with stayin' home.

Jessie knew there wasn't going to be too many Trick-or-Treaters out their way. And truth be told, she was hoping for a night to sit quietly with her own thoughts and the house to herself for most of the evening.

"Well, if you are sure you will be alright?"

"Yes, Mama," Jessie tried to shoo her mother out. "The Johnson girls will probably swing by before headin' into town, and I always love seein' the creative costumes that their mama sews for them every year. I'd hate to miss that! And Myrna Kelp will probably stop by with Ellis and Orville too. I will be kept busy enough. Honestly, Mama, this would save me from stoppin' by that party with Lydia Ruth and chancin' all of those people askin' me if I've heard from James. After that article, everyone keeps askin' me about *Guitar Ghost*."

"You sure you don't wanna talk about ghosts on Halloween?" her mother tried to wiggle her fingers spookily. "Okay, lame joke, sorry. You sure you'll be okay?"

"Positive!"

Her mother nodded as Robert walked in the room, "Carrie Grace's ready to go. She's gettin' impatient. Are we takin' her in?" he asked.

"I guess so, Jessie May wants the Charleston Chews all to herself."

"Hey, save me a couple!" her father grabbed for one from the bowl.

"Does that count as one of your two then?" Jessie smirked.

"Hardly!" her daddy was already stuffing the chewy chocolate into his mouth.

"Okay, lemme go put the left-over ribs in the fridge. The casserole dish is still sittin' on the counter coolin' from supper," Patty told Robert.

"I'm goin' to go grab a sweater. There's a little chill to the air tonight. Want me to grab you one too?"

"Yes, dear!" Patty called after her husband who was heading to their room.

"I can put the ribs away, Mama."

"No, you stay here and man your post just in case anyone comes. I'll be quick." And off Patty scooted to the kitchen.

Jessie stood in the entryway and was rubbing the smooth shiny rim of the ceramic pumpkin bowl. She loved this dish. She smiled. It made her think of so many fond memories as a kid. She sighed. *Such an innocent time then. Why can't I go back to those days of youth and innocence…when everythin' seemed so simple.*

The knock at the door startled her.

She opened the door and drew in a sharp breath. "Trick or Treat!" It was a voice she had longed to hear for so long.

The pumpkin bowl dropped out of her hands and came crashing down to the floor, shattering all over. She flung her arms around James. He winced slightly.

Her mama came rushing in to see what had happened the same time her father hurried to the door. "Jess, are you…" Patty didn't finish her question. Her hand flew to her mouth as she gasped in disbelief. There, standing in their entry way was James in an embrace with Jessie.

Tears filled her eyes. She glanced at Robert whose eyes, too, were full with tears.

Jessie stepped back and stared at James, "Is this for real? Are you really here standin' before me?"

"I am, it's really me, Jess. Either that or someone has a dang good Halloween costume of me!" and he winked.

Almost bashful, she looked down and then sucked in a quick breath when she saw the mess of ceramic shards and candy all over the floor. She turned to her mother, "I'm so sorry, Mama! I'm so sorry about your bowl."

"Oh, Jessie May! Don't worry about that bowl. That doesn't matter. James is home." She tossed her hands excitedly in the air and yelled, "James is home!"

* * *

Their bellies were full. James had come over for dinner after church and Patty had outdone herself again with the meal. Her country-fried steak and biscuits with gravy were always a crowd-pleaser. Robert rubbed his belly, commenting several times how uncomfortable he felt, "I'm full as a tick."

"You know, dear, you do that to yourself. I don't feel a bit sorry for you," Patty shook her head at her husband.

"You look like Santa rubbin' your big belly like that, Daddy," Carrie teased.

"Hey now! *Big* belly?" Robert tried to look hurt. "Well, I guess instead of sayin' 'Ho! Ho! Ho!', I should have been sayin', 'No! No! No!'" The room erupted with laughter. They lingered around the table, enjoying each other's company and conversation.

"Thank you, Miss Patty, your country-fried steak was amazin'. Mmm, mmm, how I've missed home-cookin'."

"You are most welcome, James," Patty smiled. "You know, since we are goin' to be family and all, I think you can just start callin' me Patty."

"I know, Jessie May told me that too, but I've been gone so long, it just doesn't feel right comin' back here and callin' you just Patty."

The corners of her mouth turned up just slightly, and she paused, "Well, considerin' you are goin' to be my son-in-law, I'd say it's high time," Patty shot a playful look James' way.

James turned and looked at Jessie. A smile spread broadly across each of their faces. He had wasted no time asking Robert for permission for his daughter's hand in marriage. He had taken her out Friday night – their first *official date* since he'd been back – and he'd popped the question. He had envisioned asking her Halloween night when he showed up at her doorstep, but he knew the shock of his arrival was all the surprise she could bear. He wanted to do everything right with Jessie. He wasn't certain if he should ask her so quickly since they hadn't really had much time to see each other since Monday, Halloween night. However, he decided he had waited long enough to put that ring on her finger while he was in Vietnam. Too many nights he had lain in his cot thinking about nothing else. Praying for nothing else. So, he figured after all the agonizing time they both had to endure, it was only right to not prolong it.

"Look at you two! Sittin' there grinnin' like possums eatin' sweet taters," Robert shook his head, not able to contain his own smile, "So, have you decided on a date yet?" Robert asked as he set his napkin on his plate and pushed his chair back from the table, reclining slightly in it.

"We have," Jessie said, glancing at James and squeezing his hand under the table, "We were thinkin' a summer weddin', just before the heat. I think we've settled on June fourth, it's a Saturday."

"Oh, that's a perfect time! Can I be your magnolia girl?" Carrie interrupted excitedly.

"That's not correct, Carrie Grace," Lydia rolled her eyes and was just about to correct her younger sister when Carrie interjected.

"Oh, sorry, *may* I be your magnolia girl," Carrie said proudly.

Lydia rolled her eyes, "You missed the point."

* * *

Snuggled cozy next to each other on a blanket, they gazed up at the array of fall colors on the trees above them in Eden's Pathway. The colorful canopy delicately allowed a teasing of light to sneak down on them. Jessie whispered into James' ear, "I think I'm the one who needs a cold soda now. I can hardly stand this *waitin'*."

"Well, for the record, you're the one who wants to wait for a summer weddin'. If you recall," James continued, "I originally wanted a fall weddin'. In Eden's Pathway, if you remember? And now that I think of it, we are in November and I do believe that's fall, Jessie May," he hinted with a wink.

That wink and the coy look he gave her was just what she needed, filling her with a reassuring peace that James was going to be okay. She'd been anxious for so many nights wondering what he'd be like when he returned. She recalled what Jenny Mae had told her in church about Isabelle Jenkin's brother Larry. He wasn't okay. Jessie had worried the same about James.

But now, she smiled and quietly lifted up a quick prayer. *Thank you, God, that you are so good and faithful.* She turned to James, "I don't know if November is realistic, but maybe pushin' our weddin' up would be a good idea after all." James grinned smugly. She shook her head at him, "Now, don't go gettin' too big for your britches." She inhaled a slow and steady breath and let it out. "I

368

reckon I may just have to let you get your way," Jessie conceded. "However," she paused with her own coy look, "I wouldn't get too used to that, James Theodore." And this time, it was her turn to give a wink!

Meet the Author

Chanda Stelter never envisioned herself as an author. Originally from a small town in the upper mid-west, she grew up a country girl. She was a stay-at-home mom who later went back to school to be a teacher. Teaching is her passion and focal point of her professional life, but one bizarre night – sick and not able to sleep – she would have an unexpected twist in her life's narrative. She gracefully phrases it, "God had His own plan," and playfully adds, "with a little humor along the way."

With her initial journey as an author being unforeseen, she began writing behind closed doors, still unsure of her talent and path. However, encouraged by friends and family and propelled by her acceptance towards the unpredictability of life, Chanda found herself increasingly excited to finish what she started in the middle of the night. Her love for romance, coupled with her faith-driven perspective, gave birth to her unique brand of a Christian romance historical fiction. Through her writing, Chanda seeks to not only entertain, but also to infuse her stories with messages of hope, humor, love, and faith—values she holds dear in her own life. Her writing will resonate with readers, inviting them into a world where history and romance intertwine, guided by the beacon of Christian faith.

A devoted wife of over 25 years and a loving mother of two adult children, Chanda and her husband have recently become empty-nesters. She enjoys this new stage of life reconnecting with her husband. Now they delight in the company of their house dog and two garage cats who have cleverly managed to claim the inside of the home as their own, also.

As Chanda continues her journey as an author, she welcomes readers into her world of unexpected stories, inviting them to explore the unknown, embrace faith, and celebrate the unpredictable beauty of life.

Connect with Chanda at:
guitarghostseries@gmail.com

Or follow and like her on Facebook at:
https://www.facebook.com/GuitarGhostSeries.ChandaStelter/

In the future, the story continues…

Jessie screamed out in pain and her thoughts in that moment went irrationally to her husband, *This is all James' fault and he's not even here to help me.* She was about to utter that she couldn't take it anymore when another wave of contractions came over her body, rendering her speechless. She grit her teeth and let out an agonizing groan. Dr. Banks popped his head up and said, "Okay, it's time to push."

* * *

Jessie sat cradling their newborn son in her arms, staring at his precious features while she waited for the nurse to bring James into the delivery room. Their son had dark chocolate hair, just like his daddy's. It was thick and silky to touch. With him tucked against her body in one arm, she used her free hand to stroke his soft, newborn hair with her thumb. She leaned her face down to her infant son and inhaled deeply. She took in his sweet smell and closed her eyes in tranquil gratitude. She had no idea it would feel like this to love so fully. She couldn't believe she was a mother.

Her thoughts were interrupted as she felt James' hand gently caress her shoulder. She hadn't heard him walk in amidst the bustle of the hospital staff, "Oh Jess, he's beautiful."

373

"Jamesy," she only called him that when she was truly bewitched. "Isn't Bennett perfect?" They had named him after James' father who had died of cancer when James was only seven years old. "We have a son – Bennett Robert Patterson. Look what we did together." Hearing the words off her own tongue, Jessie almost shook her head scoldingly at herself. Here just moments ago while she was in such pain, she was ready to blame James. *Isn't it funny in life*, she thought to herself, *how often when we are in pain, we want to blame someone else*. She heaved a sigh.

"Are you okay?" James asked with sudden concern.

"I'm more than okay, James. Thank you for lovin' me. Thank you for this beautiful boy we have together because of our love."

James leaned down to kiss Jessie and sat down on the bed next to her. She could smell cigarette smoke off his breath. Since he came back from Vietnam he was struggling to quit. She loved him wholly, of course, but she did not love that he was smoking. She would talk with him about that, but later. Right now, she wanted to enjoy this time together. She sat quietly with James, savoring the moment. It was mesmerizing. They were parents.

* * *